DEMON'S QUEST

HIGH DEMON SERIES, BOOK FOUR

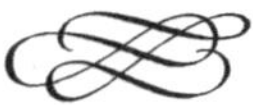

CONNIE SUTTLE

Print Second Edition (2018)
Print ISBN: 1-63478-067-1
Print ISBN-13: 978-1-63478-067-4
eBook ISBN: 1-93975-907-2
eBook ISBN-13: 978-1-93975-907-8

Published by:
SubtleDemon Publishing, LLC
PO Box 95696
Oklahoma City, OK 73143

Cover art by Renee Barratt @ The Cover Counts

To Walter, Joe, Larry, Lee, Dianne, Sarah and Mark.
Thank you.

ACKNOWLEDGMENTS

As always, this book is the result of collaboration. If it weren't for the support of my editor, my cover artist and my beta readers, it would be less than it is. All mistakes, as usual, are mine and no other's.

About the Author:
Connie Suttle lives in Oklahoma with her husband and a conglomerate of cats. They have finally banded together to make their demands, which has proven disconcerting to all humans involved.

You may find Connie in the following ways:
Facebook: Connie Suttle Author
Twitter: @subtledemon
Website and Blog: subtledemon.com

Blood Destiny Series:

Blood Wager

Blood Passage

Blood Sense

Blood Domination

Blood Royal

Blood Queen

Blood Rebellion

Blood War

Blood Redemption

Blood Reunion

Blood Destiny Series Boxed Set (Books 1-10)

Blood Recall

Blood Alliance*

Legend of the Ir'Indicti Series:

Bumble

Shadowed

Target

Vendetta

Destroyer

Legend of the Ir'Inditi Boxed Set

High Demon Series:
Demon Lost
Demon Revealed
Demon's King
Demon's Quest
Demon's Revenge
Demon's Dream

God Wars Series:
Blood Double
Blood Trouble
Blood Revolution
Blood Love
Blood Finale

Saa Thalarr Series:
Hope and Vengeance
Wyvern and Company
Observe and Protect*

First Ordinance Series:
Finder
Keeper
BlackWing
SpellBreaker
WhiteWing

R-D Series:

Cloud Dust

Cloud Invasion

Cloud Rebel

Latter Day Demons Series:

Hot Demon in the City

A Demon's Work is Never Done

A Demon's Due

Seattle Elementals Series:

Your Money's Worth

Worth Your While*

BlackWing Pirates Series

MindSighted

MindMage

MindRogue

MindMaster*

Black Rose Sorceress Series

The Rose Mark

Rose and Thorn

Black Rose Queen

Queen of Thorns and Roses

Future Wars Series

Buffer Zone

Black Zone*

Other Titles from SubtleDemon Publishing:

Malefactor

Transgressor

Underhanded*

by Joe Scholes

*Forthcoming

CHAPTER 1

"Is that what they do?" Wyatt was gripping his grandfather's arm so hard it probably would leave a bruise on the King of Karathia.

"The Larentii Wise Ones *Change What Was*—when the time is right," Lissa explained. They couldn't really see anything—Kifirin had relinquished Reah's body the moment the five Larentii and their Protectors appeared. All of them pulled the pertinent people out of the ballroom of the San Gerxon Casino. Inside a private banquet room, the Larentii Wise Ones, surrounded by their Protectors, were working with their energy over Reah's Thifilatha.

"But how will she be if they bring her back?" Wylend worried.

"The same. Anyway, that's what I hear."

"Mom?" Gavril's voice floated from behind, filled with worry.

"Son, go back out there, you need to calm your guests and let them know it's over," Gavin took his son's arm. For a moment, it seemed as if Gavril were seventeen again, instead of nearly seventy.

Gavin walked out with Gavril, while Farzi, Nenzi and six other reptanoids came rushing in.

"How our Reah?" Nenzi was nearly in tears.

"The Larentii are doing what they can," Lissa tried to reassure him.

"I felt her die." Aurelius arrived as quickly as he could—someone had taken over for him on an assignment.

"Aurelius, the Wise Ones are working on her," Lissa did her best to hold the old vampire back. Tory was on his knees as close to Reah and the Wise Ones as he could get. Norian had come and he and Lendill were in a corner with Kaldill Schaff. Norian and Lendill's father were both trying to calm Lendill.

"Something's happening," Wyatt breathed. A flash of light came and the Wise Ones gathered in a tighter knot.

"They've forced her out of the Thifilatha," Lissa sighed. "Is Kifirin still here?"

"I am here, avilepha." Kifirin appeared at her elbow. The god sounded tired. Exhausted, actually.

"Tell me what happened," Lissa demanded.

"Something that should not have been," Kifirin sighed. "That is why the Wise Ones appeared—this event was not in the timeline. Neither was Reah's child's death. Unfortunately, the Wise Ones cannot recall an unborn child."

"Then what changed it? What made this happen?"

"Someone who shouldn't have the ability has tapped into the Telling Winds to change things," Willem appeared. "Until now, only I have been able to tap into that power. I didn't see the baby's death until it was too late." Willem shivered. "I understand that Reah healed the core on Cloudsong before she came here."

"She healed a dead world? That's incredible. Kifirin, does this mean the other worlds that Zellar killed will live again?" Lissa stared up at the dark god.

"Avilepha, we cannot send her out to do these things. If she chooses to go, I will not hold her back. I think she needs protection, love. She saved your youngest, did you know?"

"He said as much." Lissa lowered her gaze. "Will she go back to him now?"

"I cannot answer that." A collective sigh drew their attention—the Wise Ones were stepping back. And then as one, they all disappeared. Tory was off his knees, but Wylend reached Reah before him.

"Erland, stay here as my ambassador," Wylend ordered, lifting Reah in his arms. "Wyatt, Corolan, Garek, with me," he added. Wylend disappeared with Reah.

"Son, let's go see what we can do to support Gavril," Erland muttered to Ry. They took off toward the ballroom.

"Mom, I need to be with Reah," Tory was at Lissa's side in as little time as it took to skip there.

"Child, Reah's mate should never wait for approval," a tiny curl of smoke came from Kifirin's nostrils. Tory was left staring at empty space as Kifirin disappeared.

"I am going. Do you wish to travel with me?" Aurelius asked. He'd not taken his eyes off the Wise Ones or Reah the whole time, listening to this conversation or that with only half an ear.

"Yeah. Let's go," Tory sighed.

"I'll see if I can bring her out." The voice was vaguely familiar, but I hadn't heard it in turns.

"Wyatt?" I stared up at the warlock who wanted to be a healer instead of heir to the Karathian throne.

"Here is my love," Wylend came into view.

"Where am I?" I felt dizzy and confused.

"In my suite," Wylend smiled at me.

"Wyatt, what can you tell me?" Karzac appeared from nowhere.

"Dizziness, probable confusion. The wounds are healed but there is still bruising around the sternum, ribs and thigh, with the sternum bruise the most severe," Wyatt said.

"Good. What else can you tell me?" Karzac lifted an eyebrow at Wyatt.

"That she should rest for at least ten days, with no strenuous activity during that time. No skipping, folding or sex. Until I say so," Wyatt added.

"Very good." Karzac smiled.

"I have a headache," I muttered, rubbing my forehead with fingers that shook.

"And a headache," Wyatt laughed. "I can handle that." He did. The pain left as soon as his fingers moved mine aside and touched my skin. "Now, you should likely eat something—clear broth and liquids at first."

"Please, no," I mumbled. "That last stuff I got was tasteless."

"See, this is the difficulty in treating a Master cook," Wyatt chuckled.

"I brought these; they were having a meltdown, Em-pah." Lissa appeared with Farzi, Nenzi and the other six reptanoids.

"Corolan, find some rooms," Wylend directed.

"Reah?" Aurelius moved Wyatt aside and sat on the edge of my bed.

"Auri?" I was weeping in his arms in seconds. All except Farzi and Nenzi faded from the room.

"She's sleeping—Farzi and Nenzi are with her," Aurelius raked a hand through his gold mane of hair. "Cried herself out, I think. Over the baby and everything else."

"She wouldn't let any of us near enough to do that," Tory grumbled.

"Torevik, what did you expect? She was troubled when you appeared to turn your back on her and the child. Gavril didn't help— he should have seen it, yet he pulled you away at every opportunity, leaving Reah by herself or with me." Aurelius gave Tory a level look.

"I didn't know what to do," Tory moaned.

"You could have gone to your father. Or to your mother or any number of other people. Yet you walked away from Reah instead. If you'd bothered to explain to her how you were feeling, it might have made a difference."

"Doesn't matter now—she won't even look at me."

"Love doesn't turn on and off, like a faucet," Corolan patted Tory's shoulder. "Keep that in mind and stand in front of her. She'll notice, I promise."

"Corolan knows what he's talking about," Wylend gave Tory a hug. "Don't give up, child. We'll make her smile again."

~

"This is good. Very good." I sipped my broth—it was seasoned perfectly. I could imagine small chopped leeks or scallions in it, with seasoned croutons added at the last moment. I said that aloud without thinking.

"And that is how I usually serve it." The cook had come to the table. Wylend had summoned him, I suppose. He was younger than I imagined and smiling at me.

"This is Radolf, who might be a very good warlock if he didn't stay in the kitchen constantly," Wylend chuckled.

"Why is there any need to be a warlock when you can cook?" I smiled at Radolf.

"Exactly what I've always said." Radolf sat next to me. "I was thinking about adding noodles to this, or pasta of some sort."

"Nothing heavy," I agreed. "Something thin and light, and not too much of it. Just enough for the taste and to entice the appetite."

"Exactly," Radolf nodded.

"Is that why the soup bowls are small?" Corolan wrinkled his nose at Radolf.

"Of course. We slave over the main course—you think we want you to be full after the soup?"

"There's a duck recipe I've been working on," I told Radolf. "How do you feel about allowing someone else inside your kitchen?"

"I won't mind if I get to help."

"Don't tire her out, son." Garek gave Radolf a look from his place at the table.

"That's your father?" I looked from Radolf to Garek. Garek gave me a blinding smile. Both had dark hair, but the eyes, noses and chins were different.

"Yes. I disappoint him constantly," Radolf grinned back at his father.

"You do not," I elbowed Radolf gently. I was too weak to do otherwise, and I had to admit that I liked Radolf immediately. It made me wonder how old he was—I couldn't gauge ages well in the Karathian race. Wylend was thousands of years old and still looked young—not much older than I.

"I think I tripped our exalted King more than once when I was little," Radolf declared.

"At least six times, running underfoot," Wylend gave Radolf a pointed look. "Thank goodness it was always in my private quarters."

"It would be too undignified for the formal hall," Wyatt agreed, smiling.

"Don't laugh, I think I tripped over you a time or two as well," Wylend grinned at Wyatt. Wyatt was only a year or so older than Tory and Ry.

"How are the meetings going on Campiaa?" I asked quietly.

"Couldn't be better—I got word from Erland before dinner," Wylend said. "The delegates who were reluctant to join were merely afraid of the Strands. Gavril has the Strands locked up at the moment —it appears they may be the first to feel the bite of justice from the Campiaan Alliance." Wylend sounded happy about that.

"And their warlocks?"

"Dead, including Nidris," Wylend said softly. "That one Gavril killed himself. Let us hope there are no others who know how to tap cores."

"I made a promise to heal the core on Thiskil," I said, looking down.

"Not until you're much, much better," Wylend said. "Love, come here and sit between Corolan and me."

"I'll bring her," Radolf said. "Come here, put your arms around my neck," he lifted me from my seat and carried me to Wylend. Corolan moved to the next chair down, giving me his. Wylend floated my water glass across the table. Water was the only thing Wyatt would allow me to drink. I'd already had my broth. The servants brought out the next course and Wylend sneaked a bite or two of his fowl to me, which was very good. Wyatt pretended not to notice. And when I nearly fell asleep at the table, Corolan tucked me against his side and let me close my eyes.

~

"Reah, we go back—Teeg need us." Farzi sounded upset. As was I, when I came fully awake.

"What does he need, honey snake?" I stroked Farzi's cheek after sitting up in bed. "Sweet man, give me a hug and a kiss before you go," I held my arms out to Nenzi. Nenzi was more than happy to give both, as was Farzi. The others came forward and got the same. Wylend had put me in a separate bedroom inside his massive suite of rooms.

I found myself wishing I could go with the reptanoids, just to spend the day with them. I wanted to be myself and feeling strong, instead of weak as I was right then. Aurelius was taking them to Teeg, then he was leaving as well. He was the last one in line for hugs and kisses. Someone would return him to his assignment—the one that had been interrupted when I was wounded. I was informed that the Larentii healed the wound I received and that was that. I hadn't thought it possible to live over what had been fired in my direction. The Larentii truly were the strongest and most talented of healers.

"Want company?" Corolan walked into my room. He'd spent the night in Wylend's private bedroom.

"What kind of company?" I asked, yawning. He laughed when I covered the jaw-cracking stretch of my mouth.

"The kind where I scoot you over, hold you against me and you fall asleep on my shoulder. Wylend is tending his court today, or he'd do it himself."

"Uh-huh." I was using another of Lissa's phrases.

"Scoot." Corolan lifted and deposited me toward the middle of the large bed. He dropped his robe on the floor and, dressed only in pajama bottoms, climbed into bed with me. "See, this isn't so bad," he pulled my head onto his shoulder. "Now, little girl, go back to sleep."

~

"Try this—it's the lightest I could make," Radolf offered the bite of crepe, holding the fork out for me. I felt a tiny bit awkward—nobody had ever fed me like that before. I was sitting on the counter in his large kitchen, swinging my bare feet while he fixed something for me as a late breakfast. His staff was busily preparing lunch—I'd slept quite late while Corolan did whatever magic he'd done to keep me napping long past my normal waking time.

"What's this?" Garek walked in and stared at my feet. I stilled them.

"No, you may move as much as you like," Garek was frowning. *Pulling* in a pair of socks from somewhere using his power, he proceeded to slide them onto my feet while Radolf fed me another bit of crepe. The crepe was very good.

"I'll put sweet cream on it next time, when we're not so worried about the diet," he said.

"This is good—it has a light, nutty taste," I said.

"Just a bit of nut spice, that's all," Radolf grinned and offered one more bite. "And I want to put some meat on those bones." He set the fork down and tapped my shoulder.

"Hasn't taken care of herself," Garek agreed. I wanted to have a talk with both of them about awful things happening over which I had no control, but they were both smiling. They knew already.

"See, cheeks still pale," Garek ran a knuckle gently down my face. I closed my eyes—they'd betrayed me by allowing a tear to slip away.

"Here, now, there's no need for that." Radolf was the one who lifted me off the island. "Put your arms around my neck, heart's love," he murmured against my ear. I embarrassed myself by sobbing a time or two against his shoulder.

"What's wrong with my little love?" Wylend was lifting me away from Radolf.

"I'm sorry," I sniffled. "I don't mean to take you away from court."

"Love, we recessed for lunch. You haven't taken me away from anything." Wylend carried me out of the kitchen. I was clutching the finest raw silk robes in my fingers, holding onto them tightly and wrinkling them, most likely, as Wylend carried me toward his suite. He could have folded us there, but he admitted that he wanted to baby me along the way.

"Here, Radolf sent this," Garek was right behind Wylend, offering me a drink of some kind. "It's berries blended with ice cream," he said. The concoction was pink from the berries and tasted like a dream.

"Radolf is a wonderful cook," I sighed after tasting it.

"His mother still grumbles that he didn't do something more important with his life," Garek did a little grumbling himself.

"Feeding people is a higher calling," I said. "Not everybody can do that, you know."

"Are we better now? Shall we have lunch in here?" *Here* was Wylend's bedroom.

"I'm having lunch now." I slurped more of my drink.

Garek had a table set up quickly, so I sat across from Wylend as he ate and he and Garek discussed several issues that Wylend was dealing with. At the moment, I was glad Wylend was handling all of it —I was feeling sleepy again.

Lok, many times great-nephew of the legendary Dragon Warlord, stared down his opponent. The flag was about to fall, signaling the beginning of his final bout in the Solstice Trials. Lok had trained most of his life in bladework, though the Falchani were turning to more modern weapons to fight their old enemies. Tradition was steeped into their bones and every child with any aptitude was still taught the art of the blade. The swords were made by hand but the craft might be dying. Lok worried that eventually—perhaps not in his lifetime but eventually, the Falchani would walk away from all of it.

Rumors swept the city—many talked of joining the Reth Alliance. The current Warlord was holding off on any decision in the matter, but it hung over their heads like a rain cloud. Lok still hadn't made up his mind about the whole thing. The flag dropped and Lok went to work, blades flying, fighting his opponent.

≈

"Lok, I grow tired of seeing you in my tents," the Lion Warlord teased good-naturedly as he handed out the prize for that year's Solstice Trials. "I'm beginning to think the others are just too soft. Is this the tenth one of these you have?" The large gold medallion was handed to Lok, who bowed respectfully to the Warlord.

"Eleven, Warlord," Lok replied, smiling. "But I don't keep track of those things."

"I'd pay you to train the advanced classes."

"I know, Warlord. I just don't think I have the patience for it."

"You've said that before. I ran out of tattoos to offer you long ago. Is there anything else I might offer instead?"

"A cup of tea?" Lok grinned.

"Done," the Warlord laughed.

≈

"They're recruiting from the Reth Alliance again—the Warlord only allows them to come once a year," Lok's cousin, Jeng, announced as he slid onto the stool at the noodle cart just inside the marketing district.

"Where?" Lok asked, using chopsticks to shove noodles into his mouth. Three days had passed since the Solstice Trials and he'd been at loose ends. Lok had done his twenty years in the Warlord's army before turning to the Solstice Trials. He was ninety-seven—in his prime for a Falchani, who lived an average of two hundred sixteen years. Nothing else appealed to him—he had no desire to run a business—that sounded boring in the extreme.

"Just outside the clothing district—there was space and an empty shop for them to set up. Today is the first day—they'll be here for three days."

Lok snorted, lifting his cup of rice wine and draining it. He spoke Alliance common, just as every Falchani his age and younger did. The Warlord had decreed it, saying that Falchan couldn't afford to remain isolated as it had in the past. Too many of their closest neighbors had been attacked in the past two hundred years. So far, Falchan had been spared, but Lok often wondered at that. They were a prime target, he felt, since they held no major weapons and their army was still equipped mostly with steel instead of Ranos technology. All it would take would be a ship filled with barbarians armed with a Ranos cannon and Falchan could be conquered.

Lok cringed at the thought of Falchan joining the Reth Alliance and slipping away from tradition, but the move might become inevitable. There were still plenty of worlds that belonged neither to the Reth nor to the Campiaan Alliance, newly-formed as it was. Still, it offered its worlds some sort of protection against an increasing threat from pirates and other filth. Just thinking about it made Lok's fingers curl, as if wishing for a sword grip. Shaking his long braid in frustration, Lok resolved to get it out of his mind.

"Cousin, they are harmless," Jeng sighed, misinterpreting Lok's actions.

"It's not the Reth Alliance that worries me."

Jeng drew in a breath. "You're worried about the pirates, too? I heard they took down the Lidrithi Government."

"When?" Lok lifted an eyebrow at his cousin, who accepted a bowl of noodles from the vendor.

"While you were hip-deep in the Solstice Trials," Jeng said, slurping noodles. He watched Lok's face carefully—Lok didn't often reveal his emotions. Lok was a throwback; everybody said so. In another time, he might have challenged and won the position as Warlord. Those days were gone. Lok's torso was covered in red dragons, in deference to his long-ago ancestor, the Dragon Warlord. All the old paintings and drawings portrayed the Dragon Warlord's tattoos. Lok had requested—and been granted—permission to have those tattoos copied onto his skin by the Lion Warlord.

"Jeng, what do you think Falchan might do if we were attacked by those pirates?" Lok's question was casual, but Jeng had studied his cousin for a very long time. Tried to emulate him, more often than not. He knew Lok's question had the weight of the universe behind it.

"We don't stand a chance," Jeng sighed, lifting a cup of rice wine to his lips.

❧

Lok examined the comp-vid. Yes, he knew how to use one—the technology had invaded Falchan in the past handful of years. The program listed all the benefits one might come to expect from the Reth Alliance if one signed on as RAA or ASD—Regular Alliance Army or Alliance Security Detail. The pay was sufficient. Training acceptable. Accommodations depended on which branch hired you. ASD sounded more fitting to his talents. Of course, he wasn't about to tell some recruiting agent what he thought. That might gain him swift passage to the worst position in the Regular Army.

"Please sit," the tall, dark-haired man offered Lok a seat when his name was called. "Lok, is it?" The man consulted the portable comp-vid in his hand.

"Yes."

"I see that you've won the Solstice Trials eleven times."

"Yes." Lok displayed no emotion with his one-word answer. No indication of the eighty years of training he'd put into those brief trials, just to come away with a gold medallion, the Lion Warlord's image stamped on its surface.

"And you've come away from your military service with top honors."

"Yes."

"Are you serious about coming to work for the Reth Alliance?"

"Yes."

"What are you hoping to gain from signing on with us?" That question made Lok's dark eyes widen just a fraction.

"You want the truth?"

"Yes. Of course."

"I hope to gain knowledge that may protect Falchan someday. From pirates or other invaders. I hear they've stepped up their attacks on non-Alliance worlds. Falchan may be vulnerable. I wish that to be otherwise."

"Do you know who I am?" The dark-haired man asked Lok.

"No idea. A recruiter. That's all I know."

"I am Lendill Schaff, Vice-Director of the ASD. Welcome to the Reth Alliance, conscript Lok."

~

"He did not call her that."

"He did. Our son has made a choice." Garek knew the arguments would come—Keetha argued about everything. Belittled Radolf for desiring to be a cook. Even his position as Head Cook to the King of Karathia didn't mollify Keetha's thwarted ambitions where her son was concerned. Radolf had expressed his interest in Reah—to the King and to his father. Knowing what his mother's feelings were likely to be, he hadn't approached her.

Garek, wanting to soften the blow when it came, brought it to her attention instead. Wylend had accepted the news—he'd guessed at it already and had no problem sharing his mate with Radolf. And Reah— she bloomed like a shy flower around Radolf. If they talked of cooking, they were both in rapture. Keetha wanted to squash her son's feelings.

"Neither of them will get children. She has a High Demon's marks on her neck. That means that only he will father her children. This is the worst possible news. Tell Wylend I will not stand for this. It's bad enough that he brings something like that to Karathia and parades her around on his arm. He already has an heir. Who will give us heirs, Garek? Any ideas on that?" Keetha's hands were firmly positioned on her hips as she glared at her Karathian warlock mate. Garek was a trusted lover to their King. Keetha didn't mind that—it elevated the entire family's importance on Karathia. Now, her son was not only a cook—he wanted that filthy High Demon as a mate!

"Keetha, I never imagined that you might be racist," Garek said softly.

"Radolf never wanted filth for his mate before," Keetha nearly shouted.

"You say that about the King's intended?"

"I'll say it about any of them marrying into the Karathian race!"

"Erland is mated to the Vampire Queen."

"She's a Queen," Keetha snapped. "Even if she is a nasty blood drinker, she's a Queen, and a powerful one at that. And she's Wylend's granddaughter. This—this High Demon—has nothing. What will she offer Radolf, Garek? Tell me."

"I never thought you a social climber before, Keetha. This is opening my eyes a little."

"I will not sit still while our son sends the family into oblivion by not reproducing."

Garek wanted to point out that having only one child had been Keetha's choice, not his. He held his tongue. "Erland's son was born by surrogate," he pointed out instead.

"If you suggest such an unnatural act to me again, we will part ways, Garek," Keetha hissed. "You see that Wylend chose the heir born naturally instead of that one."

Garek drew in a breath. Keetha was dancing around treason. "This conversation is getting us nowhere, Keetha," Garek sighed. He'd wanted to smooth the way for Radolf. He'd stirred up the insect's nest instead. He would go to Radolf and ask him to hold off speaking to his mother about Reah for a while. Perhaps a few full turns might do the trick. Garek folded away from his mate as she lifted a finger to make another point.

"Sex tomorrow," Wyatt grinned at me. I wish I didn't embarrass so easily over things of that nature. But I do. I felt my cheeks grow hot. Wyatt laughed. Nine days I'd spent at Wylend's palace, receiving deferential treatment from Wylend, Corolan, Garek and Radolf.

Radolf and I prepared the duck recipe I'd dreamed up in my head. It had turned out very well. With only a minor adjustment here or there, it would be worthy to serve in the finest restaurant. I'd come to enjoy my time with Radolf like treasured jewels. We laughed, talked and cooked inside his kitchen. Wylend, whenever court didn't take him away, would appear there, tasting whatever it was we were cooking. He accused us of putting extra pounds on his frame, ate whatever we offered and disappeared. In the nine days I'd been there, I think half the palace found their way to the kitchen on some errand or other. They never went away empty-handed.

Wylend made arrangements to bring me to his bed the moment Wyatt released me. "Here, try these strawberry tarts," Radolf handed a saucer to Wyatt, along with a fork. "Your cheeks are still pink," Radolf grinned at me.

"I'll get you," I threatened.

"I'm so scared," he waggled his fingers at me.

"How many Falchani recruits did you get?" Norian set his comp-vid on the breakfast table and peered across it at Lendill.

"Six," Lendill replied, selecting a roll from a heaping plate and pulling the butter dish over. Norian and Lendill were currently working from offices in Ildevar Wyyld's palace, for different reasons. Norian didn't want to come near Gardevik Rath or his son. Lendill was there because Reah wasn't on Le-Ath Veronis.

"What did you think of them?"

"I brought three into the ASD immediately. One of those even you'd be proud of."

"In training?" Norian grunted.

"Yes. Do you think Ildevar will offer membership into the Alliance again?"

"I haven't asked him." Norian sipped his tea.

"One—the best one—worries that those pirates may attack Falchan."

"A reasonable fear. They took Lidrith, and it was better armed."

"But Lidrith isn't home to a race of warriors, born and bred," Lendill pointed out.

"True. Are you training the one you're so proud of to combat pirates?"

"Absolutely, among other things," Lendill grinned. He had plans to visit Reah later. Had asked one of Lissa's Falchani to fold him to Karathia. Drew was glad to offer.

Radolf and I had just placed the ox-roast in the oven. I'd wanted to serve it to Wylend and the others—Radolf wanted to learn how to prepare it. We both got our wish. I was washing my hands at the sink when a woman appeared in the kitchen. Now I knew where Radolf got his eyes, nose and chin.

"Mother, what are you doing here?" Radolf sounded unsure, suddenly.

"I just wanted to look at the filth you've chosen for yourself," his mother snarled. I almost dropped the towel I was using to dry my hands—her voice was filled with hate. And what was she talking about? She already knew Radolf was a cook—he'd said she was still dealing with his decision over that.

"Reah is not filth," Radolf hissed right back. "Leave, mother, before you destroy everything."

"I'll not leave. Not until she tastes what a Karathian Witch can do to her." I blinked as light formed around her hands. The blasts were hurled in my direction seconds later, only to dissipate into nothing before they reached me.

"Keetha, leave. Now you see why Wylend is wise to select Reah as his mate," Garek appeared beside his son. "Power of any sort cannot be used against a High Demon—they are immune. Leave, Keetha. Do not make this worse than it is already."

"I will not," she snapped. I was staring at her now. What was Garek saying? That Wylend was using me, because power wielded by his kind had no effect? Was that what I was—a shield for him? I blinked stupidly at Garek and then at his mate.

"That's not all I have to say," Keetha seethed. "You'll never give my son children. I don't care how much he wants you. You'll never be welcome in my home or in my family, you stupid filth. Leave my child alone!"

"What is the meaning of this?" Wylend was suddenly in the kitchen and thundering, his anger more than evident. I stared at him in confusion. Had it all been for show? Had they courted me—treated me as they had, to reel me in as protection for Wylend? And Radolf? What was this? I sobbed and skipped away.

CHAPTER 2

"What. Have. You. Done?" Wylend was glowing, his power gathering as he stalked toward Keetha. Only now did she realize the extent of the foolishness she'd committed.

"I didn't know she'd just," Keetha's voice trailed off and she shrank back from Wylend's anger. Radolf stood, stunned. Garek, the spineless fool, wasn't doing anything to protect her from Wylend. Keetha had never despised her mate more.

"Your power is removed," Wylend hissed, the light around him blowing outward. Keetha shrieked as she felt her ability fall away. "I'm holding back from killing you because I love Garek. That is the only reason you're enjoying life now, Keetha. I suggest you not forget it. You are banished from the court and the palace. Do not," Wylend bent over her, his voice deadly soft, "come within my sight again." He waved an arm and Keetha vanished.

"Find Reah," Wylend snapped. "Find her. Immediately." Several ran to do his bidding.

~

Renegar had shown me the old palace on Beliphar; had told me I could use it if I wanted. That's where I was, huddled in blankets on the wide bed. Everything in this wing was placed in stasis. The fabrics, walls, roof, food, everything was pristine. No dust touched any of it. None of that mattered. Was Wylend using me? Why had Radolf's mother called me filth that he'd chosen? Where had that come from? Where? It didn't matter; I was homeless again. I should just get used to it. Nobody wanted me for me.

"You have such a low opinion of yourself." Kifirin sat on the end of the bed. A tiny curl of smoke filtered away from his nostrils.

"What opinion should I have, mighty god of the Dark Realm?" My voice dripped with sarcasm.

"You are loved, and not just by the ones you left behind moments ago," Kifirin said. "I exercise patience with you as a gift. Do not push me, daughter of my heart."

"Or you'll what?" I snapped. "Have me beaten as a child? Used up by the ASD? Kill my unborn child?"

"Reah, do not. I would hold you, if you would allow it. I see now that you do not know how to truly accept love. It was withheld when you were young, so now you know not how to deal with it as an adult. I will consider this. What I want to tell you is this. Your father loves you now."

"What? Are you crazy?" I was probably well on my way to being burned to a crisp for calling a god crazy.

"Reah, time has no hold upon my kind. Six lifetimes of penance your father served for his treatment of you. Just before Edan Desh was scheduled to be released from his prison, I switched his current spirit for one six lifetimes from now as he lay dying upon another world. That Edan never had a child, although he longed for one. This Edan you might love. Might take your troubles to. Sit in the shelter of his arms. He searches for you, little Demon. To offer apologies."

"And I'm just supposed to skip right to him and call him father?" I couldn't believe what I was hearing.

"I ask that you give him a chance. He is not the man you knew. Through six lifetimes, he has done many things to protect children. That was his punishment. Think on this, little Demon. How many will you punish by withholding your love? Yes, some have mistreated you. Take what they have to offer. Give them the opportunity to make amends. Forgiveness is difficult for you; I know this. Allow them to treat you gently now, in recompense for harder times before."

"Well, stupid me—is that all it is?" I snapped. "I have a hard time forgiving? Listen to yourself. Did you wonder when you were six what you did to make your father hate you? At least I thought Addah was my father then." I hugged myself to keep my hands from shaking.

"No. The one who made me gave me love." Kifirin disappeared.

"Sure. Disappear when you don't have a good answer for something." I wiped wetness from my cheeks.

Lendill cursed. In multiple languages, the last of which was Elvish. Many books described Elves as benign creatures—tall, beautiful and soft-spoken. Lendill could tell them with certainty that when Kaldill was angry, he could make anyone blush with the words from his tongue. Lendill had learned from the best.

"Where the fuck is she?" Lendill asked for perhaps the tenth time. Drew stood nearby, arms crossed over his wide chest, his eyes hooded and a slight scowl on his face. Had he known it, he looked very much like Dragon, his father, at that moment.

"No idea. We can't trace a power signature from a High Demon," Corolan sighed. "Wylend is so furious he is still locked in his suite, attempting to calm himself. I sent a message to Erland on Campiaa, asking that he and the Queen watch for Reah."

"None of the rest of us have the ability to find her either," Lendill muttered, raking fingers through his black hair. Corolan explained— twice—what had happened. Lendill had no idea that someone else was expressing interest in Reah. Now, Radolf, Garek's son, had folded away from Karathia, leaving his father distraught. They'd lost his trail after a while—Radolf was powerful enough to scatter the signature. Corolan couldn't have said anyone knew of Radolf's ability to do that until now.

"The bitch has been punished?" Lendill asked. Radolf's mother had caused this. Lendill was glad she wasn't present—he was tempted to strangle her.

"Her power removed and banished from the palace and the King's sight. He'll kill her if he sees her again," Corolan nodded.

Three days passed. Three days. I ate little and slept less. The bed was where I stayed most of the time, crawling out of it finally on the morning of the fourth day and dragging the sheets off. A laundry room lay next to the kitchen, meant to clean the kitchen towels, napkins and tablecloths from the tables. I used it to wash the sheets, towels and my own clothing—I only had what I'd worn when I left Karathia. I wandered around, wrapped in a towel while my clothes dried. I ate a little; there was fruit and dried pasta. I put a dish together, only eating a bit of it. I intended to keep my promise—I was going to heal Thiskil's core as soon as I was dressed again. No matter that the promise was made to one who'd helped kill my mother and my daughter. I made the promise. I would keep it.

Thiskil had been destroyed ten turns after Cloudsong's destruction. Still, I recalled Renegar's words and chose six stars. A kitchen timer sat beside me—it would tell me when a click passed so I could switch sources from which to pull energy.

"Very wise." A Larentii appeared and sat beside me shortly after I turned full Thifilatha. This was not Renegar—I knew that immediately. His eyes were bright and piercing as he looked up at me. Standing at well over eight feet, normally I would look up to him. At fifteen feet in full Thifilatha, I now looked down upon him.

"Welcome, honored Larentii," I inclined my head in a slight bow to him. He gave me a dazzling smile.

"I came to observe," he said, still smiling.

"You are welcome to do so," I replied and focused on the first star.

"You glow when you do this, did you know?" The Larentii was still there when the core was healed and sealed up again.

"I've never seen myself when I do this," I sighed. I was nearing exhaustion—the recent neglect of my body most likely was to blame. I had no idea if I'd have sufficient energy to skip to Beliphar.

"I will take you," the Larentii offered. In a blink, I was inside the massive kitchen. "You should eat and then rest," he said while I plopped onto a chair I'd dragged in earlier. I nodded, holding my head in my hands. A headache was coming on.

"I will go now," he added.

"What's your name?" I asked, looking up at him. You'd have thought the sun broke through clouds when he smiled.

"Nefrigar," he replied before folding away. He was back in less than a blink. "Now is a good time to visit Falchan," he was still smiling when he disappeared again. It reminded me of a child's story that Gavril had given me to read once, in an attempt to teach me his mother's native language. A cat had disappeared, leaving only his smile behind. I'd forced my way through the book. I could still read some of it, but speaking the words eluded me for the most part. I took Nefrigar's words to heart, however. When I was strong enough, I was going to Falchan.

Gavril cursed. And then cursed again. Things were going so well for the fledgling Campiaan Alliance. He'd thought to visit Reah. Now, through Erland, he was learning that someone had upset Reah on Karathia and she was missing again.

"I think, after Keetha called her filth and told her to stay away from her son, Garek made it worse by making it sound as if she were a shield for Wylend, when he meant that she wasn't a likely target for any witch or warlock if they wanted to get to Wylend by harming his mate," Erland explained.

"She didn't wait for an explanation, she skipped away immediately. Radolf left right behind her. Now, they can't find either of them."

Erland was angry on Wylend's behalf. Who'd allowed that foul woman into the palace to begin with? When Erland returned to Karathia, he'd do some questioning.

"Child, we have meetings to attend this evening," Dee, sitting nearby, thought to bring Gavril's attention back to the present. They'd met inside Gavril's private study. Once belonging to Arvil San Gerxon, Gavril had removed the garish and ostentatious from the spacious room, opting instead for the tasteful and understated.

"Gavril, we'll find Reah. She's turned up every time in the past—I don't believe this will be any different. Take pride in your accomplishments. You've formed an Alliance from nothing. And you've convinced Wylend to come aboard. The Reth Alliance courted him for centuries. This is no small accomplishment, son."

"I know, Uncle Erland. I was hoping that Reah would be with me tonight. At the ball."

"Wylend has scrapped the date for his marriage as well—since we can't say for certain when we'll find her. I can't believe the Wise Ones brought her back for nothing."

"Yeah. You're right," Gavril rubbed the back of his neck in a frustrated manner. How the hell could he apologize to Reah if he couldn't find her to offer the apology?

I waited two days before going to Falchan. In that time, I gathered enough gold coins from Beliphar's abandoned treasury to do for a bit and put a wardrobe together. I packed two sets of leathers I'd purchased, and the rest was plain but nice and would last. I couldn't predict how long I might stay, but I wanted to experience as much of Falchan as I could. With my large bag in hand, including my pilfered gold, I skipped to the world I'd dreamed about when I was a child.

The capital city of Cedar's Falls was lovely and crowded. The streets, still the same after centuries, were narrow and lined with carefully placed flat stones. Kiosks dotted the streets and alleys, competing with more permanent buildings lining the street. Everything drew my eye—red flags snapping in the afternoon breeze over a storefront, a rice wine bar called The Dragon's Breath had customers inside and out, while another shop sold jewelry. What pulled me was the ringing sound of a hammer on steel far down the way. Someone was crafting metal. I hoped they were making a sword. Hastily I jerked my rolling bag behind me as I walked in that direction.

"This is incredible," I breathed. An artisan was indeed fashioning a blade inside the dim smithy. Tools hung on walls, ready for use. The forge was in the center of the room and the sword maker had just taken the heated metal out to hammer. The blade was still in the rough stages of manufacture, and I understood that the steel would be folded and beaten, folded and beaten, many times before the craftsman would be satisfied. Then, the steel would be wrapped around a core of iron, forming the heart of the blade.

Sword making on Falchan was a highly respected art and the blades were quite expensive, taking months to create. I'd seen what Drake and Drew had, although theirs had been created by Grey House. Just as complicated a process was employed there, only at the end, one of Grey House's Master Wizards placed spells on the blades. The least expensive of those kept the blade sharp and prevented rust. Drake and Drew's held protection spells. Those spells protected the owners from harm in some way. I could never hope to afford even a knife from Grey House. It still angered me that Teeg kept the one that Great-Aunt Glinda had given me. I wanted it with me now.

"Does this fascinate you?" An assistant carried in a basket of charcoal for the fires.

"Yes," I stared at the traditional fold in his dark eyes, his black hair braided down his back and the leather apron he wore over loosely-woven black pants. He wore no shirt, revealing the tattoos of a wildcat of some sort, running up and down his arms. He had no chest or back tattoos—he hadn't earned them. On Falchan, every tattoo had to be earned. One did not go out to find an artist on a whim. Fathers usually approved their son's or daughter's first—after their child had passed their weapons classes or distinguished themselves in some way. After that, military commanders gave permission for tattoos as they were warranted. A chest or back tattoo, in old Falchani lore, denoted exemplary service in battle.

Once, as a special demonstration, Drake and Drew's father and uncle had sparred in full leathers for visiting dignitaries on Le-Ath Veronis. I'd stared, spellbound, as the two warriors went after each other, as if it were a dance. Drake and Drew, sitting next to me, had explained that any one of those blows would be deadly if the opponent weren't ready to block it. Dragon, his sons and his brother fought with two blades each. Not every warrior had that talent or ability.

"You're welcome to watch as long as you don't get in the way. Visiting?" The assistant eyed my bag.

"Yes. I've looked forward to this for a very long time."

"There's an inn just down the street," he jerked his head in the direction I'd come. I'd ignored what I walked past, once I heard the ringing of steel.

"I'll look into it." He'd known to speak common Alliance; I was an obvious outsider. I knew a few words in the Falchani language, but not enough to do anything other than embarrass myself.

I watched for nearly a click, but the folding and hammering was repetitive. I went looking for the inn. "One gold piece, one Eight-Day," I was told. I handed over a gold piece for a Falchani week. Meals served there cost extra and I could have paid for those in advance, but I wanted to taste what the streets had to offer instead of limiting myself. That's what took me out again, searching for food after hefting my bag onto the small bed inside the tiny but immaculate room.

Sliding onto a stool outside an open-air restaurant, I watched the proprietor make rice noodles. He flattened and steamed the rice mixture before brushing oil over it and placing another layer on top of the first. After steaming all of them, he set about cutting the noodles in thin, even strands. I'd done something similar with traditional pastas. At least they were traditional where I came from. The noodles went into a broth he'd prepared as it was ordered, cooked together for a short time and then served with a small spoon and a flourish.

"Do you have any chives, green onions or leeks?" I asked, gesturing over my bowl of noodles.

"Some here," he set a small bowl down next to me. I sprinkled the finely chopped green onions into my bowl and tasted the best rice noodles I'd ever eaten.

"This is exceptional," I said. The cook merely nodded, as if he got that compliment all the time. "How much to teach me how to make?" I asked.

"You want to learn?" He quirked a black eyebrow at me. The tattoos on his arms were falcons, their beaks open in silent screams as they prepared to strike an unseen enemy.

"Yes." I nodded enthusiastically at the cook's question.

"Finish dinner. Then learn."

"All right." I smiled for the first time in several days.

"Soak rice first. During night." I nodded as he drained rice with a bamboo colander. "Now, grind down fine." He showed me by grinding the rice against a stone slab, using another stone fashioned to fit both hands. He handed the stone to me; I set to grinding. He grunted in satisfaction—I'd done something similar before.

"Texture like this," he pinched some in his fingers, so I'd know what to look for. I nodded. We coated a flat pan with oil before spreading the first layer. He was surprised and pleased that I'd been watching him before. I did it exactly as he'd done. We ended up with usable noodles afterward. Then we turned to the broth. He made a quick version, but I asked him about making a reduction.

"You make, I taste," he smiled.

"All right." I went looking to see what spices he had while bits of beef cooked into a broth. Taking out the beef, I chopped it finely, appreciating the knives the cook had to work with. Adding the beef bits back to the broth, I threw in several spices and let it simmer. While we waited, we made two more batches of noodles. He introduced himself, too—his name was Flyer. No surprise—he did have bird tattoos.

"Reah?" He rolled the sound of my name on his tongue.

"Yes. Or Re, if you prefer." I sliced more noodles under his watchful gaze, and even put a bowl together for a customer who walked up. Flyer collected the money while I offered green onions. We served a crowd after that, and I put my broth to the test.

"You try, no charge," Flyer apparently knew this customer. He smiled and nodded as I placed the bowl in front of him, using my broth and the noodles we'd made.

"Mmm. Mmmmm. Yes. Flyer, this your best ever," the customer was eating quickly. Flyer was now studying me carefully.

"Where you learn to cook?" he asked.

"My family owned restaurants," I told him the truth. "I've just never made rice noodles before."

"You like job?" he asked. "Last helper go off to army."

"Maybe," I smiled at Flyer.

That's how I ended up working a food stall with Flyer. He was older—nearing one hundred eighty turns. Gray was finding its way into his hair, and while he was normally busy, we were even more so when I showed him how to take good chunks of beef, braise it and slice it thin as a whisper before dripping sauce over it. We served that with a bowl of noodles for an additional charge. People would line up during mealtimes just to get that.

Since Flyer's business was a permanent building, he lived in an apartment above the restaurant. Normally he kept the inside portion closed during spring and summer months, but we opened it up when business threatened to block the narrow street outside. My only complaint was that we had to deal solely with river-caught fish—there was no ocean nearby and Falchan still relied mostly on ground transportation. I would see the occasional horse and rider go past the restaurant. Still, the river fish was good—I designed a special sauce for it with the available ingredients, along with a light, fish stew.

"I not like fish much before," Flyer said.

"It has to be cooked right away," I said. They also didn't have much in the way of refrigeration. Flour was also difficult to come by—it was grown on plains far from Cedar's Falls. Flyer said that we might get some at a good price when the harvest started. I nodded my understanding—flour was a precious commodity on Falchan.

~

Two months went by and I found I was happy. It was a pleasure to wake inside my tiny bedroom that Flyer had cleared out for me over his restaurant. The room was included as part of my pay, he said. He was also fascinated by the fact that I never needed a bathroom. "Some races are like this," I explained. He nodded. Flyer was a wise man, I decided. Had seen much of life and it gave him a patient perspective.

The late summer afternoon was winding down and Flyer and I were preparing pans of noodles when we heard screams outside and then a shadow darkened the street.

"What the fuck," I muttered, setting my pan of noodles on the counter and rushing out the door. What I saw infuriated me.

"No," Flyer whispered right beside me. A huge pirate ship floated overhead. Right then, I was thankful it was only one.

"Flyer, if I don't come back, I loved working with you." I kissed him hastily on the cheek and skipped away right in front of his eyes.

This was a first—skipping inside a moving vehicle. It turned out to be a simple thing. Pirates, if they are unprepared, are easily taken down. There had to be around a hundred or so and they were concentrating on powering up the Ranos cannon, readying their ship to take Falchan away from its people. I could only change to my smaller Thifilatha—the ship's ceilings were too low to do anything else. They thought to attack me by hand.

That, of course, was a mistake. If they touched me, they burned. Burned as if acid had been poured on their skin. I watched their flesh melt with satisfaction. Greed and subjugation were their only goals; I was showing them how to die instead. When they ran before me, after I'd smashed the console controlling the Ranos cannon, I chased or skipped after them. In half a click or less, all were dead. Now, I faced the problem of a floating, directionless ship that hovered over Falchan.

In all the vids I'd seen, the ship always had some sort of self-destruct that the hero employed to get rid of the nuisance. This had no such thing. Now what? I had none of Lissa's ability to turn the thing to mist and destroy it in that way. What could I do? The people below were likely still screaming and frightened. Therefore, I did the only thing I could think of.

Dragon? The former Warlord had never gotten mindspeech from me. Probably didn't know I had it. Hoping he wasn't engaged in something important, I'd decided to contact him. If he couldn't help, perhaps he could tell me what to do instead.

Reah, I never thought to hear from you. Many search for you—where are you?

On a pirate ship floating over Falchan, I replied. *I killed the pirates, now I don't know what to do with the ship.*

A comforting mental chuckle came through, making me sigh and relax my shoulders. I hadn't been sure of a welcome, or if he'd respond at all. He was beside me in moments.

"Change back, I'll get us off and then send it far enough away that they won't see when I destroy it," he grinned. He *Pulled* clothing from somewhere so I could dress quickly, then folded us to the ground. I watched, standing beside the First among the Saa Thalarr, while the ship disappeared. "It's dust now," Dragon looked down at me and smiled.

"Reah?" Flyer came up beside me. "What you are, Reah?" Flyer looked worried.

"She's High Demon, sir cook," Dragon said in Falchani. I understood that much, at least. "Reah killed your attackers. Those won't bother you again."

"You look familiar," Flyer squinted at Dragon.

"The Dragon Warlord, at your service," Dragon inclined his head and disappeared.

"Flyer, do not have a heart attack," I said as he clutched his chest. As it turned out, that wasn't why he gripped the front of his shirt.

"The Dragon Warlord," Flyer said reverently.

"Absolutely," I sighed. "Never mind that Falchan just got saved by a High Demon; *that* was the Dragon Warlord." I took Flyer's arm and steered him toward his shop.

~

"Reah, where you go?" Flyer watched as I packed my bag.

"Flyer, I hate to leave, but you will likely have about a dozen visitors in very little time. All looking for me. No, I'm not a criminal," I held out a hand at his worried expression. "I have mates, I guess. And they tend to show up if they know where I am. Just feed them a bowl of noodles and charge them double." Bag in hand, I kissed Flyer's cheek for the second time that day and skipped away from Falchan.

~

"Are you kidding?" Gavril got the news from Drew. "Your father saw her there?"

"She killed a ship full of pirates who were armed with a Ranos cannon. Dad can't lie, you know. Well, neither can we." Drew grinned. "Dad got rid of the ship for her—she didn't know what to do with it afterward."

"What the fuck is going on?" Lendill and Norian appeared. Norian could fold, Lendill couldn't. Lendill had dragged the Director along for that reason. Drew was forced to tell the story a second time.

~

"I have the information from Drake," Erland brought the news to Wylend.

"She was on Falchan? All this time?"

"She healed Thiskil's core early on, but you already knew about that. She was working in one of those noodle shops that are all over Falchan's capital city."

"Then let's go. We'll see if she's still there." Wylend's face held determination, so Erland didn't try to deflect the King of Karathia.

⁓

Flyer wasn't surprised when eight men showed up at his shop, all looking angry and out of sorts.

"Reah said you might come," Flyer nodded at Wylend, Erland, Gavril, Dee, Tory, Aurelius, Lendill and Norian. "She said to serve you noodles and charge you double."

"She's not here, is she?" Tory said. He was the tallest of all those assembled, standing nearly seven feet in height.

"No. She disappear. Poof." Flyer flicked his fingers.

"Figures." Lendill muttered angrily.

"Did she say where she was going?" Gavril asked.

"No." Flyer shook his head. "Best cook. Crowd get angry now. I lose same as child."

"Farzi and Nenzi will go crazy," Gavril sighed.

"Are we going to have noodles?" Dee asked. All eight of them took a seat at the counter while Flyer served bowls of noodles.

⁓

"Hello, Nefrigar." He'd appeared like magic shortly after I skipped to Beliphar.

"Greetings, Reah. It was a good time to visit Falchan, was it not?" The skin around his bright-blue eyes crinkled as he smiled at me.

"Yeah. I just can't go back or the horde will find me for sure."

"If that is your choice," he lifted a vase from the bedside table and examined it carefully—it was crystal of some sort and likely worth a lot. Just about everything was that remained inside the deserted palace.

"Are you hungry? You must be after eliminating the pirates."

"A little." I'd gotten used to regular meals, living with Flyer.

"Then come." Nefrigar folded us away.

When I complained that I wasn't dressed properly to go inside the restaurant—I had no idea where we were, after all—Nefrigar used power to dress me. "This is nice," the tunic was purple silk with embroidery at hem and cuff, the loose pants matching. Silver shoes, matching the embroidery, peeked from beneath my pants.

"Would you like jewelry?" Nefrigar smiled.

"That's all right, but thank you for the thought," I said. My nose was pulling me inside the restaurant—good smells of baking bread lured me along. I hadn't had good bread while on Falchan.

Nefrigar didn't order—Larentii fed on sunlight. Instead, he watched, somewhat amused, as I ate veal in wine sauce and several pieces of bread. "I'm too full to move," I sighed, refusing dessert. Strangely enough, Nefrigar paid for my meal. He handed over a credit chip. Where do Larentii get credit chips? Do they manufacture them with their power? I thought about asking, but since I didn't really know Nefrigar, I held the question back.

"Bardelus is a good place to visit right now," he said after taking me back to Beliphar.

"Bardelus? Why Bardelus?" They weren't part of the Alliance, either. Neither Reth nor Campiaan.

"Little one, perhaps you should broaden your horizons," Nefrigar smiled and disappeared.

I dithered for two days, then, worried that I might be missing something, I gathered the gold I hadn't spent on Falchan and skipped to Bardelus.

CHAPTER 3

*A*lliance common was spoken for the most part, but in certain portions of Grithis, a city surrounded by forests and farmland on Bardelus, there were ethnic communities where other languages abounded. Purchasing a comp-vid first thing, I set about navigating my way through the city. Gold was accepted everywhere. They'd tried to put their own version of the credit chip in place, but since they were non-Alliance, it fell through.

My first thought was to find a place to stay. Going through advertisements for hotels and inns, I discovered that businesses weren't held to any sort of standard. A photograph on the comp-vid might be very different from the reality. I discovered that from the first three inns I visited, none of which resembled the images on the comp-vid. I'd chosen them because they seemed reasonable in price. I was learning my lesson quickly—Bardelans were notorious liars and they expected to haggle over everything.

"I refuse to pay your price," a customer pounded his fist on the clerk's desk in the fourth inn I visited. The desk shook precariously while a small cloud of dust rose from the filthy counter.

"Seventy-five, then," the clerk countered, giving a price five silvers less than previously mentioned.

"Seventy," the thick-fisted customer pounded again. I wondered if dust and rat droppings would sift down from the ceiling. They did. "And you agree to clean my room."

"No. Room cleaning is a separate charge," the clerk sniffed. At that moment, I was hoping he might inhale some of the dust. He did, sneezing four or five times in rapid succession.

"Seventy, and you clean my room," the customer snapped, raising his fist.

"All right, seventy with room cleaning," the clerk jerked his hand out, catching the customer's fist.

"I'll stay for free, if you allow me to clean the rooms and this pig-sty you call a reception area," I offered. Both the clerk and the customer turned to look at me, complete shock on their faces.

"This is not a pig-sty," the clerk huffed, offended.

"No? See this?" I pointed, I wasn't about to put my finger in it. "Rat droppings. You have rats. Do your customers know this?"

"You have rats?" The customer was now swearing and about to pound the desk again.

"Sixty, and your room cleaned," the clerk whined.

"Sixty and she cleans the rooms," the customer jerked his head toward me.

"And I stay for free in exchange for the cleaning," I added.

"All right." The clerk went to find keys, muttering under his breath the entire time.

"Very nice, I wouldn't have thought to throw in rat droppings," the heavy-handed customer smiled as we walked toward the stairs. No elevator here, unfortunately. I not only had my key but a master and information that I shouldn't go into any room before nine bells and the cleaning supplies and equipment were in a janitor's closet on the first floor.

"When would you like your room cleaned?" I asked the man. He was well dressed, with reddish-brown hair that was a bit long and curling around his ears. He was also dressed better than most I'd seen in this section of the city, in a matching jacket and pants in dark brown over a tan shirt. No ties or other neckwear were worn on

Bardelus. I got the idea it was just too formal for their way of thinking.

"I'll be going out every morning by seven bells. Any time after that will be fine." He had light-brown eyes, lips that might smile now and then if he allowed it and the nose of an aristocrat. Wondering what brought him to this inn, I nodded as he opened the door to his room. Mine was farther down on the opposite side. I was surprised that my room was as clean as it was when I walked into it.

Getting rid of the rats and vermin was my first objective—I'd learned a trick during my tenure with the ASD. When I went Thifilatha, small or large, I frightened small animals and insects. Any insect thinking to get close to my gold scales was burned. They stayed away. Same thing with rats, mice and other vermin. I'd once chased a criminal through rat-infested sewers while in my smaller Thifilatha. The rats were running before me. They helped bring the culprit down —they were knocking him over after a while and racing across his back in their efforts to escape what they saw as a larger predator—me.

Skipping into the dark, cluttered and stinking attic later, I turned to my smaller Thifilatha. You should have heard the squeaking and shrieking as tiny feet scrabbled across boards and stored items, making a hasty retreat from the worst danger they'd ever smelled in their short lives. I have no idea where they went and I had no care to know—I just knew they wouldn't be back until I moved out. This boded well for the restaurant downstairs—I saw it was closed on my way in.

Skipping back to my room, I went to check out the bathroom. I wasn't satisfied with the cleanliness of it, so I went in search of cleaning supplies. Except for the cracked and peeling floor tiles, it was as clean as I could make it when I finished.

Then I skipped into the closed restaurant. I found the reason for the closure—the clerk knew very well they had rats—the writ of closure was lying on the bar, citing vermin and unsanitary facilities as the reasons. It gave three moon-turns for the problems to be addressed before the license reapplication process would be forced. A moon-turn remained before it was completely condemned and additional fees would have to be paid to apply for a license from scratch. Squaring my shoulders, I began to clean. Now that the rats were gone, things should be simple.

~

"Edan, I am giving a small salary increase," Addah said, pushing a comp-vid across his desk toward his second-born. "Your pastry is quite good and your salads please the guests."

"Thank you," Edan ducked his head respectfully. The salary increase worried Edan, though. What might Aldah do if he learned of it? Was this just a game Addah played, attempting to pit his children against one another? Edan had checked employment listings only that morning—a new restaurant was opening and every shift and position was available. He intended to apply on his afternoon break.

~

"You want what?" The desk clerk, whom I learned was also the owner, stared at me in shock.

"Only a few fittings and fixtures. It should be inexpensive—I can do the work. The rest of the restaurant is clean."

"But I will have to call the inspectors and hire a cook."

"You have a cook," I said. "You only need two assistants."

"You—cook?" The man almost hooted. Briefly, I considered slapping him before coming to my senses.

"It costs nothing to bring the inspector back. All we have to do is repair the sink."

"Fine. Repair the sink. Then prepare a meal for me. I will decide if you can cook." The man was short, although taller than I, with graying dark hair, a thin moustache and narrow brown eyes. He looked much like the rats I'd chased from his inn.

Good, inexpensive fare was my goal—the inn didn't draw the customer base to support expensive dishes. I used fowl, pork and beef to prepare three dishes. I'd spent my own money on the meat, too. Rat-face, whose name was Neidles, approached the food with trepidation, although his nose might have twitched a time or two. He tasted the pork dish first. I'd wrapped the loin around a stuffing and then surrounded that with a crust before baking. It was moist, succulent and exactly the kind of fare that would appeal to the locals.

Neidles didn't say anything, chewing and swallowing before going to the fowl. The fowl was prepared with a simple sauce and potatoes on the side. It would go well with a good green salad, but I didn't want to push it. The beef I'd sliced thin, breaded and quick-fried before sliding the medallions over a light sauce. All dishes were inexpensive to make. Neidles paused to go back and take a second bite of the pork dish, then back to the chicken before moving on to the beef. I think his knees gave way on the beef dish. He was moaning in pleasure by that time.

"Will you call the inspector?" I asked.

He couldn't speak, his mouth was full. He nodded enthusiastically instead.

"Good. Let me know when you're done; I'll clean up and we'll discuss assistants."

Three six-days later, we were open for business. The inn's guests were the first to arrive—they could smell the food on their way in and out. Once they got a taste, word spread quickly. I had two assistants, Harne and Nari, who thought to be lazy at first. I disabused them of that notion.

"You will not leave a mess," I snapped at Harne. "Laziness will not feed your customers or keep a kitchen clean. The inspector passed us, but he will be back, you can place money on that bet," I untied his apron. "Change your apron daily. More often if it becomes soiled. You lure your customers with your sanitary practices as well as the taste of your food. We will have both in this kitchen."

Nari was better. She watched me closely whenever I prepared anything, then did her best to copy it. Harne, after learning we would not tolerate his reluctance to work, (and after I threatened to let him go) poured himself into the work. He cleaned. He chopped and sliced.

He stirred, sifted and rolled. And once he'd gotten a taste of the pastry, he focused on that.

Neidles had to hire additional help after another three six-days. And that's when I started seeing reports of missing children. Mostly it was young girls, ages nine to seventeen, but occasional boys would disappear, ages twelve to twenty. Grithis was a large city, boasting more than seven million in the city and surrounding boroughs. A missing child here or there was to be expected, but these were disappearing frequently in twos and threes. Children who went out to play together never returned. I became worried when the numbers neared fifty. Someone or something was preying on the children of Grithis.

Neidles came in on off-day, which was First-Day for all of us. I intended to do a bit of sleuthing into the mystery of missing children. Neidles wanted to make sure he was wringing as much of a percentage from the wait staff as he could.

"Neidles, you employed them, you go over the figures with them," I snapped when he hauled out his comp-vid to go over all four employees' tip records. He backed away from me; I had no patience with him right then.

"I can fire you," he said.

"Go ahead. Find someone else who'll cook and clean for a pittance." I was making little from working as a master cook in his small restaurant. I controlled the recipes. I oversaw the purchases of meat and vegetables. All the receipts and records were dutifully turned over to Neidles at the end of every six-day. "I'll go get my things now. I'm sure someone else will hire me and I won't have to clean," I shot over my shoulder as I walked out.

"No, no, you do not have to clean now," he was beside me suddenly. "I will hire someone else."

"Good. I have plans for today," I said, trying to walk away from him.

"With a man?" He sounded petulant.

"No. I intend to enjoy the day," I said and left him standing in the entryway. I'd cleaned that, too, found a rug in the attic to put along with other, small bric-a-brac to dress up the place. Neidles only had to count the money. His inn was filling up more often than not, after my arrival. If he'd pay to have new tile laid in his bathrooms, it would be even better. I didn't mind the work, but it was becoming overwhelming with the demands of the kitchen. At least it helped take my mind off the troubles I'd left behind. I was too tired to let my thoughts chase each other at night, now.

I found two things when I did my sleuthing—one, the places where the children were disappearing weren't far from the inn, and two, the heavy-fisted guest was there ahead of me, poking around.

"I'm surprised to see you here," he said as I stared at the small alley where three eleven-year-old girls had disappeared.

"Same here," I nodded.

"You're not from here, are you?" he asked.

"No."

"Where from, then?"

"I was born on Tulgalan," I replied. I didn't see that it hurt anything.

"Before you accuse me of having anything to do with those disappearances, they started before I arrived; the local officials were afraid to report it. Now, rumors are flying so they have to give out the numbers," heavy fist said.

"Why would they do that?" I asked quizzically, staring into his light-brown eyes.

"Grithis is a commonwealth and not under the Prime Minister's thumb. There are six commonwealths left on Bardelus, running their own private government. Like a separate country, you might say. Grithis has been corrupt for a very long time. You saw the state of the inn when we moved in. I thank you for the cleaning and the food in the restaurant. I haven't eaten that well in a very long time. Plovel," he held out his hand as he introduced himself.

"Reah," I couldn't help smiling as I took his hand.

"Well, Reah, I would very much like to get to the root of these disappearances, but I keep running into tall and sturdy walls."

"It worries me," I said. "Do you think it is slavery or sex rings taking them? Have any traces been found at all?"

"Not much," he replied. "Come over here. The locals botched the scene when they investigated. If you can call what they did an investigation," Plovel muttered. He was right—they'd walked right through the area numerous times, destroying any evidence that might be had. The crime scene was next to a brick building that showed signs of aging. Mortar was missing between bricks. I knelt to examine a brick that appeared loose. It came out in my hand.

"What have we here?" Plovel knelt next to me and peered inside the hole. A tiny doll, a child's cheap metal ring and string jewelry were all inside.

"This was their hiding place," I sighed. The neighborhood was poor and indicative of the toys the girls left behind. "Did anybody see anything?"

"A woman across the street says she saw four girls playing here before the disappearances were reported, but we've determined she was mistaken—only three were taken."

"Did she give descriptions?" I asked.

"I have those in my room," Plovel said. "It sounds as if you've done this sort of thing before."

"I may have, once," I hedged. Plovel would probably know it anyway. He seemed quite shrewd. "Who sent you?" I asked.

"I work in a special unit for the Prime Minister. The same thing happened in two other commonwealths before hitting this one. The PM wants this investigated and the perpetrators stopped before they attack United Bardelus."

"I see," I nodded. "I'd like to get this finished as well—I don't like children disappearing."

"Perhaps we can combine our forces?" He smiled as he offered to work with me.

"Perhaps. I'll certainly share information if I get any. In the meantime, I think Neidles is becoming jealous. Probably not a good idea to allow him to see us talking."

"I wouldn't suggest it anyway. We can have general conversations in the restaurant. I can send anything else by comp-vid."

"Good." I passed my ID number off to him, and he gave his. It was a relief to have someone else working on this, as it seemed a bit overwhelming. I did plan to skip into the local constabulary, however, just to see if I could access the records they had.

~

"Why are you doing this in the dark?" Nefrigar appeared beside me, scaring me witless as I scanned record after record of child disappearances at the local constabulary, downloading them into my comp-vid.

"Nefrigar, what are you doing here?" I hissed. He smiled, his blue eyes almost glowing in the semidarkness.

"I came to see if you wanted anything."

"Honey blue, I wish I could do this faster," I muttered. "I don't want to come back here if I can help it, and those fool guards outside could come in to piss anytime."

"Did you just call me honey blue?" That amused him, I think.

"Honey blue, I called you honey blue. Now stop talking so I can think." I rubbed my forehead in frustration.

"Here." He tapped my comp-vid with a finger, downloading everything in a blink. I stared at him in shock. "You asked. I gave," he was smiling again.

"Thank you," I whispered in reverent awe. Larentii ability was worthy of anyone's amazement.

"I'll fold you to your room, you don't have to skip," he said, and took us both.

~

"Yes, I do have a criminal record, but that is behind me. My incarceration information is included," Edan tapped the business manager's comp-vid.

"You've worked for Desh's number one for the past four months?"

"Yes. That information is also included and verified with pay records."

"You're Edan Desh. The one who used to win the awards."

"Yes, but my staff had a great deal to do with that," Edan said. "And now my cooking skills are somewhat rusty after five years of being away from the kitchens."

"I understand. I have a spot for an assistant cook. If you want it, you will start in an Eight-Day unless you need longer to give notice."

"No, I will be expected to leave as soon as my notice is given," Edan said. "I will be ready to go to work when you say."

Edan turned in his notice that afternoon. Just as expected, Addah ordered him to gather his things and leave the restaurant. He threatened Edan, too, just as Edan threatened Reah years ago. Vague memories of what the other Edan had done shamed him and gave him nightmares.

Ilvan was weary of going through restaurant kitchens, searching for code violations, all while smelling food cooking on the stove and watching others prepare it. His fingers itched at times to move someone aside and take over. Especially if he found them doing something wrong. A new restaurant was opening and he was interested. His interview was scheduled for the following day. Ilvan had more lift in his step as he walked to work.

"She's torturing us. That's what she's doing," Gavril grumbled, going over records with Dee.

"Focus, child. We have the trials for the Strands tomorrow."

"I know. Do you think anyone will come forward? We've tripled the guard around them."

"Perhaps you should ask your brothers to come. I can't imagine anyone getting past them."

"I hate to do that. It shouldn't be necessary."

"Your choice."

~

Plovel, if you don't ask how I purloined these records, I will not be obligated to answer, I sent the message on my comp-vid, along with copies of the records I'd filched the night before. Security was much too lax in Grithis. The city was ancient and beautiful, but it was falling to ruin around its citizens. All taxes gathered were lining corrupt officials' pockets—I could see it clearly.

Greed abounded among business owners and commonwealth officials alike. If Neidles became any greedier, he would burst with it, I think. I had to show him the difference between a bad cut of meat and an acceptable one before he slashed my food budget. The farmers and ranchers came in two days per six-day to sell their goods, and I preferred to buy directly from them.

They weren't much better off than the commoners walking the streets, trying to stretch insufficient paychecks to feed their children. And children were still disappearing. Plovel and I were going through record after record, trying to make sense of all of it. Poor research and botched forensics only hampered our investigation.

~

"Neidles, now is not a good time," I muttered when he appeared in the restaurant, asking yet again about the cost of the meat I'd purchased. "Do you want this restaurant to stay open? Already you charge more than is needful. The customers only return because the food is good."

"Supply and demand," Neidles pointed out. I wanted to shove a copy of the Alliance regulations in front of him, showing that it was illegal there to price gouge. To Neidles, gouging was a high art and one at which he excelled. If I were a true commoner living in Grithis, I would be planning my move to United Bardelus immediately.

"What are your plans for tomorrow?" Neidles ignored my frown.

"I intend to sleep late, then do my laundry. Wash my hair. Off-day is the only day I have to do those things."

"You wouldn't consider coming out with me?" He smiled slyly, pulling at the neck strap of my apron suggestively.

"I am very sorry, but I came to Grithis to get away from my mates. I am not looking to replace them," I snapped, my voice harsher than I'd intended. Neidles jerked his hand away as if he'd been burned.

"I will make you want to go out with me," he huffed and stalked away.

"I'd like to see you try," I muttered.

~

"If Neidles knew you were here, he'd throw both of us out," I said, offering a sandwich to Plovel. He was poring over his comp-vid while I did the same inside my room. It was past midnight and we were both exhausted.

"Reah, you make the best food," Plovel smiled tiredly. "If I weren't married, I'd ask you out."

"If I didn't have mates, I might consider it," I said. "Besides, we're not right for each other. I enjoy working with you, though."

"Exactly what I was thinking," he grinned. He needed a wife willing to stay at home with his children. Slightly plump, I imagined, and smiling easily. He didn't need a scarred and wounded High Demon mate.

"We're missing something here, I just don't know what it is," I grumbled.

"You're tired. You worked all day. Let's call it a night and start fresh in the morning."

"All right." I nodded. Plovel sneaked away after making sure nobody was watching. It wouldn't do to cause a scene with Neidles.

"Ilvan Desh?" The business manager lifted an eyebrow.

"Yes. I worked at Desh's number two before working as a restaurant inspector here in Targis."

"Ah. It says here your specialty is pastry and desserts?"

"I can make other things as well. These I would qualify as a master in."

"Very well. You start in an Eight-Day. Is that sufficient time to give notice?"

"Yes. It is all that is required by law." Ilvan nodded, rose, took the offered hand and walked out of the restaurant. The building was nearly finished and the sign, proclaiming it Dee's Restaurant was being hung as Ilvan walked out the door.

Lersen Strand still had friends. He'd provided for them in the past, now they were returning the favor. Something was in the works, Lersen knew. Mental messages had been passed to him although they seemed garbled—he couldn't send and could barely receive, though the sending was quite strong. The mindspeech messages had come at the direction of Hendars Klar, an old friend of Lersen's father, when the old man still lived. Lersen imagined that Hendars might withhold assistance if he knew Lersen had arranged his own father's death. Lersen sighed and hunched his shoulders at the thought of his father's murder—there was no need for his involvement in that crime to be revealed unless it benefitted him in some way.

Meanwhile, Hendars had found formidable allies somewhere, and the plan was to send in a team powerful enough to collect Lersen and his cousins before the trials started. At least that's what Lersen understood from distorted mindspeech. Rumor had it that Teeg San Gerxon could understand mindspeech perfectly and could send and receive. Lersen didn't believe it. Teeg San Gerxon wasn't any better than Lersen Strand. Lersen still wanted Campiaa, but he might have to settle for putting his own alliance together. Hendars was on Bardelus as near as he could tell, and the rescue would likely be launched from there. Lersen settled back on the narrow cot inside his cell, impatiently waiting for his rescuers to arrive.

~

"Remember when you told me that a witness saw a fourth child when the three came up missing?" Plovel and I were at it again, cups of strong tea and coffee at our elbows as we read through records.

"I remember," he nodded.

"Here's another one," I said, handing my comp-vid over. "This one said he saw three children playing, when only two disappeared."

"I wish we had a better way of correlating this gibberish," Plovel grumped, taking my comp-vid away and staring at the information.

"Yeah. If I had ASD equipment and the records had been filed correctly to begin with, I'd have this done in three ticks." I looked up to find Plovel staring at me, his mouth open.

"I'm former," I muttered.

"You used to work for the bloody ASD?"

"Yes, and bloody is an apt description," I sighed.

"They kicked you out?"

"No. They'd love it if I signed up for another stint."

"Why are you here again?"

"Well, I was upset with the King of Karathia. After I was upset with Norian Keef. After I was upset with Teeg San Gerxon. After I was upset with Torevik Rath, Lendill Schaff—I guess that's all of them. I'm not upset with Aurelius."

"You just named the Director and Vice-Director of the ASD."

"Yeah. But I'm only married to one of them. Inadvertently, of course."

"You know, I'm not even going to ask which one. And the King of Karathia?"

"I was only engaged to him. That may be off, now."

"Teeg San Gerxon?"

"Also married to him. Inadvertently, of course."

"All right." Plovel breathed a calming sigh. "Shall we get back to it?" We both started reading records of child disappearances again.

~

"We're quite happy with your progress, Lok. You may be sent out soon on an assignment, just to see how it goes," Lendill nodded to his newest and best Falchani recruit.

"Good." Lok seldom smiled—Lendill was getting used to that.

~

"Reah, I know your comp-vid came from here and it has a blocking chip in it—the local government doesn't want the people to get feeds from United Bardelus or anywhere else, for that matter. Since you mentioned Teeg San Gerxon earlier, I thought you might be interested in this." He handed his comp-vid over. I stared at the headline for the longest time.

"The Strands escaped?" I think my voice squeaked, I was so shocked.

"Yes. It says here that several were killed when the Strands managed to break out of their prison. With help, obviously."

"Does it say who got killed?" My heart was suddenly doing triple time.

"It doesn't mention names—it just says six. Probably guards and such."

"May I use this?" I didn't wait for permission, I was busily clicking keys, working my way through password after password to get into ASD files. Lendill hadn't locked me out. Yet.

"Here it is," I whispered, scanning the list of names. I breathed the biggest sigh of relief—I hadn't recognized any of them. I'd been terrified that I'd find the reptanoids listed. That would break my heart.

"Nobody you know?"

"No." My heart was stuttering toward a more normal rhythm. I erased the information and handed the comp-vid back to Plovel. "So the local government is looking to control their masses by preventing them from seeing that life elsewhere might be much better?"

"The news vids tell them lies—that life is actually worse in other regions. If Bardelus has a sphincter, Grithis is it."

I hadn't bothered to watch any news vids except those regarding missing children. I was going to pay more attention from now on.

"Somehow, they managed to find the locating chip we planted and deactivated it, but that was after they found their way into this sector," Gavril pointed to the spot on the map. He'd worked this out in advance with Norian and Lendill. They suspected that others might be involved, but even Gavril's compulsion hadn't been able to penetrate the elusive information in Lersen Strand's mind before he'd escaped. Something very powerful had blocked it.

"What's there?" Norian studied the map.

"Hilfri and Bardelus," Lendill said.

"I saw a kid crying in the park on Clover Street," Harne walked into the restaurant yawning. He had a new girlfriend and stayed up late the night before. Figures.

"What was the problem—was he lost?" I asked, ignoring the yawn and the reason behind it.

"No—his mother was with him, taking him to school. He said he didn't want to go by the playground. He said there were ghosts there."

"Ghosts? Really? That's odd," I said. The few times I'd been by the playground, it was usually full, with mothers more watchful now than at other times. The playground seemed a safer place than letting the children run in the streets.

"I couldn't figure it out, either," Harne shrugged and went to get eggs out of the cold-keeper.

"Have any children been snatched from the playground on Clover Street?" I asked Plovel later as he ate his breakfast. I'd pulled the pot of coffee and went to refill his cup myself.

"None that I've run across," he buttered his breakfast roll before spreading it liberally with fresh-made jam.

"Harne said he saw a child crying as he went past it this morning. The child was telling his mother that the playground was haunted."

"That's strange—that playground is generally full when school is out."

"I know."

"I'll go by there today and look around," he said.

"Good. Let me know if you find anything." He nodded, so I took the coffeepot and freshened up other customers' cups as well. Never hurt to play it safe, by paying attention to all the customers as equally as I could. I was trusting Neidles less and less as time went on, and I'd never trusted him from the beginning.

CHAPTER 4

"There's trouble in Grithis." Lendill passed the comp-vid to Gavril.

"Children disappearing? You think that sounds like Lersen Strand?"

"We don't know who he's allied himself with. How can we know what to expect from them? I'm assuming he's still with his rescuers, anyway."

"He has to be—can't see the Strands doing anything else besides cozying up with other criminals."

"I still don't understand how you didn't get some of this information out of the Strands. I thought your compulsion could cut through steel."

Gavril laughed. A hollow laugh. "Too bad that doesn't work very well on Reah."

"You wouldn't try, surely."

"No, but I've thought about it."

"My father says it's next to impossible for Reah to trust. He says it was beaten out of her as a child. That fucker had twenty-six other children, and not one of them stood up for her. Six other wives and not one thought

50

to take in the orphan. Monsters walk in daylight, Gavril Tybus Montegue. Every single day." Lendill tossed his comp-vid onto Gavril's cluttered desk. Normally it was tidy and neat—now, it was littered with comp-vids.

"Reah trusts the reptanoids."

"She loves them better than anyone else, I think," Lendill sighed.

"And they've been going crazy since she disappeared. If I hadn't sent them to Birimera for a change of scenery and to check on the crops, they might have gone down with the others. I could've had them down there, guarding the Strands when they were sprung."

"We couldn't predict that," Lendill pointed out. He'd lost three of his, Gavril had lost the other three. The Strands were wanted in the Reth Alliance just as much as the Campiaan Alliance. They were now free again and likely plotting revenge somewhere with who knew what sort of criminal element. Lendill figured they'd fled to either Hilfri or Bardelus, and his money was on Bardelus.

"Where should we start looking?" Gavril said, turning toward the wide window behind his desk. It looked over the well-kept grounds of the San Gerxon estate.

"I'm for going to Bardelus. There are six boroughs there that aren't part of United Bardelus. Each borough is a law unto itself, with Grithis being the worst. Greed, kickbacks, payoffs, bribery, you name it, it's happening there. Prime territory for the Strands, don't you think? The child disappearances are just an added worry."

"How many children?"

"Hundreds. At least that's what my operatives are picking up from the secure transmissions. Could be more—it's hard to track that sort of thing."

"What's the population of Grithis?"

"Around seven million. Plenty of people to prey on."

"Could be a slavery ring. Is it mostly girls?"

"Mostly. With a few boys here and there."

"Sex rings, then."

"Could be. That's the common thought running through the ASD. We're keeping an eye on it, in case it filters into the Alliance."

"Dee!" Gavril shouted. Dee stood in the doorway in less than a blink.

❧

"I sat on a bench in the park and watched the children this afternoon," Plovel said as he ate a late supper. "Used amps to listen to conversations."

I nodded. Amps were tiny sound enhancers utilized by spies everywhere. You could pick up a conversation from quite a distance. "Hear anything?" I asked.

"A group of little girls saying that a friend heard crying. Of course, that could be rumor. You understand how that sort of thing gets around. The scare factor." Plovel shook his head. "Did you know there used to be a building on that site? One of the mothers told me. It makes sense—the park is the right size for a building there and it lines up with warehouses on either side."

"Honestly, I hadn't thought that much about it until Harne came in with his story this morning. Now we have ghosts and crying children. This is crazy." I walked away from Plovel's seat at the counter when I heard Neidles' footsteps outside the restaurant.

"Reah, how are you?" Neidles seated himself two stools down from Plovel.

"Good," I said. "Are you hungry?"

"Yes. What do we have tonight?" I passed a menu over that listed the day's specials.

"You made beef in wine sauce?" Neidles lifted an eyebrow, no doubt calculating the cost of the wine in his head.

"It only took four bottles and it was inexpensive," I sighed. "Is that what you want?"

"Yes." I went to put a plate together for him. I served it with rice since potatoes were more expensive than the dried grain. It irked me that Neidles thought constantly of the bottom line instead of the quality of the food served.

"This is good," Neidles shoved food in his mouth. He had the manners of a Harlooni pig. I didn't let him see when I rolled my eyes.

"Reah, you may leave work early if you'd like to come walking with me," Neidles gave his mouth a perfunctory swipe before grinning at me. I wanted to cringe.

"While that sounds tempting, I have to put the marinade together for tomorrow's fowl dish," I said. Neidles left shortly after.

"Are we having fowl marinated in something for tomorrow?" Plovel chuckled and pushed his plate over.

"We are now," I muttered.

"Do you mean to tell me that my son is cooking for the Queen of Le-Ath Veronis?" Garek stared at Erland Morphis.

"Yes. I mean to tell you that and yes, your son is cooking for the Queen. My mate." Erland grinned. The grin alone could stop traffic at nearly any intersection.

"Well, at least I know where he is, now. I'm sure he did that because his mother insulted her. The Queen. Your mate." Garek glared at Erland.

"Keetha insulted Lissa?" Erland raised an eyebrow.

"Keetha insults everybody. I've learned to accept her criticism as a compliment."

"And what does she say about me?" Erland asked.

"That you're ugly." Erland laughed so hard he snorted. Garek laughed, too, and slapped Erland on the back.

"Any word on Reah?" Wylend walked in.

"Nothing, love." Erland pulled Wylend's head to his shoulder. "But we're still looking."

"I think about Reah every time I make this," Ilvan dipped into his fish stew. Once he'd learned that he and Edan would be working together, they'd formed a truce of some kind, and even had good conversations. Few of those conversations involved their shared past. Ilvan was surprised that Edan was so patient now. Something had changed in his older brother, who now treated fellow employees as equals instead of hired slaves. The head cook, a man called Silmor, seldom shouted at the help—there wasn't any need for it. Ilvan found that to be a welcome change. And, after a lengthy training day, Ilvan had put Reah's recipe for fish stew together for the staff.

"This is excellent," Silmor tasted his bowl of chowder. "We could sell this." Ilvan and Edan smiled at one another.

~

"So, they just tore down the building and put a park here." I surveyed the playground equipment. It needed paint and upkeep, in my opinion. Pipes were rusting and swing seats needed to be replaced.

"Probably hauled dirt in from somewhere," Plovel agreed. Our morning had begun extremely early—the sun was barely up and the spring winds were cold that blew across Grithis. I would have to go back and start the breakfast menu. Neither of my helpers had progressed enough to handle a meal on their own.

"I'm surprised they bothered. The way things are with the current politicians, they'd have left the concrete slab and let the children play on that." The more I saw of Grithis' government, the more I hoped the people would rise up and topple it.

"They had to bring in something—All these buildings have basements." Plovel pointed to the other buildings still standing on either side. "It had to be filled in and capped before the dirt is spread over it. That's standard across the planet."

"Ah." Still, I was surprised they bothered. "I wish I could stay but I have to open the restaurant. Good luck." I patted Plovel's arm and turned to go back to the inn.

I spent the rest of the day cooking and working the restaurant, only noticing while I was closing up that Plovel hadn't come in for the evening meal. He always did that, just to check in if nothing else. That had me worried.

"Have you seen Plovel?" I asked after I locked the restaurant, finding Neidles right behind me.

"Seen him? Not recently. I'll tell you where he is if you'll come to my suite." Rat-faced Neidles had done something and my breath caught in my throat.

"You'll tell me where he is now, and I'll not be coming to your suite, now or ever." I always carried my knife with me. Always. That knife was now at Neidles' throat and he was staring at me, frightened out of his wits.

"I had him arrested," his voice quavered, but that didn't keep the contempt out of it. "I've seen you two together. Don't think for a tick that I'd let that happen."

"Why was he arrested? Why?" I backed Neidles against the wall. "So help me, if they've harmed him, I'll cut your balls off." I hissed the threat at him, standing on tiptoe so my face would be in his.

"I-I told the authorities I saw him take a ch-child."

"You fucking moron," I snapped. "Find another cook, Neidles. We're done." If that didn't shock him enough, my skipping away certainly did.

"No one is allowed to see the prisoner," I was told by a constabulary officer every bit as loathsome as Neidles. Perhaps worse.

"You mean nobody sees him who doesn't pay first," I hissed. "Where is he?" I held back from gripping his throat in my hands.

"In the cell around the corner." The man was smiling now—he thought I was about to offer a bribe. He was dressed in a wrinkled uniform and sported oily brown hair. His eyes were washed-out blue, his mouth narrow.

"You disgust me," I snapped at him and skipped away. I heard his scream even as I appeared inside Plovel's cell. They'd beaten Plovel already—he had a black eye and a broken nose. His clothing was dirty, too, as if he'd been knocked into the dirt several times.

"Reah?" Plovel sat dejectedly on a rusty bunk that had no mattress. How anyone was supposed to sleep on that was beyond my comprehension.

"Plovel, can you stand?" I asked.

"I think so, why?"

"Because I'm getting you out of here. We have to hurry." I grabbed his hand and helped him up—I could hear shouting and running feet as I placed my shoulder beneath Plovel's arm and skipped away.

"Where's your office—where you work, Plovel?" I'd skipped us to the capital city of United Bardelus. It was called Bardelus Prime, for the Prime Minister.

"What? How did we get here?" Plovel peered around him, confused. "Am I dreaming?"

"No, hon. Tell me where to take you. I think you need help."

"Office on Lawgiver Street," he muttered. I had to ask three people who passed us before I got good directions. Skipping is only an exact science if I know precisely where I want to go. I did the best I could with what I had to work with.

"Where's your office?" Plovel's feet were dragging and I was taking much of his weight as we walked across marble tiles toward an elevator.

"Third floor. Anybody there will help," his speech was slurred. They'd hurt him worse than I thought.

"All right." I didn't bother with the elevator; I took him directly to the third floor by skipping. As soon as we got inside a reception area, people were shouting and calling for medical assistance.

"This may be the armpit of this section of the galaxy," Gavril muttered, looking around him. Lendill had given coordinates on where the children were disappearing. Gavril, Astralan and Stellan had brought Lendill along to look for their quarry.

"You think we need a place to stay, boss? There's an inn over there." Astralan jerked his head toward a two-story hotel that looked less run-down than its surroundings.

"Sure. We'll see if they have rooms and then we'll ask questions," Gavril agreed. There didn't seem to be anyplace that might meet his expectations as far as places to stay went.

"He looks like a rat," Stellan muttered to his oldest brother as Gavril approached the front desk and the clerk who stood behind it.

"We need two rooms with two beds each," Gavril said.

"I have two that just came open; I'll move in the extra beds right away," the clerk replied. "That will be one hundred silvers per room each night."

"Out of the question," Gavril snapped. "You will take fifty for each room and you will tell me anything you know about the child disappearances and any other criminal activity that you know of." Compulsion dripped from his voice, causing the clerk to go blank-eyed immediately.

"Harm Reah," Plovel's words were forced, "I'll fire all of you." That caused the female agent to take her hands from my arm. Did she think I'd done this to Plovel? Why would I haul him in if I'd beaten him? Some people just didn't think in times of crisis.

"He needs medical attention now," I snapped. Someone was already communicating on a comp-vid. I rode with Plovel to a nearby hospital, too, along with three agents.

"What happened? He didn't say we couldn't question you," the female agent said as Plovel was hauled into an emergency ward.

"The constabulary in Grithis happened, after some moron said Plovel had something to do with the child disappearances," I said.

"That's eight hundred clicks away," she scoffed.

"I'm not local," I said. "I can get around quickly if I must."

"I don't believe you. You're involved in this."

"Sure, and the moon is made of yogurt," I said, grabbing her arm and skipping right back to Grithis. "See—they're still having a fit over his disappearance." We stood outside the constable's station in the moonlight, staring at the window of Plovel's cell. I could see the shadows of people still milling around inside it. "If you don't mind, I'd prefer not to stay here." I took her arm and skipped her back to the hospital.

"How did you do that?" The agent stared at me, just as the two men we'd left behind were also staring. They'd seen us disappear and reappear.

"Do you have your head buried in the sand all the time? You should know that some races are capable of this."

"Yes, but, none of them ever come here," she said.

"I'm here now. And I want to know if Plovel is getting good care." I walked up to the reception desk. I heard all three agents whispering furiously behind me as I asked the aide what was happening.

"He won't let us treat him until he speaks with someone named Reah," a nurse or assistant walked toward us.

"That's me." I was led into a treatment room.

"Reah, it's underground. They didn't fill it in. Those children are under the playground." Plovel was gripping my wrist so hard it hurt. "I was looking for the entrance when I was arrested."

"I should have killed Neidles," I muttered. "Will you be all right?"

"I've been worse."

"I'll go back," I said, and skipped away, no doubt causing medical personnel to gasp.

Of course, it was still dark and I was wearied as I stared at the deserted playground. Is this why the children said it was haunted and they could hear someone crying? The sound traveling upward, somehow? I began walking the perimeter of the grass that outlined the play area. If there was an entrance, it was hidden well—I walked around it three times without finding anything. There was one way I might deal with this, although I was trusting what Plovel told me and skipping in blind. Just as a precaution, I went in as my smaller Thifilatha.

"We're sorry, the food is usually better. I think Neidles fired the cook," a harried Nari informed the newest guests. Four men had come, all looking much too wealthy to be there, she thought, as she served sandwiches and bowls of soup.

"It's all right," Gavril reassured the girl, who seemed close to tears for some reason.

"No, it's not all right—I was learning so much from Reah, and now Neidles has chased her off." She wiped tears away, then stared at Gavril as he dropped the spoon into his soup bowl.

"Describe her," Lendill demanded while Gavril struggled to find his voice.

"This tall, long white hair," Nari held a hand up at the proper height.

"What happened? Do you know where she went?" Astralan asked.

"No. Stupid Neidles kept saying he was going to force her to go to bed with him. I guess she told him off and he fired her."

"I'll kill him," Gavril's hands clenched into fists. He was rising from his seat to go in search of the proprietor when the explosion occurred.

The old basement had been wired against intruders, and the ones who'd captured and held the prisoners folded away somehow—I saw flashes of light, six to be exact, while ducking debris and shrapnel as it flew toward me. My scales are very hard while I am Thifilatha—it was what saved my life. If I'd been in my normal form, I might have died.

Speaking from experience, only Ranos technology can effectively pierce my scales.

Children, locked inside cages and abandoned, were now screaming and crying while I straightened up. I'd been correct earlier; the authorities hadn't bothered to fill in the basement. They'd capped it to make it look as though it had been filled in, but it was hollow and empty beneath the playground until the kidnappers had located it and used it for their own purposes.

I knew what had caused those six flashes of light, too—no High Demon would ever be fooled by that filth. Ra'Ak. They were feeding off the children of Grithis. Most likely with human assistance. I stumbled over debris and jerked open cage doors, carefully lifting out seven children and skipping them aboveground. I heard sirens and knew I needed to leave—the culprits were long gone—who knew where they might go next?

"Who's there?" A voice shouted. The children began to weep louder. I skipped away.

~

"Tell him it was the worst kind of monsters, feeding on children," I passed the comp-vid to the female agent. "He has the code to get into it—I left information here for him." I tapped the comp-vid. "I'm going to attempt to follow that filth. They need to be destroyed."

"But where will they go? I can send agents out if I have some idea." She was begging me to tell her something.

"I don't think they'll stay on Bardelus. I think they're long gone from here," I said. "I saw them. They won't want to remain here if they know I know about them." I didn't say that any Ra'Ak was afraid of a High Demon. Ra'Ak held no power against a High Demon. I'd already killed several. They wouldn't wait to see whether I intended harm or not. That was a given. "I only found seven children alive," I added.

"Thank you for your help," she said.

"Tell Plovel to get in touch via comp-vid—he has my code," I said, and skipped away.

There wasn't any need to go back to the inn—I figured Neidles had already sold my belongings for what they might fetch, the rat-faced asshole. I skipped straight to Beliphar instead.

"Where are her belongings?" Gavril gripped Neidles's shirt in his fingers. He and the others had arrived at the blasted playground in time to see Reah disappear. Gavril and Lendill had both cursed, long and hard, while Astralan and Stellan rounded up frightened children and turned them over to the authorities. Gavril knew by scent alone that the Strands were in league with Ra'Ak. Lendill was on his comp-vid immediately, putting up bulletins across the Alliance regarding the dangers they might be facing. Gavril was placing compulsion on Neidles again, to learn what he could about Reah and to get her things back.

"I have her things," Neidles voice was flat.

"You will give them to me." They followed Neidles to his suite, where all of Reah's clothing and such had been gathered. The two warlocks lifted the bag and boxes. "If you ever bother Reah again, I'll kill you," Gavril promised, before nodding to Astralan, who folded all of them to Campiaa.

I slept for the better part of three days. I had no idea how tired I really was. Meals were the only thing I climbed out of bed for—nothing else gathered my attention. On the morning of the fourth day, Nefrigar was sitting on the side of my bed when I woke.

"Hello, honey blue," I rubbed my eyes to bring him into focus. He smiled. "Are you acting as my agent?" I asked. "You show up every time I don't have anything else to do."

"Is that what an agent does?" He stood when I slipped off the bed and followed me into the kitchen.

"They find work for their clients," I nodded, putting the kettle on for tea. "But they usually take a percentage. Well, even if you did, the percentage wouldn't be much, Neidles didn't pay a fair wage." I put tea in the pot while waiting for the water to heat.

"I have no need of wealth or currency." He leaned against the counter and watched me work. I sliced bread and placed it under the broiler. Toast sounded just as good as anything else for breakfast. Food was running out—I would have to restock the kitchen.

"What do you need?" I looked up at him.

"Something that keeps my interest," he was smiling again.

"Ah. I'm the new toy."

"Toy?"

"Something to play with."

"That sounds as if you believe I might lose interest, or use you for frivolous reasons."

"Yeah. I guess that's right," I sighed, pulling my toast out of the oven.

"Little one, I do not believe that will happen. I came to tell you that a position opened up on Tulgalan in a new restaurant. They are searching for an Eight-Day cook. This might be a good position to hold while you search for the ones who fled Bardelus."

He could be right—an Eight-Day cook was the cook who worked one day per Tulgalanian week, so the others could have the day off. At times, Eight-Day cooks had specific specialties they served for the midday and evening meals—Tulgalani loved to take their families out to eat on Eight-Day. With seven days left to hunt the filth feeding off children, it could be an ideal situation. "It pays well," Nefrigar added.

"It'll have to—I'll be forced to rent something to stay there."

"You will do fine," Nefrigar waited until I finished my meager breakfast before folding me to Targis.

Using one of my credit chips, I rented a cube. The cube was actually a rectangle—most of them were, but the slang term was used all the time. My apartment was only one room, with a tiny kitchen on one end, a bed on the other, with a microscopic sitting area in between.

Clothing was also a necessity—fall was approaching quickly and Targis was cold from the beginning of the ninth month, running through the end of the year and into the fourth month of the next. I used up even more of my credit chip for that, and all this before I even interviewed for the position. It didn't matter, I could support myself for a short while if necessary off my hoarded credit chips. It would mean I could hunt Ra'Ak scum indiscriminately.

"Yes, we're still interviewing." I spoke via comp-vid with the restaurant manager. It surprised me that it was called Dee's—that's what Teeg had called his assistant. It didn't matter—Teeg and his assistant were on Campiaa, if they weren't hunting the Strands. I'd done some research when I reached Targis—the Strands were still on the loose. "I have time this afternoon if you'd like to come in," the voice continued.

"I'll be there," I agreed. I'd never gone through a formal interview before—people had tasted my cooking and that was that.

"It won't bother you to be an Eight-Day cook?" The man identified himself as Wroth, the business manager for the restaurant. Owned by a corporation, he'd said. I didn't ask him to explain.

"No, that leaves me time to pursue other interests," I said. "My last job was nearly round the clock, the demand was so great. This will allow me to do other things. Hobbies and such. I'll do research. Perhaps write a little." I didn't say it would be information on my investigation; he didn't need to know that.

"Will you cook something now? I was too busy to have lunch earlier." Wroth wanted evidence of my skills, since most of the experience I'd listed was on non-Alliance worlds.

"Do you have yaris fish?" I asked. I was hungry, too, and hadn't seen yaris fish in months. Wroth smiled.

"You're hired," Wroth mumbled around his second bite. I was using one of my simpler aliases from my ASD tenure. Reah Silver was the name and ID I'd given. I was hoping that Lendill didn't have tendrils out, searching for hits on any of the false IDs he'd given me through the years.

"Good. Do you have a preset menu or will it be left to me?" I asked.

"Both—some items will be served every time, but you can offer up to three specials every Eight-Day. Send the information to me via comp-vid if you can't come in—I'll let you know if we can't get the meats or vegetables ahead of time. We have a very good buyer. Feel free to go out with her anytime, if you have something specific you want."

"What's her name?"

"Teira. Here's her code." Wroth handed a card with a number over.

"All right. I'll contact her—I'm particular about the fish and beef," I said.

"You'll be paid every second Eight-Day, and records and receipts are due at the same time. Silmor, the head cook, has a list of duties," Wroth handed over a comp-vid. "This is yours to keep your records on—make sure you communicate with Silmor on any issues that crop up or if repairs need to be made. He'll let you know if there are any problems with your work or your crew. You'll have two assistant cooks and six helpers, in addition to the waitstaff."

"All right," I nodded, accepting the comp-vid. I'd not heard Silmor's name before and wondered where he was from.

"Will you make yaris fish as a special on your first day? I'll come for that," Wroth smiled.

"If you want. I'll ask Teira to buy it. Are oxberries available?" I asked.

"I'll see." That question piqued Wroth's interest, I could tell. Eight-Day was two days away. I had plenty of prep work to do if I were to do my best for my new employer.

~

"We're worried that this will filter into the Alliance," Norian stood before the huge screen in the meeting room. Sixteen agents sat at tables, scanning the information gleaned from spotty records concerning the Bardelus child disappearances.

"These monsters eat humanoids," Norian went on. "We currently have reports of child disappearances on sixteen Alliance worlds since these creatures disappeared from Bardelus. And we have it on good authority that these may be allied with Lersen Strand and his cousins, in addition to other criminals. What we need is intelligence gathered. Do not approach any of these yourselves; they will kill you easily. We have no weapons against them; we can only pass the information we receive on to others, who may be able to combat this threat. Now, let me repeat this—if you want to die, go ahead and attack them. Your death will be most swift, I assure you. While they appear to prefer the tender flesh of children, they are not above the occasional adult humanoid, tough skin and all."

"What do they look like?" An agent raised her hand. Lok, sitting at a table in front of her, turned to see who'd asked. She didn't interest him—she was of medium height with light-brown hair. He preferred women from Falchan—warriors who could spar with him. Tall, black-haired and tattooed was his ideal. He turned around in his seat and stared at the image of a monster on the vid-screen.

"They don't always look like this," Lendill Schaff stood and spoke, now. "They are shape-shifters of sorts, and can appear just as humanoid as anyone here. Some with sensitive noses can scent them, but we do not have that luxury among us. Search for evidence of missing children. We especially want information from witnesses who report seeing an extra child with those reported missing."

"What? Are you suggesting that one of those things poses as a child to lure others away?"

"It's possible," Norian said. "We must consider every possibility at this point, including one that they may be using a kidnapped child to do the same thing—as a lead-away."

"That's sick," the female agent muttered. Lok felt the same, only he didn't voice his opinion aloud.

"We expect all information to be funneled to us as quickly as possible," Lendill went on. "We will coordinate all of it here and send pertinent data back to you. We will be searching for similarities and differences in all cases. Meanwhile, if you discover that the perpetrators are local and humanoid, apprehend them and hand them over to local authorities. Make sure your ID chips are up to date, just in case."

"Remember to keep yourself hidden from these creatures, they are capable of mindspeech with one another," Norian said as the agents rose from their seats. "What one knows, they all will know, including your names and your images. Safe journey."

Lok lifted his leather jacket from the back of his chair—he'd been assigned to Tulgalan. Settling his comp-vid inside an inner pocket, he walked out behind the others.

Lendill told him it would be cold already, and destined to get colder when fall turned into winter in Targis. Lok pulled the collar of his jacket up—this one wasn't lined with his favorite sheepskin. He'd switch jackets as soon as he arrived at his apartment.

"Your key chip." The clerk handed the chip over after verifying Lok's rental. Lok barely nodded to the man and went for the stairs instead of the elevator.

In the four months since he'd worked for the ASD, he'd not found a single person to spar with. His training had been done on Toris, where most ASD agents received their basic instruction. ASD agents moved to Le-Ath Veronis after that, but Lok had come directly from basic training to an assignment. Lendill told him that he'd be moved to the vampire planet when this assignment was over. Lok huffed at the idea. Vampires. They actually existed.

The furnished apartment was more cluttered than Lok liked. Too much of the frivolous, he decided, taking in the four-room residence.

He had a kitchen, a sitting room, a bedroom and a bath, all paid for by the ASD. Tossing both bags onto the bed, he stared out the bedroom window at the city of Targis.

"Master Cook Silmor? This is Reah, the Eight-Day cook," I identified myself through my comp-vid. I could see his image, just as he could see mine.

"What is it, Reah?" He sounded tired.

"Is it possible to ask one of your helpers to put six scoops of rice to soak before they leave tonight? I want to make a rice noodle soup," I said. "If not, I can come down and do it before you close for the evening."

"I'll get someone to do it for you," Silmor said. "Allee!" He shouted a name over his shoulder. I heard a faint reply. "Put six scoops of rice to soak," Silmor shouted again. Another faint reply. "It's done," he smiled slightly. "Anything else?"

"No. Thank you, Master Cook Silmor," I said. He terminated the call from his end. He was older—more than a hundred, but had no gray in his reddish hair. He had a thin face and didn't appear to be overweight—from what I could see, anyway. He'd smiled—always a good sign. Perhaps we would get along, he and I.

We ran out of yaris fish before the dinner rush was over. Dee's was quickly gaining a reputation, even against Desh's and the Star Gazer. I would have to tell Teira to get more fish next time. The lamb dish was almost as popular, served in an herbed citrus sauce. And the rice noodle soup? Anyone who tasted it was telling everyone else at the table how good it was.

My two assistant cooks were cousins—Oris and Danis. Both men, they looked to be related, with blond, dandelion fluff for hair, cut short, of course. Blue eyes and full lips that smiled—a lot—

rounded out their features. Three helpers were female; three were male.

"Cook Reah, there's a man out there, asking to speak with the cook!" One of the waitstaff—a young woman—rushed into the kitchen, her face glowing pink.

"Does he have a complaint?" I asked, pulling off my apron. I wasn't dressed well enough, really, to go out in the dining area, but a customer was asking. I had to go. "Show me," I said, motioning for the girl to lead me to the proper table. I almost stopped dead, my breath catching in my throat, when I saw the man in question.

Falchani. No doubt about it, with the inscrutable scowl that many of them wore. I had no idea if he wanted to complain or ask how a dish was prepared. His face might be quite handsome, if the scowl were removed. Thick, black hair hung down his back in the traditional braid, his black eyes staring as we approached. I thought to smooth my tunic and didn't—he was watching.

"Sir, is there a problem?" I asked.

"You prepared these noodles?"

"Yes."

"They're good. Who taught you how to make them?"

"Someone named Flyer. On Falchan." I didn't want to lie to the man.

"You learned from Flyer." His words were a statement, not a question.

"You know him?" I asked.

"I ate there more often than not," the man replied.

"I'm glad you enjoyed the food," I nodded respectfully to him.

"You could carry rice wine."

"Sir, I'll ask if it might be available." The more I stared at him, the more I wanted to know him better. That was a first for me. Before, men always approached me. I didn't go to them. Ever. He had the blackest eyes, and I imagined if he ever smiled, it would be like the sun breaking through a cloud. I found myself wishing to see that. "Call ahead, next time, and I'll let you know if we were successful in obtaining rice wine."

"Do you serve these noodles every day?"

"No, I'm only the Eight-Day cook—I don't believe the regular staff knows how to prepare rice noodles."

"Will you serve it next Eight-Day?"

"This was a special, and those are expected to rotate," I said. "But if you call the day before, I can arrange to make the noodles for you."

"Make the noodles. I'll come." I watched his face—he wasn't giving even a hint of emotion.

I did something then that I'd never done before. Or will ever do again. "Perhaps—perhaps you'd like to have dinner with me sometime?" I was shocked by my forwardness.

His eyes widened the barest fraction. "I prefer my women taller, with dark hair." My face burned immediately. Now I knew how young men felt, asking someone out for a first date.

"Of course you do," I muttered. "Enjoy your meal." I turned and walked away with as much dignity as I could muster.

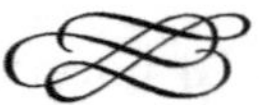

CHAPTER 5

I was never so glad to wipe off the last counter and get the last dish put away as I was that night. The waitress who'd taken me to the Falchani's table shot sympathetic glances in my direction now and then. I was glad when she turned in her count for the evening and left with the other waitstaff. Silmor had left a message for me, asking for a marinade to be put together for the steaks stored in one of the meat keepers. I put the marinade together and set the meat soaking in it, going over and over my embarrassment. Did I say I liked Falchani? Right then, I didn't.

"Riding the bus?" Oris grinned.

"No. I'll walk," I said. And I would. Right to the nearest dark and secluded spot. I'd skip to my cube from there. My temporary home was across town, in the lower middle-class portion of Targis. It was the best I could afford.

"Be careful, then. We heard there are girls coming up missing. Three, just last week," Danis said. "And with you so, well, not tall," he wasn't sure if he were insulting me or not.

"Don't worry. I should be fine," I reassured him. Three girls were missing? When had that happened? Of course, I'd been buried in meal planning and such, but that was no excuse. I'd have to be better than this.

We set the alarm and locked up the restaurant, my assistants going one way while I went the other. I skipped as quickly as I could.

Later, I sat with a cup of tea at my elbow while I read through the ASD records of the three missing girls. These girls hadn't been taken together—that was the only thing different. They'd disappeared on three consecutive days, too. Were the Ra'Ak attempting to steer us away from their trail by changing tactics? Hunching my shoulders and then relaxing them, I worked to get the kinks out. They ached. Not just from the work but from tension and embarrassment. My face went warm every time I thought about my invitation to the Falchani customer. I'd never do that again. Never. *Ever.*

My eyes were almost closed when I pulled up information on fifteen other worlds, all having to do with child disappearances. All recent. "Fuck," I mumbled. I was too tired to keep looking. I had to sleep.

"Tell me why." Gavril sounded hurt. He had photographs in front of him, taken by Dee's restaurant buyer, Teira. All the photographs Dee handed to Gavril were of Reah. Dee owned all sorts of businesses, restaurants being one branch of them. Kifirin had come to him with this project, just as he'd come to him fifty years before, bringing Gavril to him to raise and teach.

"Kifirin," Dee stated flatly. "So I built this. For her. He says not to go rushing in. She needs to settle and get comfortable. Make friends. I hired the best I could—ones who will treat her carefully. You'll get regular updates. Share these images with the others, with the same warning. Step back for now. We'll woo her. Slowly. Build her trust, if we can."

"And did Kifirin say why we shouldn't go rushing in?"

"He says that makes her run. So don't. Make offers, instead. Tell her that you'll be waiting, if she needs or wants anything. Or just to talk. She's renting one of those minuscule cubes on the eastern edge of Targis. You own a luxury apartment building on the west side, not far from the restaurant."

"I do?"

"You do, now. You can offer one of those apartments as a place to live. Rent free."

"Of course rent free," Gavril growled. Dee recognized that growl. His Teeg was frustrated.

"It's either this or go looking for her again," Dee said.

A thick, cream-colored envelope waited on my tiny kitchen table when I got back from doing my grocery shopping on First-Day. Worried, I opened it while placing perishables into the keeper.

Dearest Reah, we know where you are. The first line of the letter made me draw a shaky breath. *We will not push or demand—we realize now that this would be a mistake. There is no need to run; we will not approach you unless you wish it. All of us will be available if you need or want anything, including sitting down to talk. Wylend wants you to know that Garek worries that you misinterpreted his words—he only meant that you would be less of a target if someone wished to get to Wylend by harming you. He would never use you as a shield—he wishes to protect you instead. Lendill worries that you will not tell him if you need supplies or information such as he can give. Torevik sends his love and his sincerest apologies. Aurelius sends his love, as do I. I also wish you to consider this—I own the Crown Apartments on the west side of Targis. It would please all of us if you'd consider moving into one of them—we would worry less if you would do so. Unit # 927 is available; all you have to do is ask the concierge for the keys. Your clothing and any other belongings we could gather are already there. We make no demands, Reah. The choices are yours to make.*

My love forever—Chash.

I was weeping helplessly at the end. And later, when my face didn't look such a mess, I skipped to the west side of Targis, searching for the Crown Apartments.

"Your keys, lady." I thought the man was going to bow or something when he handed them over. He led me to the lift and rode up with me. Luxury? I'd be wallowing in it. Real estate was at a premium on Targis' west side. Addah lived in this part of town, now—I'd checked. The apartment had expensive tiles laid, with rich, handmade rugs, beautiful artwork, a sumptuous master suite with a huge bed, two more bedrooms and the kitchen of my dreams. The cabinets were already stocked with dishes, pots and pans. Exactly what I would buy for myself, if I could afford it. I wanted to weep again. I may have brushed away a tear or two while the concierge showed me through the place.

"Will you be moving in right away?" he asked. I could only nod.

"You won't get the rent back," the clerk said when I turned in the keys to my cube later. It had taken two trips to get everything out of it.

"I know." I walked away from him and my tiny cube with no regrets.

My next surprise came when I went to put my clothing away in the new apartment—another envelope waited in a lingerie drawer.

Reah, use this. It will be funded by all of us. Love, Chash. It was a credit chip, strung on a chain. And then, when I walked into the huge closet —it was as big as my cube, perhaps larger, even—there were notes attached to some of the clothing.

Reah, it was a wrench allowing this to leave my closet. I had hopes of seeing you inside my suite at times, searching for something suitable to wear —Lendill.

Reah, I kept some of your things—they bear your scent and I couldn't part with them—Chash.

Reah, this is my favorite dress. You wore it when you graced my arm at the harvest ball, remember? I love you—Wylend.

Reah, come and skip rocks with me. Please?—Tory. That note was on a pair of faded jeans. I recalled the first time we'd done that—Tory, Rylend, Gavril and I. More tears came.

My love, you are my treasure. You know that—Aurelius. "I know that, Auri." I sat on the floor and wept, even when there shouldn't have been any tears left to fall.

I used my codes to get into the local constabulary's records on the three disappearances in Targis. Very little evidence had been collected —I found vid images where all three girls had last been seen. I was forcing myself to work at this—I'd almost succumbed to huddling inside my new apartment instead. The notes—they'd been so loving. There'd been no demands from Teeg, and that's what I was used to from him. I wanted to talk to him. Ask him about Farzi and Nenzi. Ask to speak with them, tell them I was all right. Would he settle for talking or would he be as he was, only waiting for me to make the first move and then pounce like a cat, playing with a mouse but never truly letting it go? I shook my head, hunched into my knee-length wool coat against the cold wind and skipped to the location where the first girl disappeared.

Dusk was settling in so I would have to hurry if I expected to see anything. Only a few fibers from the girl's jacket had been left behind for the authorities to collect, and those had been caught on the brick of a building near a street corner. She'd been walking home from a friend's house; they'd spent the afternoon together. The girl was fourteen and taller than I, according to the records.

Bending over, I examined the brick carefully—I could see where it had been scraped for possible DNA samples.

"Lose something?" I whirled to see Mr. *I prefer taller women with dark hair.*

"I lost nothing," I snapped. "But some parents lost their daughter. I was looking to see if the authorities missed anything."

"As if you'd know," he said.

"Wait, is that sarcasm? I thought you were the master of the flat and uninflected."

"Do you treat all your customers this way?"

"No." My voice was sullen, now. "Do you treat all cooks this way?" I went back to studying the brick, wondering what he was doing there. I moved down toward the corner—the brick that held the fibers was several feet from there. Reaching the corner, I turned, going down the narrow alley between buildings. Nearly fifteen feet down, I found it. More fibers. They'd missed this.

"Fuck." His voice was right behind me. He'd seen it too, shortly after I'd found it.

"They dragged her around the corner and into this alley," I muttered, looking around. Seven days had passed since the abduction, but I pulled the small, ultra-bright penlight from my pocket and searched the alley anyway. Tulgalan doesn't use paper anything, so there was very little litter. The Falchani was breathing over my shoulder the entire time. Wanting to give him an elbow in the ribs, I chose silence instead.

"What's this?" I pulled a collapsible metal wand from my pocket and lifted the piece. It looked to be a few links from a chain. Metal bracelets were popular among young men on Tulgalan at the moment. The Falchani was staring at the evidence, too, before hauling out a comp-vid and tapping out a rapid message. The alley was swarming with local police in no time.

"And just who are you?" A detective leaned over me. Mr. Falchani had pulled out a badge—he was a private investigator. Go figure. I— for the moment, anyway, was just a cook for Dee's restaurant.

"She's ex-ASD." Norian Keef sauntered into the alley. I wanted to kick his kneecap. Break it, too. I'd just been thinking of Lendill and wondering if I were going to have to play that card to get myself out of this. Instead, Norian showed up. *Lendill can't fold. I can*, came the mental message. "This is sloppy work if your employees missed this before," Norian went on. "I ask one of my former employees to check on this and what do we find?" Norian had already whipped out his credentials, cowing all of them. The Falchani faded away the minute Norian showed up.

"We'll handle this from here—no need to call in the ASD," the detective snapped.

"Then don't force us to do your work for you," Norian grabbed my arm and hauled me out of the alley.

"Reah, they're touchy as hell about this," Norian said as soon as we got out of hearing distance. "They don't have any leads. I know you were on Bardelus—that idiot innkeeper described you. You know what happened there. I also know that you don't work for me anymore, but if you can file a report, I'd be more than grateful and it may help us track the scum responsible. Lissa is ready to go if we find Ra'Ak, and if it isn't Ra'Ak, we need to know that, too. Our agents—all of them, could be putting their lives on the line needlessly if we don't know what we're dealing with."

"I'll file a fucking report, Norian," I said, jerking my arm from his grasp.

"Reah, I didn't mean to be rough with you, little girl. Lendill is about to go crazy without you. Please consider throwing him a bone now and then. And file the report." Norian disappeared.

I filed the report. In official ASD form and fashion, sending it to Lendill and copying Norian. Was I supposed to send a personal message too? I couldn't think of anything to say.

"I hope we have more ox-roast. We've already run out of the oxberry dessert," Oris placed the last salad on a tray for the waiter to take to a table.

"We've got five more servings," I said. The restaurant was packed and people without reservations were turned away—it was nearly closing time. I'd suggested we send the ones we turned away through the door with a small dessert and a sampling of our other dishes. That turned grumbling into surprise. Many of them we took reservations from for the following Eight-Day.

"The man with the long braid is back, asking for noodles," a waitress rushed into the kitchen. I'd held some back, just in case.

"What else does he want?" I asked.

"He wanted to try the ox-roast. I told him we might be out." She gave me a wry expression.

"I'll put his dinner together." She actually helped, putting a light salad on a plate and taking it to him as I threw rice noodles into broth and cooking that while plating up the ox-roast.

"There you go," I said, loading it onto a tray for the waitress to carry to the Falchani's table.

"He wants to talk to you again," the girl winced.

"I want to bust his nose," I muttered, making the girl laugh. I hefted the tray up and carried it to his table.

"I had to wait two clicks to get in here."

"I told you to call ahead," I said, settling the tray on a stand and handing off his noodle bowl, followed by the plate of ox-roast.

"I thought you were making that up."

"I never lie about food," I said. "Is there anything else?" I swept the tray off the stand.

"Ex-ASD?"

"That's what the Director said. And he's not high on my list, unless it's the list of people I never want to see again."

"What's the problem with Director Keef?"

"Where do you want me to start?"

"Start with the most recent."

"My dead daughter," I snapped and walked away.

"Tread lightly around Reah," Lendill said. Lok had contacted him as required, and reported on the alley incident. Lendill had already received Reah's report. "Reah has special talents, so don't ever underestimate her," Lendill went on. "Too bad you don't have mindspeech—she'd be a good contact if you ever got into a tight spot."

"She doesn't look big enough to get herself out of a tight spot."

"I think the last person who thought that had a knife to his throat in less than a blink. Don't fuck with her, Lok. She'll be armed and most certainly dangerous. Harm her and I'll see you kicked out of the service."

~

"Sorry, we're completely booked," became a byword on the third Eight-Day. This time, we sent a waiter down the line of hopefuls with a comp-vid and a tray, passing out samples and taking reservations. The Falchani learned his lesson; he had a table reserved every Eight-Day for the next six moon-turns. I found that out by checking the reserve list. His name was Lok—he'd never bothered to introduce himself.

"Are you going to force me to serve you every time? Is this your way of torturing me?" I asked, setting his bowl of noodles down, followed by the pork special.

"It wasn't my intention; I just thought you might want to talk."

"Not particularly—I have a restaurant full of guests. Didn't you notice?"

"Now who sounds sarcastic?"

"I always sound that way. It's normal."

"Then we'll talk when you're not working."

"Oh, did I grow three hands taller and dye my hair?"

"You don't dye it?"

"This is my natural color," I said. "I have to go to work. Sorry to disappoint you and all." His face showed no emotion, but his black eyes followed me as I went to the next table when a guest waved at me.

"It's a Falchani recipe. I went there to learn how to make it," I said when the guest asked about the noodles.

"You're the cook?"

"Yes," I smiled at the man. "I learned to make these noodles from an old Falchani man named Flyer, who was like a father. He let me stay in a small room in his home over the restaurant. He has one of the most popular noodle restaurants in Cedar's Falls."

"Where else have you cooked?" The man's eyes were dancing.

"I've cooked at the San Gerxon on Campiaa. I've cooked for the King of Karathia and the Queen of Le-Ath Veronis."

"Does the Queen really have fifteen mates?" The man's female companion asked.

"She has seventeen, two of whom are Falchani," I laughed. Drake and Drew would be so proud.

"And how was the King of Karathia?"

"He was well the last time I saw him, although he may have been in a bit of a snit when I left."

"If you're taking your cooking away with you, I can see why," the man laughed.

"Can we get a photo with you?" The woman asked.

"Sure." We got one of the waiters to snap the image, after the two had squeezed together while I stood behind them, smiling the best I could. At least I was dressed better now—the clothing Teeg had left in my closet saw to that.

"Reah, this is Wroth." I hadn't heard from him since I'd gone to work at Dee's.

"Hello, Wroth, what can I do for you?" He'd contacted me through comp-vid.

"You can come down to the restaurant," he said. "I'd like to speak with you."

"I'll be there in half a click."

I ran through the shower, cleaning up and dressing in record time. I'd gotten to bed late the night before—I was planning short trips to other worlds where children had come up missing, in addition to working on Tulgalan's disappearances. Now, Wroth wanted to talk. Was it because I was giving out samples to people we had to turn away? Had Lok complained or some other nameless, faceless individual? I was shaking when I skipped away from my apartment.

"Reah, I wanted to see you because of this." Wroth pushed a comp-vid across his desk. I stared at it in shock, and then stared at Wroth in shock. The vid-news contained a photograph of me posing with the two guests from the night before. When the restaurant ratings are done each year, nobody knows which food critics will be sent out to sample a restaurant's fare. This man had come every Eight-Day since I'd started cooking for Dee's. And he was the critic designated to handle the ratings this turn. Desh's still held top honors this time, but Dee's had gotten critical acclaim for their Eight-Day menu.

"He says that if you were the head cook, Dee's would have taken the top honor, hands down."

"Oh, dear," I sat back in my chair, shivering. I liked Silmor, although I'd never met him. Now, this would ruin everything. I could wave good-bye to any working relationship with the man.

"Reah, Silmor has known from the beginning that you are a better cook. I'd like you to take the Master's exam." Wroth's words came from far away.

"I need to think about it," my voice quavered as I stood. Just when I had my legs under me, something came along and knocked me down again. Silmor might say that to his employer, but he was still head cook. He could make my life unbearable. Wroth watched as I turned away from him, ready to walk out the door. Two people stood in the doorway, and the sight of them made my vision turn dark and then go black.

I dreamed I was crying. Someone was singing to me. That had never happened. No nanny, even, had ever sang for me. Addah wouldn't hire someone like that. Not ever. He'd hated me—a tiny babe he'd been saddled with when my mother had the temerity to die after being poisoned with a drug that made her bleed out. I'd never seen her. But the two men standing in the doorway had. One of them had even helped kill Raedah, after raping her. But then Kifirin had told me this wasn't the same man. That his spirit had been traded, somehow, for that of a future lifetime. How was that possible? The gods could shuffle your lives around like pieces on a game board?

"Hush, Reah. Shhhh." I trembled when I woke and I was crying—I wasn't dreaming it. And the one who held me might have been the last person I'd thought to do so. Edan Desh's face was over mine. Crooning to me.

"She's awake now," Ilvan gave my face one last brush with the cold, wet cloth before taking it away.

"Thank the gods," Wroth said.

"Reah, you're so small. I don't have that memory," Edan lifted me off the floor. He'd been crouched beside me, there on the floor between Wroth's desk and the door to his office.

"Reah, Edan and Ilvan are Silmor's assistant cooks," Wroth said softly. I could only stare in shock, first at Edan, then at Ilvan.

"We're not going to hurt you," Ilvan said softly.

"Can you stand up, baby?" Edan asked. Why was he calling me that? I shivered.

"It'll take time," Wroth said. "Silmor, come in here, please." Now I would know. I always knew when somebody was lying. "Silmor, Reah thinks that things will change after this review." Wroth tapped his comp-vid after Edan set me on the floor. He still had a steadying hand under my elbow.

"Reah, I came out of retirement for this job. And as soon as I can, I'm going back to retirement. You're not hurting me at all," Silmor declared. I blinked at him. He wasn't lying. But why? Why had he come out of retirement for this job? I didn't understand.

"Don't worry about it, Reah. You look shaken. I'll get someone to take you home." Wroth looked worried.

"I'll be fine," I said.

"Don't you want someone to go with you?" Edan actually seemed troubled. I couldn't reconcile that with the Edan I'd known before.

"What were you—when Kifirin came to take you?" I asked instead.

"I don't know you. The other one I knew too well." Ilvan blinked at my words—he had no idea.

"Come." Edan steered me out of Wroth's office. "I was a pediatrician," he said, his arm around me, walking me toward the employee's entrance at the back of the restaurant. "I see he told you."

"I'm glad you got a second chance this time, but it has to be difficult, with the criminal record," I said, turning the knob on the back door. "I'll have to get used to the fact that your face won't be connected to physical pain from now on."

"Reah, I think if there were any way that I, or Kifirin or some of the others could take some of our mistakes back, we would. Instead, we have to go forward and try to put things behind us."

"I need time to think," I rubbed my forehead. I had a headache.

"Go home and lie down. Sleep if you can."

My head was throbbing so badly, I took the bus home. Of course, Lok was waiting outside the door to the Crown Apartments.

"The concierge wouldn't allow me inside unless you approved my visits," Lok grumbled.

"I have a terrible headache," I muttered, brushing past his wide shoulders. He followed me inside the building anyway.

"Ms. Silver?" The concierge had a question in his voice.

"It's all right," I waved a hand helplessly. Lok and I rode the elevator to the ninth floor.

"This is yours?" Lok looked around when I opened the door.

"No. It belongs to one of my mates."

"One of your mates?"

"Yeah. You'd think I'd have painkill around here somewhere," I sighed, heading toward the bathroom.

"What does this mate do?" Lok was still looking around—he'd followed me right to the bathroom.

"He's the founding member of the Campiaan Alliance."

"You're married to Teeg San Gerxon."

"Yeah. Anyway, that's what he says." I was going through drawers and cabinets. There wasn't any sort of medication anywhere to take for a splitting headache. "Why are you here again?" I looked up at him.

"I wanted your help on this investigation. There's information on the bracelet links you found in the alley."

"Fuck," I muttered. "There's a drugstore on the corner." I grabbed his arm and skipped us there. Lok stared while I attempted to read labels. "Damn," I sighed, pulling three different brands off the shelf and heading toward the self-pay chip reader.

"How the fuck did you do that?" Lok was still staring and cursing, now that we were back inside my kitchen. I poured water in a glass and took three times the recommended dosage. It would take at least that much to have any effect.

"What do you know about me?" I asked. "I checked your records, you're ASD. Active."

"Lendill said you were special. He just didn't say how special," Lok grumbled.

"Ah. Lendill. One of my other mates. Inadvertently." I wet a towel in the sink, squeezed the water from it and went to sit on the sofa, the cloth over my eyes.

"You're married to Lendill Schaff."

"Inadvertently."

"Fuck. The links are from a bracelet that girl wore—Andree Wirth," he said her name. "A boyfriend gave it to her. They found DNA on those links and they can't identify it."

"Probably Ra'Ak," I muttered. "I couldn't find anything on those other two girls. It's as if they were snatched from the air."

"I looked too—same thing."

"Did they talk to the boy?" I asked.

"He was home—his parents confirmed it. They said he'd given the bracelet to Andree."

"Did you talk to him?"

"Didn't see any need."

"Well, if we get the opportunity, I'd still like to question him."

"I know where he goes to school."

"Good enough."

"What else are you planning to do?" Lok asked.

"Before I was slapped into the past earlier, I was planning to go to

Pridded."

"There's already an agent there."

"You think that'll stop me?"

"I see that was a stupid statement," Lok admitted. "When will you know if you're going and will you take me with you?"

"Are you a sadistic slave driver? Because I assure you I already have one of those," I pulled the cloth away to look at him. He smiled. Actually smiled. It was like the sun breaking through a cloud, just as I imagined it might be.

"Oh, now you want to be seen together," I snapped, slapping the towel over my eyes again.

"I do prefer taller women. With dark hair. I can change my ways."

"Don't bother. You've already fucked up the vision."

"What vision?"

"You're not going to shut up, are you?" I pulled the towel away again. "Let's go." I grabbed his arm and skipped us to Pridded.

CHAPTER 6

"This is it," Lok said. We'd arrived at a warehouse, with parts of it still in use. I could hear hovertrucks backing up for loading down the way. "These kids come here and trade prescribed meds after school," Lok added. "The one who was grabbed forgot her purse and ran back for it. They never found her."

I was looking around the area—I could see markings on the floor. "What are these?" I asked.

"No idea," Lok said. I walked around them—they were spaced evenly apart—in the form of an equilateral triangle. "Looks like something from those old witches' tales."

"Then let's see if we can get an expert's evaluation," I said. *Wylend?* I sent.

Love, what do you need?

I just need a little advice, I returned. *Do you have someone who can come to Pridded?*

Where on Pridded?

Shoordeed Warehouse in Parid.

Wylend and Erland both came ticks later, surprising Lok.

"Wylend, Erland, this is Lok, ASD," I introduced Lok to them.

85

"Love, I wish you would call me more often," Wylend pulled me against him and kissed my forehead.

"Can you do anything about a headache, and do you know what these are?" I pointed out the symbols on the floor.

"May the stars never fail," Erland said. "Who did this?"

"We don't know yet," I said. "But this is where one of those children disappeared."

"This is forbidden spellwork," Erland said, walking around the triangle of symbols. They'd been drawn on the concrete with colored chalk.

"What does it do?" I asked. Wylend put his fingers on my forehead, causing the throbbing to go away.

"It's a transference—you trade one body for another," Wylend said softly.

"Like Nidris did for his brother?"

"No," Erland shook his head. "That was a simple spell, making someone look like someone else. With this, you're moving a spirit into another body. You're trading souls around. It's called soul-shifting."

"That's not scary or anything," I said, feeling cold all over.

"It doesn't last long—both bodies begin to die quickly; that's why it's forbidden," Wylend said.

"What's the purpose in it, then?" I asked.

"It's the ultimate disguise," Erland told me. "If you're sitting in jail, awaiting execution, you trade off with your jailer, who's executed in your place. But in order for you to stay alive, you have to keep trading bodies before the one you currently inhabit dies. You leave a trail of dead behind you."

"Unless those dead are consumed by monsters who have a taste for flesh," I suggested. "Before they die, of course. Has anybody checked on those children we found on Bardelus?" Erland whipped out his comp-vid and punched keys.

"That's not good," Erland muttered. Lok was following the conversation, his usual scowl plastered across his face. "There's only one left out of the seven, and he's dying. They haven't managed to save any of them."

"This just gets worse as it goes along," I sighed. "Wylend," I dropped my head against his shoulder, "who would know how to do this?"

"Reah, I will have to do research and get back to you, love. Will you not come home with me now or visit soon?"

"I'll try to visit soon," I said.

Keep your promise, Erland's voice sounded in my head.

"Tomorrow," I said.

"Good. Very good." Wylend leaned down to kiss me. Erland removed the markings with power and he and Wylend disappeared.

"Are you married to him as well?" Lok asked dryly.

"I'm only engaged to Wylend," I huffed.

"We have multiple mates on Falchan. It is rare to see the *ai yevu*."

"The single mate?" I asked, translating the phrase into common Alliance.

"Yes. The direct translation is *my only*."

"So," I said, changing the subject, "we have someone who's trading souls with child after child after child, possibly because the Ra'Ak has a taste for the young and tender," I almost gagged when I said it—it made me feel so ill.

"Sounds like a Karathian or something similar," Lok observed.

"Yes—something just like that," I sighed. "Is there anything else we need to see here?"

"I think we found more than enough."

Lok filed his report from my apartment; I sent one to Lendill as well. I got a response right away, in the form of Lendill Schaff.

"Reah, this is disturbing—are you sure of Wylend and Erland's information?"

"Lendill, ask them yourself—they weren't lying. They just didn't know right away who might be able to do this sort of thing. There's no doubt about those children on Bardelus, there's only one of the seven left."

"Fuck." Lendill flopped onto the sofa next to me. "Reah, do not stand in front of another bullet, I beg you," he put his arms around me.

"Honey, I sure don't want to do that," I muffled against his shirt.

"Good. Come to bed with me?" He murmured softly. We left Lok munching on a sandwich in the sitting room and closed the bedroom door.

"Reah, we only got the once," Lendill undid a button, placing a kiss. His mouth was warm as he nipped my collarbone. I remembered the time before with Lendill—in his office. This was our first time in a bed. He didn't disappoint. Whatever it is that he has, it comes through when he fucks. I was begging him, I think, before all was said and done. He gave me everything I asked for, and then some.

∾

"Reah, I have to go," Lendill gave me a gentle kiss early the following morning. "Norian is here to take me back."

"How did you get here in the first place?" I asked sleepily.

"Larentii," he said. "I'll see you soon. Send mindspeech." He kissed me again and walked out of the bedroom. When I got up later to have my morning tea, I found Lok sitting on my sofa.

"Have you been here all this time?" My fists were on my hips.

"You have two extra bedrooms. I borrowed one. You have plenty of room; I'm thinking about moving in. It'll be easier to communicate."

"And you decided that."

"Yes."

"Unbelievable." I shook my head and went off to make tea.

"I don't have any Falchani black," I said, handing him a cup of my brand. It wasn't as strong as what the Falchani normally got.

"This will do; I have some black in my hotel room. I'll bring it when I move in."

"Uh-huh," I muttered. I ended up skipping Lok to his hotel room three times, to move his things, and then he had his cup of tea while I prepared lunch.

∾

"What is this? It's very good."

"It's evil, that's what it is." It was; a sandwich made of ham and thinly sliced fowl, with a good white cheese in between, dipped in batter then deep-fried. I didn't make it often—I could hear arteries clogging just by looking at it. You could dust it lightly with confectioner's sugar if you wanted—I preferred mine with a bit of fresh jam.

"You call this the evil sandwich?"

"Yes, the evil, heart attack inducing sandwich," I agreed, taking another bite. Lok laughed at me.

"What are you doing?" I'd hauled out my comp-vid and went looking through dates of death for the six children on Bardelus, discovering that the seventh had died overnight.

"Look," I pushed it toward him, "these children died around three days apart. That means that the one doing this has to move on to a fresh victim every third day."

"Sounds logical," Lok stuffed the last of his sandwich in his mouth and chewed thoughtfully, going over my research. "They all died around mid-afternoon," he observed.

"Shortly after school was out," I said, agreeing with his assessment. "This is the extra child that some witnesses are reporting —the one who's doing this, that is." I pulled my comp-vid back and sent a quick message to Plovel, telling him that we were dealing with the culprits in the Reth Alliance, now. Then I sent the same message to Lendill, asking if it were possible to warn all children to be wary of strangers approaching—including other children they didn't know.

"That'll be hard for the teens to accept—they love to interact with those they don't know." Lok said, watching as I put the message together.

"Let's go to Farrahn," I said. "Just to see if there's anything there." Lok nodded, so I skipped us there.

"How many of those creatures are there?" Lok asked as we made our way through a playground where three children had disappeared.

"I saw six power flashes when they got away on Bardelus," I said. Lok whipped out his comp-vid and sent that message. "They didn't know?" I asked, trying to remember if I'd sent that information to

Lendill earlier. I guess I hadn't. He would probably yell about it when I saw him next.

"He's asking if you forgot to tell him something," Lok turned his comp-vid around so I could see the message.

"Yeah, he'll yell the next time I see him," I grumped. Lok's black eyes gleamed with humor; he was enjoying himself. It was times like that when he reminded me of Dragon. I kept that information to myself.

"Look—chalk smudges," I pointed out the blue dust on the floor of the old gymnasium. "What do they use this for?" I looked around—there wasn't anything apparent.

"According to my records here, the teens gather at the end of the week and drink alcohol," Lok said, consulting his comp-vid.

"Why haven't they torn this down?" I looked at the ceiling, where old tiles and insulation were dangling precariously. Windows were broken or vandalized, brick crumbling—the place was a hazard. And now, three teens were missing and likely doomed if not dead already. Actually, likely Ra'Ak fodder already; these had been missing eleven days. I shook my head. "Lok, we need to find these things and the humans who help them."

"I agree," He nodded. "Are we ready to go back, now?"

"Yeah."

What do you wear to a tryst with the King of Karathia? I dithered after getting a bath and primping. Wylend and I had never had sex. Something always got in the way. Now that it was a planned thing, I got shaky over it. The dress he'd labeled his favorite was for a formal affair, in black silk. It did look good in contrast to my white-blonde hair, piled on top of my head. I remembered wearing jewels he'd said belonged to his mother. She died in the coup that killed his father.

I still had the tunic and loose pants in purple that Nefrigar had manufactured somehow. I slipped into that, along with the silver shoes that matched the embroidery. I hadn't seen my patron Larentii for a while and it made me wonder where he was.

I'd broiled a steak for Lok before going to get dressed, and he'd even cleaned up the kitchen after he ate. He'd settled in the media room afterward to watch the news vids for anything new that might come along.

"I'll be back tomorrow," I told him before skipping away.

"Here's my love, now." Wylend smiled at me. "You look beautiful." I'd skipped into his sitting room and found Corolan there with Wylend.

"Little girl, you don't know how we worried over you," Corolan sighed, leaning down to kiss me before folding away.

"I have champagne on ice, love," Wylend settled me on the wide sofa and poured a glass for me. I love champagne. This one was perfect. "Are you nervous?" he asked me.

"Um-huh," I nodded as I sipped my drink.

"It's just me, love. Nothing here to be frightened of. Do you think I won't know how to treat my Reah?" Wylend removed his jacket, and then his shirt. I'd never seen him without a shirt. He was muscular—more so than I imagined. "I work out with Corolan and Garek," he smiled at me. "It's not all sex with them, you know. And if you ever want either of them, all you have to do is say it."

"They're not obligated," I muttered.

"They know that. They want you, Reah. I think Corolan has a permanent erection around you."

"Wylend, Corolan's erection isn't the one I'm concerned with, right now."

"Is it mine that you're focused on?" Wylend leaned in to kiss me. And then kissed me again, touching my mouth with his tongue. When I parted my lips for him, he took full advantage. "Yes," a thrust with his tongue. "See," another thrust. "Here," he took my hand and placed it over the bulge in his pants. They were quite tight, there. "Rub this,

Reah. For me." He guided my hand; he was still kissing me and pushing me back on the sofa. "Undress me. Please."

I fumbled with the button, and then three more buttons, freeing the erection we'd discussed earlier—he hadn't bothered with underwear. His hips and thighs hard with muscle, I had a bit of difficulty pushing his pants down. Wylend didn't care. Once they were lower than his knees, he pushed me back all the way and kicked them off, not caring where they landed. Now, his hands were under my top, fingers stroking ribs and the underside of my breasts. In a flash of movement, the top was over my head and gone.

"These are perfect," he lowered his head to a nipple and nipped it with his teeth. Grinding his erection against me, he sucked the nipple into his mouth before turning his attention to the other one. Had I thought this to be slow? Wylend was nearly frenzied. His hand at the small of my back, he worked the tie loose and pulled the silk pants down.

"These—you must buy more of these," he whispered, kissing the top of my lacy panties. I would have to—he ripped them away with power. "Are we ready, Reah?" Two fingers slipped inside. "Ready enough," he sighed and took me swiftly.

"So beautiful." I woke later to dim light in Wylend's bedroom. Corolan lay beside me on Wylend's huge bed. I frowned—when had Corolan come?

"I haven't come. Yet," Corolan murmured, reading my thoughts and brushing my left nipple with a knuckle. "Tell me if you don't want this, little girl. The stars know I do." Corolan leaned down and kissed me. His loving was slow and erotic, making me crazy after a while, and I was begging him with my body to increase his pace. Smiling down at me, he gave me a little before backing off again. Corolan had my hands in his, both raised over my head. He refused to let me use them while his body worshipped mine. That's the only way I can describe it. His skin against mine nearly drove me wild. Now I knew why Wylend wanted Corolan in his bed. Corolan thrust faster after I begged him to do so; I came, and then came again, crying out with the pleasure.

"Yes, that's what I wanted to hear," Corolan said softly, before his thrusts increased and he took his pleasure as well.

"Sleep, Reah." I moaned when Corolan left the bed early the next morning. I did sleep, for perhaps another click or two, before someone else lifted me from the bed and carried me to Wylend's private bath.

"Father will not come to you, because he knows I desire this." Radolf had come from somewhere, and he carried me into the shower after using his ability to turn it on and set it at the right temperature. I was a little sore from the night before. Radolf took care of that, loving me in the shower and then meticulously washing my body. Wylend found us huddled together in bed, my head on Radolf's shoulder while he sipped tea that had been left in the bedroom for us.

"We wore our little Queen out, Radolf," Wylend chuckled.

"I can't move," I moaned.

"You don't have to," Radolf murmured. "The palace will wait on us today. They'll feed you by hand if you wish it, heart's love." Radolf was stroking my hair when my heart seized.

"Fuck!" I shouted and skipped away.

Lok had two blades out, facing Ra'Ak spawn on school grounds. These spawn no longer resembled the humans they'd once been; they'd changed already. Students, ranging in age from twelve to fifteen, were huddled against a fence at Lok's back while teachers pressed against them, trying to keep them calm. Lok didn't know to take their heads and there I was, clad only in a towel, staring at nearly a dozen hungry spawn.

"Reah!" Aurelius appeared, tossing a Ranos rifle to me. I started shooting the moment it reached my hands.

~

"Nice outfit," Lok commented dryly after the spawn dusted.

"Don't be an idiot," I muttered, pulling my towel up and attempting to secure it better. "We need to check every one of those students. If any one of them can't speak when normally they do, then they were bitten."

"I'll help," Aurelius went toward the crowd still huddled against the fence. Norian, Lendill, Gavin and Tony showed up to help, just as the local authorities did. Gavin, Tony and Aurelius would know if any of those children were spawn, just by *Looking* or sniffing. They sorted three out of the crowd. I felt ill.

"We can't kill them here," I was brushing tears away. The students had been traumatized enough already. "How did you know to come?" I turned to Lok.

"I came to speak with Andree's boyfriend. He was one of those you just shot. And what did you call them?"

"Those are Ra'Ak spawn. So, Andree's boyfriend really hasn't spoken to anybody since the incident, has he? His parents covered for him and this is what they got." I shook my head. "You have to cut their heads off, or shoot them with a Ranos pistol or rifle. That's the only thing that will kill them," I added.

"I watched the boy turn into that creature the moment I called out to him," Lok said. "And then he charged me. I was wearing my blades beneath my coat." He had a long coat lying on the ground nearby. "I cut several of them; they surrounded the boyfriend and all turned at the same time. Everybody was running and screaming."

"Can we go now? I'm a little underdressed," I complained.

"And turning blue." Lok lifted his coat and wrapped it around me.

Auri, I'm going to the apartment. Come by when you're done, I sent.

I will. I grabbed Lok's arm and skipped away. He made tea for me this time, while I was dressing in the warmest fleece I could find. I was still shivering when he handed the hot drink to me after I scrambled onto a barstool.

"Reah, you're still shivering, love," Aurelius appeared, followed by Lendill, Norian, Gavin and Tony a few ticks later.

"I'm trying to warm up," I said, sipping the tea. Lok made it stronger than I did, but that was to be expected—he was Falchani.

"Gavril says that the core must be repaired on Campiaa," Gavin sat on my other side.

"I know. I was going this week." I'd always been frightened of Gavin, for some reason. He never let you see what he was thinking and that always worried me. Aurelius was his vampire sire, and Gavin was Teeg's father. Either way, I had to deal with him.

"Am I something to be dealt with?" He tilted his head slightly and looked at me. Gavin was a Spawn Hunter, just as Aurelius, Tony, Drake and Drew were. He could lift thoughts from heads just as easily as the rest of them.

"You scare the bejeezus out of me," I admitted, using one of Lissa's terms. Chash and I used to laugh over that one—we never could figure it out.

"He scares you? Reah, I just watched you shoot eleven of those creatures in four ticks." Lok shook his head.

"Yeah? You're not married—inadvertently—to his son, either."

"Is that what you call ours, too? Inadvertent?" Lendill looked at me while reaching for the sugar across the island. I stared in amazement as it moved on its own, slapping into his hand.

"Uh, honey, you just pulled the sugar to your hand," I pointed out.

"Well, maybe I'm not such a disappointment to my father after all. Now, back to the question." Lendill was like a bulldog. A handsome bulldog, but a bulldog, all the same.

"What would you call it?" I said. "You show up with your father, you're both speaking a language I don't understand and then he says *say yes, Reah.* I say yes and boom! We're married. Isn't that inadvertent? And before you start," I turned to Gavin, "Arvil San Gerxon demanded that Teeg and I marry. I'd say that was inadvertent, too. And you still scare the bejeezus out of me."

Tony started laughing. Maybe he could. Maybe he'd never been afraid of tall, dark and brooding.

"I do not brood." Gavin declared and sipped his tea.

"Child, she can't interpret what you don't show," Aurelius told Gavin over my head.

"Reah, how would a High Demon stack up against a Spawn Hunter?" Tony was only chuckling now.

"I have no desire to find out," I snapped. If I had anything suitable at hand, I might have thrown it at him.

"What's a High Demon?" Lok was watching and listening with his usual inscrutability.

"Reah." Several voices said at the same time.

"Reah, it is decidedly inconvenient to have to search constantly for you." Corolan showed up, his arms crossed over his chest.

"You could have sent mindspeech," I said, trying to make myself smaller.

"Would you answer?"

"Yes. All those times, you would have gotten something from me, if you'd just bothered."

"Stars have mercy," Corolan rubbed his forehead.

"Who is this?" Lok said.

"Corolan, uh—what's your title?" I asked him. I couldn't say concubine; that was demeaning and didn't fully explain what he was. Well, now he was my lover, too, and I still didn't know how to explain it.

"Special advocate to the throne," Corolan looked at me. "Reah, I want to glare at you. Perhaps chastise a little. Wylend has court, or he would be here himself."

"I know. But leather pants over here can't be alone for a click without getting into trouble." I jerked my head in Lok's direction. Lok lifted an eyebrow at my statement but remained silent.

"And you should consider explaining things to Radolf, he thinks he did something wrong," Corolan continued.

"Oh, for heaven's sake, is he still there?" I asked.

"He's probably in Queen Lissa's kitchen on Le-Ath Veronis, preparing a meal. Badly."

"Let's go," I slid off the stool. I didn't know he'd taken another job. Truly. I thought he was still cooking for Wylend. All of us, Lok included, were taken to Le-Ath Veronis by Aurelius, who volunteered.

"Honey, what's this about you cooking a bad meal?" I stood in Lissa's palace kitchen staring at Radolf, who was grumbling and stirring batter—much too hard.

"Reah, where in the universes have you been?" Radolf dumped the bowl onto the island and nearly ran toward me.

"I had to go kill Ra'Ak spawn. You didn't do anything wrong."

"Heart's love, don't scare me like that again." Radolf put his arms around me and rocked me gently.

"Hon, just send mindspeech next time, all right? I'll answer, even if I'm mad."

"I will. I don't suppose you'd help me cook?" He stood back and looked at me.

"I'm starved. I haven't had anything to eat all day. What are you making?"

"Ox-roast. And I'll feed you something while it cooks."

"Sounds good." I wrinkled my nose at him.

"I love you," he said, leaning in to kiss me. And in front of at least eight other witnesses, I told him I loved him, too.

Radolf, Corolan, Aurelius and Lendill were all there, sitting and eating tiny sandwiches and fresh oxberries while Radolf cooked and I offered advice. Radolf teased me. Fed me a berry. I sat between Aurelius and Lendill, with Corolan on Auri's other side. I wasn't surprised when Tory walked in and sat beside Lendill.

"Baby, why didn't you tell me you were coming?" He sounded hurt.

"I didn't know until a few minutes ago."

"Will you sit with me?" I looked at him and sighed.

"Yes." I slid off my stool and went to him. Lok, who sat apart from us at one end, watched the whole thing with hooded interest.

"Do you know about the Dragon Warlord?" I asked him, even as Tory pulled me off the stool beside him and settled me on his lap.

"The Dragon Warlord is my many times great-uncle," Lok sniffed. Tory pulled my hair back and kissed behind my ear. He knows that drives me crazy and initiates the linking.

"Really?" I was starting to feel it, heat suffusing my body. "Drake, Drew, is your father available?" I gasped and sent mindspeech at the same time. Drake, Drew, Dragon and Crane all appeared in the kitchen. "Lok here," I was breathing with difficulty while Tory kissed down my neck, "is your many times great-nephew, Dragon." Lok stood up, startled.

"My many times great-nephew?" Dragon's inscrutability could eclipse anyone's, Lok's included. And Crane was right behind Dragon in that respect.

"How is the Dragon Warlord here?" Lok whispered.

"Uh, somebody else explain," I breathed when Tory's hand brushed a nipple through my fleece shirt. Tory skipped both of us to his bedroom.

"Reah, baby, I just," Tory was pulling my clothes off as fast as he could. Then his came off. Tory is perfect. Perfectly proportioned for his height, with wide shoulders and well-muscled everything. He never finished his statement. Both of us were so heated by the time we were undressed we made love as quickly as we could. High Demons had what was termed the linking, and the desire feeds off itself until lovemaking is a frenzied affair. We both fell asleep afterward.

"I am First among the Saa Thalarr," Dragon held out his hand. "We are an immortal race, chosen to combat the Ra'Ak."

"Reah killed eleven spawn earlier," Lok nodded.

"Reah is High Demon. They have the ability to fight spawn and the Ra'Ak as well. It is the way they are made. Saa Thalarr also have ways to fight them. We are recreated for that purpose."

"Is this the Crane General?" Lok nodded toward Crane.

"Yes." Dragon smiled. "And these are my sons, Drake and Drew. I have another son, Dragon Taylor, but he is with his mate at the moment."

"I haven't had anyone to spar with for months," Lok winced. "I feel out of practice."

"We can take care of that," Crane grinned maliciously. "Easily."

"Baby, wake up," Tory kissed me gently.

"Huh?" I cracked an eye open.

"Baby, I love you. And I'm an idiot. Tell me you'll overlook that." Tory rubbed his nose tenderly against mine.

"Tory, what will you do if it happens again?"

"If I make you pregnant?"

"Yes. I don't even have an empty birth control chip, now. Karzac removed it since it was drained."

"If you get pregnant again, I'll be screaming with happiness from the top of the palace. Your grandfather will hear me and jump for joy."

"Denevik. I keep forgetting about him."

"Baby, he knows you're not used to this. He would like to see you, though. Just so he'll know you're all right."

"I don't know what to do with all of you. It's too much, almost."

"Don't worry about it. We'll give you as much space as you need. Come on, let me love you again, then we'll go to dinner."

"Thank goodness," Lissa muttered when Tory steered me into the dining hall later. We had quite the crowd and Lok was sitting with his ancestor. He looked like Dragon and Crane had given him a workout. They weren't ones to allow laxness as far as bladework was concerned.

"Did they beat you up?" I gave Lok an innocent look.

"Pretty much."

"Good."

"Completely unsympathetic," Lok said. His dark eyes sparkled with humor, refuting his statement. Who could hope to meet an ancestor they'd admired greatly, and have them appear, alive, well and able to spar with them? Lok was lucky. Extremely so.

"When will you heal Campiaa's core?" Gavin was back to a previous subject.

"I'll go tomorrow." I'm sure I was a huge disappointment to the old vampire.

"Gavin." Lissa slapped his hand lightly.

"Reah, you remind me of Lissa," Gavin sighed. "You have no need to be frightened of me. Do you think I might harm you?"

"Emotional harm is still harm," I said, lowering my eyes to my plate. "I always think you disapprove of me." A tear fell before I could stop it. "I think I should go now." I pushed my chair back and stood.

"I will come with you." Aurelius was beside me in a tick, motioning Tory back to his seat. He folded me to his home on the light side of Le-Ath Veronis. "My child does not disapprove of you," Aurelius settled me on the sofa overlooking the floor-to-ceiling plate-glass windows. The sun was setting over the ocean, and it was beautiful.

"But he always looks at me as if I'm not adequate in some way," I brushed away another tear.

"I think he worries that you are at odds with Gavril. Gavril is his only son—he never made any vampire children. Gavin has suffered too, Reah. He thought his son lost to him, and in a way that is still true. Gavril left at seventeen. Now, he is nearly seventy. Gavin was robbed of those years with his child. Just as you were robbed of your friend."

"My best friend," I said. "Chash is gone forever, and now there's a hard-nosed vampire in his place."

"Then you know how Gavin feels. Lissa, too. Child, all of you were cheated in some way. Gavril is different now, and that will never change. There is a chasm between all of you that might never be bridged or repaired."

"Kifirin," I muttered angrily.

"Gavril is at fault, too, although he made his request at such a tender age. Asking a god for something such as this holds a danger he didn't realize. I think that young boy is still there somewhere inside Gavril, but he is a prisoner now, that Teeg San Gerxon will only allow to come out now and then. You are the key, Reah. I think you are the one to bridge that gap for your Chash. Convince him to surface, once in a while."

"He held me captive, Auri. He knew I was pregnant, and still he was hauling me around, using me as a shield against those warlocks. How am I supposed to feel about that?"

"I believe that pains him more than you might imagine. He thought to keep you safe as best he could while he used you, thinking that your comfort would be seen to during the later months. He didn't know the child would be lost, Reah. None of us did."

"Is Jes still in the dungeons?"

"No, love. He was sent to Evensun nearly two months ago."

"He was damaged, Auri. Mentally."

"I know." Aurelius' voice was soft. His arms came around me, hugging me tightly as the sun slipped below the horizon.

CHAPTER 7

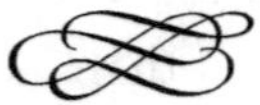

"*L*ove, must you go?"

"I promised I'd go to Campiaa and heal the core." Aurelius had coaxed me into his bed the night before. Now, the sun was up again and I was getting dressed after my bath.

"You could go later." Aurelius slid an arm around my waist. "Or have breakfast with me."

"I don't feel hungry."

"You didn't eat last night."

"I know. I feel queasy. I'm worried I'll run into Teeg. I want to see Farzi and Nenzi, but that means asking Teeg."

"And you don't want to ask him for anything."

"No."

"Don't you love him at all, Reah?" Aurelius' voice was soft. Persuasive.

"How do you want me to answer that question?" I moved away from him. I wasn't sure about my feelings where Teeg was concerned. What did I owe him? What did he owe me? What could he hope to get from me now? Teeg killed Nidris, then I'd tossed Teeg aside while the Ranos launcher was fired at me. I had no memory of that rocket piercing my flesh, I only knew that it had and that the Larentii—I couldn't say which ones—had saved me afterward. The eternally curious boy that Gavril had been was now Teeg San Gerxon, the King Vampire with nearly unlimited knowledge and inexhaustible resources. He knew almost everything. *Except how to get his mate back,* an inner voice insisted.

"Auri, I'm going," I said, pulling his head down for a kiss.

"Do you know how much I worry about you?" His hands cupped my face and golden-brown eyes gazed into mine with concern.

"I don't know what to do about that. Even though I'm out of the ASD, I feel guilty if I'm not out there, trying to do something about the Ra'Ak and the spawn and the rogue warlocks. I wake hyperventilating sometimes—did you know?"

"The only reason the Saa Thalarr and the Spawn Hunters aren't out seriously hunting this bunch is because this is outside the norm. Usually they camp on a planet and we go in disguised and hunt them down. These are moving around, and even now Belen and the others are deciding what to do about it. This shouldn't be your worry, it's just you're the one who can do something about it. You and Lissa, perhaps. We live by a structured set of rules, and we have to be sent after the enemy. So far, we haven't been sent."

"So, I'm the rogue and can move about freely," I sighed. "Just as well, I wouldn't want Norian breathing over my shoulder again."

"Reah, he knows he hurt you. And it eats at him. He's a good man; he thought he was doing the right thing. It isn't like Norian to sit still when something can be taken care of right away."

"And we saw where that led." I was ready to go.

"He didn't know Nidris was still free. Nobody did. You and your baby paid the price."

"So you just expect me to forgive right here and now? Is that what you want? Act like it never happened?" I wanted to cry. And shout. At Aurelius, and he hadn't done anything wrong. Maybe in time, I'd drop the anger and guilt I felt over the whole thing. But right then, the pain was still too fresh. If I said I forgave Norian, I'd be lying. I wasn't ready to forgive him.

"No, Reah." Aurelius pulled me against him and hugged me close.

"No, my precious love. If there were any way I could make this pain less, I would. I can only hope time will take some of it away."

"Then it can't pass soon enough, Auri. I want to crawl out of my skin sometimes, just so I can be free of it."

"I know that feeling." Aurelius kissed the top of my head. "Send mindspeech, my darling, if you need help. If I cannot come, then I can ask someone else. I am not without resources, love."

"I know." I skipped away before I broke down completely.

Campiaa was busier than ever when I landed in the casino at the end of the half-moon bay forming casino row in Campiaa City. Teeg didn't own this one, so I considered it neutral ground. I thought about getting something to eat before healing the core, but because my stomach was still queasy, I decided against it. I'd eat afterward. Instead, I went in search of the spot where the core was leaking.

Breathing a sigh, I stared at the place on Teeg's private grounds. Trust Nidris to make this as difficult as he possibly could. Tall trees surrounded the small clearing and I could see leaves turning brown already, although it was early summer on Campiaa. I would have to sit down and then turn or my Thifilatha would be obvious to everyone.

I'd skipped onto Teeg's property—I wouldn't have gotten past the guards or over the wall if I hadn't. Feeling exposed, even with trees around me, I undressed and folded my clothing, setting it to the side before dropping cross-legged onto the grass. The grounds were meticulously kept—Teeg made sure of that. Only the best for him, all the way around.

Sighing, I made the turn, my head just beneath a heavy, overhanging branch. "We'll have you back to normal in no time," I promised the brown leaves hanging down around me. Closing my eyes, I focused on Campiaa's daystar.

Boss, she's here and healing the core! Astralan's mindspeech came to Gavril while he was meeting with the President of Avendor, an important member of the newly-formed Campiaan Alliance.

Avendor grew the much desired gishi fruit that sold on the black market for more money that most drugs. Gishi fruit was delicious and only grew on Avendor. Their climate and volcanic soil saw to that. And, since Avendor was outside the Reth Alliance, it was considered contraband. Until now.

President Phires of Avendor wanted to maintain a high but fair price for his planet's produce. The Reth Alliance was working out shipping and trade agreements with the Campiaan Alliance, in an effort to ensure that standards were maintained in the growing and manufacturing of goods and services for importation. Gavril's eyes may have widened a fraction, but he didn't betray himself to President Phires when the mindspeech came from Astralan.

Go and see if she needs help, but stay back just in case, Gavril cautioned. *Let me know if there's anything I can do.*

Will do. Astralan cut off the mindspeech. He and Stellan folded to a prearranged location—they'd known for some time where Nidris had tapped the core.

Campiaa hadn't been harmed that much, but I still felt weary and ill after I made the repair and sealed off the core. Then, it seemed to take every bit of strength I had left, just to come back to myself. I saw my little pile of clothing and reached out for it, but my vision swam and then everything went black.

~

Boss, she fainted after healing the core. Stellan sent mindspeech this time; Astralan was busy shouting orders to the medical personnel who'd strapped Reah to a gurney, preparing to take her inside the San Gerxon palace.

I'll be there quickly, Gavril sent, standing and thanking Phires for the meeting. Things would work out with Avendor, but Gavril wanted to be elsewhere swiftly. Gavril thought he might shove Phires out the door before all was said and done. Instead, he handed the President off to Galaxsan, who smiled and talked with the President, leaving Gavril standing just outside his private study. Gavril folded away as soon as Phires turned the corner.

"How is she? What happened? I thought this wasn't possible anymore," Gavril was talking worriedly from the moment he appeared, rushing toward the gurney and the med-techs pushing it.

"I think she's fine—her blood pressure and vitals are all good," Astralan passed on the information he'd gotten.

"I'll be the judge of that," Karzac growled, appearing from nowhere and shocking the med-techs.

"He's a physician, you have nothing to fear," Gavril placed compulsion in a relieved tone.

Two of three straps were torn away before Karzac could calm me down. I'd wakened tied to a gurney and it brought back bad memories. The fact that Teeg was talking and issuing orders hadn't helped. I didn't have a broken arm and leg this time, or fractured ribs. I could move and I did, scaring three people half to death.

"Reah, calm down, baby, you're only strapped down to keep you from falling off the gurney, I promise," Teeg had his hands held out, attempting to bring me back to reality.

"Young one, please let me handle this," Karzac's face came into view. That's when I sighed and relaxed. If Karzac had come, then things were all right. "Reah, tell me what happened. When did you eat last?"

"Yesterday." I cringed, knowing the lecture was coming. I wasn't wrong, but it wasn't loud or hurtful.

"Reah, you are small. And thin. You have little reserves. You cannot go without eating; your metabolism is higher than that of humanoids. Do not do this again, little girl. You will harm yourself."

Teeg was handing out compulsion to the attendants, telling them to forget I wasn't humanoid. Karzac just growled low and didn't say anything. And to top it all off, they pushed me right into Teeg's bedroom and transferred me to his bed. I might have come right out of it again if Farzi and Nenzi hadn't shown up. Teeg dismissed the attendants, Farzi and Nenzi fretted on the far side of the bed while Karzac went over me, Teeg right behind him and Astralan and Stellan behind him. Astralan got a glass of juice from somewhere and I was sipping it after only a few moments while Karzac checked me over.

"Low blood sugar, mostly," Karzac pronounced. "And exhaustion. You need more rest than you're getting. Now, I should get back." Karzac patted my hand, his eyes crinkling a little with his smile. Then he disappeared, leaving me with Teeg and the others.

"Reah, don't scare us like that," Teeg settled on the side of the bed.

"I need to go home," I said, trying to move around him and get off the bed.

"No, Reah, stay." Nenzi was begging.

"Sweet man." I held my arms out to him. I had him and Farzi in bed with me in a blink.

While Farzi and Nenzi snuggled on one side, Teeg slipped off his shoes and wriggled in on the other. "Go find a sandwich," Astralan said to someone. I was eating in Teeg's bed not long after that, with Teeg's arms around me while I ate and Farzi huddled against my side and Nenzi curled in my lap as lion snake. I was stroking his head between bites and then kissing Farzi once in a while. I missed my reptanoids.

"I don't know where it came from, or why it's coming now." Lendill pointed his finger and a square of silk cloth went up in flames, turning to cinders in a blink. This was one of many exercises his father had set for him when he was small, attempting to coax out any ability Lendill might have. Norian stared as Lendill went through exercise after exercise. He burned things. Made water out of air. *Pulled* objects to him. Sent them away. Made them disappear.

"Have you tried folding?" Norian stared at Lendill.

"I'm afraid to—in case I only do it halfway. I could kill myself."

"I don't think it works that way," Norian almost smiled. "I didn't succeed the first time—you have to picture where you want to go. If it works, you go there."

"All right—how about over by that chair?" Lendill pointed to a chair inside his office—the one he kept at Ildevar's palace.

"Do it," Norian nodded. Lendill focused on the chair. Nothing happened.

"Close your eyes and picture it," Norian suggested. Lendill closed his eyes. And in a blink, he was standing next to the targeted chair.

"Holy gods," Lendill muttered in shock, frantically checking to make sure he still possessed all his limbs.

"I don't know why it's coming now, either," Norian shrugged. "Maybe you should practice a little more, then tell your father."

"What am I supposed to tell him? That I can do a child's tricks now? Since I'm two hundred forty-six? That'll impress my brothers."

"Better late than never, don't you think?" Norian chuckled. "Surely they're not that bad."

"You don't know Faldill and Reldill."

"You're right, I don't," Norian said good-naturedly. "That's why you need to tell your father first, and ask him to keep it to himself if it'll just shame you in your brothers' eyes."

"Easier said than done," Lendill sighed. "My father has always been an open communications proponent."

"You mean everybody blabs everything at the dinner table?"

"You don't understand, Keef." Lendill used Norian's last name— he'd done that since they were best friends in college. "My father is older than the dirt on Wyyld, I think. Nothing embarrasses him. He talked about sex when I was six. Went into detail when I was eleven. I think my mother threw food at him over that conversation."

"And there I was, looking up pornography on my comp-vid at that age," Norian grinned.

"What, with all those faked sounds and everything?" Lendill slapped Norian on the back.

"It took me months to figure out that the woman was supposed to be having a good time."

"Then you would have benefitted from my father's explanations," Lendill laughed.

"Come on, let's see you burn something else," Norian snickered.

"Reah, wake up, sweetheart."

"Huh?" I was warm and comfortable. I didn't want to wake up. I was in a cocoon where nothing might harm me and pain was far away. Waking would bring it back.

"Sweetheart, I want to talk to you." *Teeg.*

"Teeg, what do you want?" I turned my head to look at him; his arms were still around me and Farzi and Nenzi, now both lion snakes, were coiled and pressed against my other side.

"Reah, I've stepped back. Given you room. And all that does is make my heart hurt. I don't know how much longer I can stand this. Constantly worrying about you is making me crazy."

"You mean you're upset because your pet slave isn't here to stand in front of you?" I snapped, louder than I meant to. Farzi and Nenzi stirred. Lifting a hand, I reached out to slide fingers down smooth scales. Farzi blinked a slitted eye in my direction. I stroked his head.

"Reah, you were never that. Never. I needed your help, and I kept you with me the only way I could. After we parted on Birimera, I knew you were upset. Rightfully so. I wanted to get you away from there and away from here, because upheaval was bound to follow. It took the better part of three years to get this place anywhere near safe. And then Zellar pops up and starts tapping cores. I know what that can do—he and his Green Fae apprentice tapped Le-Ath Veronis long ago. They would have killed it, too, if something hadn't intervened.

Did you ever wonder what happened to the Green Fae? Corent is one of the two who survived. The rest emptied themselves, trying to repair what one of their young did, after he listened to Zellar. If Le-Ath Veronis hadn't been repaired by an unseen hand, the planet would have died, just like Cloudsong and Thiskil. You were the one who might get me close to Zellar's trained brood, right after we were lucky enough to get a lead on him and kill him. I wish I'd known you were coming after him, too. I'd have stood back and let you have that filth. Instead, you were handed back to me, and I'm sorry to say I used you shamelessly."

"You might as well have shackled me, Teeg," I said angrily. "With that stupid chip, and then pretending you had Chash."

"I did have Chash. Always and ever. With me. Inside me."

"Yet you wouldn't tell me the truth. What kind of relationship do you hope to have, Teeg? I can't trust you, can I? From the moment you took my friends away after Arvil died. Then planting that chip and threatening my friend. You knew I was pregnant, and you didn't say anything. You think I can just look past all that and say sure, all's forgiven?"

"What were you going to do with them? Your friends?" Teeg held a hand over Farzi's head.

"I was going to take them to Niphrin. I was going to turn them loose, Teeg. Let them choose their own lives. Arvil bought them from Zellar. Did you know that? Don't you think it's time they had their freedom? Choose what lives they want to live?"

"Niphrin was a good choice." Teeg lay back on the pillow next to me. "A mix of jungle and civilization."

"And it's Alliance. On the very edge of it, but still Alliance. I gave them credit chip bracelets—what I could scrounge from whatever Arvil gave me. It was enough to give them a start somewhere."

"And what if they wanted to stay with me?" Teeg asked.

"Then you might have asked them that. Just to see what they wanted. All their lives they've been owned, Teeg. I know that feeling all too well. Edan used to threaten me after a beating. Tell me he'd kill me if I ran away or told anyone. I thought I was getting away from all that when the conscription notice came. Only I traded one set of shackles for another, didn't I? Edan is no longer the Edan I knew. Kifirin traded his soul with an Edan six generations into the future. He was a pediatrician and dying when Kifirin made the trade. I can't even hate this Edan, Teeg. He and Ilvan work the regular shift as assistant cooks at the restaurant where I work. I don't know what to do with that. I have a grandfather I have no idea how to deal with. A father now who wants to be close, only I cringe every time I see his face. Then there you are, Teeg. Aurelius is hinting that I should just forgive everybody and forget the past. Tell me how to do that, Teeg. Tell me." I was brushing away tears of frustration, there at the end.

"I can't fix the past, Reah. All I can do is try to make the present and the future better. Try to see that your days are happy ones, instead of the misery you've had in the past. And I admit my part in that. I didn't have time to explain everything to you and hope you understood. I needed your help so I took it the quickest way I could get it. Tell me I hurt you, Reah. That I meant you harm."

"You did hurt me, Teeg. Whether it was intentional or not, I can't answer that. The end justifying the means, I suppose. That won't make me trust you. The friend I had—the best friend I ever had—is gone. He would never have done these things to me. Let me out. I need to go home. I'm trying to chase down those fuckers you let get away from you. They're hiding behind Ra'Ak, did you know that?"

"Yes. I do know that." Teeg raked fingers through his dark hair. At least he showed emotion at times, when his father didn't. "And Erland told me that they have some sort of warlock or power wielder with them; one who has performed a soul-shift. Erland says he's targeting children, because that's what the Ra'Ak prefer to dine on."

"Yes. They're such lovely creatures," I muttered. "I want to kill all of them."

"We think the Strands are in league with an old ally of Lersen Strand's father. His name is Hendars Klar. I've already passed that information to Lendill. I've got people out looking, Wylend has people looking and Norian and Lendill have people on this. Baby, ask for help if you need it. I know the High Demon in you is equipped to handle a Ra'Ak, but there are six of these. Can you stand against all six at once? Think about that. It makes my heart seize up, considering it. And those fuckers—the Strands—you already know they can get their hands on Ranos pistols, rifles and rocket launchers. How many of us will go down if you do, sweetheart? Wylend, all he and Corolan talk about when they're alone is you. And I hear that Radolf, Garek's son has already identified you as his mate. Lendill, well, his eyes follow you if he thinks you're not looking. Aurelius—you should know how he feels. Tory's Thifilathi knows you're his mate, even if he doesn't at times."

"He's too young."

"Who?"

"Tory. All the other High Demon males were thousands of years old before they were mated. Tory was in his late twenties when he put these marks on me." I tapped the back of my neck.

"Reah, I think my brother grew up fast after we lost the baby and nearly lost you. Mom said when the moon was full he was on top of the palace in full Thifilathi, howling in grief."

"Then maybe I should talk to his Thifilathi instead of to him. I still need to go."

"I fantasized about you."

"What?" Now I was staring at Teeg in confusion.

"From the time I was twelve. I knew even then. And when puberty hit, wow. Reah, I couldn't help it. When you'd put your head on my shoulder and go over my assignments with me, I was sniffing your hair and wondering what it would be like if I kissed you. I envied every night you spent with Tory or Aurelius. Spied on you, too, when you were with them. I know it was wrong, but Reah, I couldn't help it. I was so crushed with love, I couldn't stop myself. I thought Kifirin had forgotten that I'd asked to help you when I was twelve. Only he didn't. I wanted that summer we were going to spend together to convince you that we could be more than just friends. I wanted you so much by that time it was making me crazy. I know better than to ask Kifirin for anything. Ever again. He made me pay. And still I don't have what I wanted. You'd walk away from me, right here and now, and not look back. All that work. All that effort, doing what Kifirin said I should do, and the reward is still far from my grasp. I was a fool, Reah. Still am, where you're concerned."

Farzi shifted under my hand. I stroked his head. I knew he and Nenzi were listening. "Teeg, what do you want from me? How are we supposed to go forward from here? With so much between us?"

"I don't know, sweetheart." He tightened his arms around my shoulders. "Don't leave me, Reah. I'm begging. I can't face immortality if you're not with me. All I can see in front of me is empty blackness if you don't want me."

"Teeg." I rubbed my head—a headache was coming on.

"I love you, baby. I know I haven't been the perfect mate. Far from it. But I never for one tick stopped loving you. Never stopped hoping we'd have a good life if we could get over these bumps. Those bumps hit you harder than they did me. I know it. Say you'll at least give me a chance. Give it some time, my love."

"Teeg, I'll give it some thought. And I'll give you some time. All I ask in the meantime is for you to give Farzi, Nenzi and their brothers all the options you can and see what they want to do. If they want to stay with you, that's great. If Nenzi wants to open his own vehicle repair shop or sell new ones, I hope you'll set him up. And if Farzi wants that plantation on Birimera, then I think he deserves it."

"I'll take that under advisement," Teeg sighed.

"Good. Honey Snake," I lifted Farzi's head and kissed the top of it. "I love you. So much. Nenzi—sweet man, I love you, too. More than I can say. Be safe, and tell your brothers the same." I skipped away.

"You hear that?" Teeg ran a finger down Farzi's scales. "You have something I may never get."

Lok set the bottle of painkill down in front of me. He'd been having a cup of Falchani Black when I skipped into my kitchen. I just slid onto a barstool and held my head in my hands.

"Here." He set a glass of water beside the painkill.

"Thanks," I said and shook out a handful of the tabs.

"What gave you the headache?" he asked.

"Teeg San Gerxon."

"Ah. And that would be the one who owns this building."

"Yeah. Anything new on our quarry?" I popped the tabs in my mouth and drank most of the water to wash them down.

"Two more planets have been hit. I was hoping you'd take me tomorrow so we can poke around."

"I'll take you, but Eight-Day is the day after that. I need to get back at a decent hour."

"I want my noodles. I'll get you back at a good time."

"Good."

"What do you want to eat now?"

"What do we have to cook with?" I started to slide off my stool.

"No—stay right there. I'll find something." He did. It was a steak that he shared with me, with stir-fried vegetables. Simple but decent. I ate it. I watched him, the dark braid swinging down his back as he cleaned up the kitchen afterward. Yes, I still found him attractive. His black eyes were an old fantasy for me. I shoved that thought aside. Teeg's eyes had been the same for me once. Now, I couldn't say how I felt about him. And Lok had already told me what he wanted, and I wasn't it.

"Thanks for dinner, it was good," I said. "But I want to go to bed." I wanted a bath, too, but I wasn't going to tell him that.

"Here." A cool cloth was placed over my eyes. I'd been sitting in the tub, leaning back, my neck braced by a rolled up towel, my eyes shut tight, worrying over everything. I'd been so caught up in my thoughts, pulling this way and that, I failed to hear Lok when he walked into the bathroom. I thought to cover myself—the water was clear and I didn't like bubbling soap. He'd already seen everything, I suppose, so I didn't bother.

"Thanks." I said. The cloth on my forehead did feel good.

"You need to meditate," Lok said after a while. He'd sat on the floor, right next to the tub. "Clear your mind of all thoughts. It'll be hard at first, but it gets easier. Picture blackness. That's all. If something intrudes, force it out and focus on the blackness again. See only that. Emptiness. Black. Void." His voice had gotten softer on each word. I did struggle at first, just as he said. But then it got easier. And after a while, I fell asleep.

"Focus on the void," Lok's voice soothed as he lifted Reah from the tub. Wrapping her in huge towels he'd placed on the bed, he covered her up and left her sleeping.

CHAPTER 8

"Reah? Pretty girl?" Corolan sat on the edge of my bed.

"Cory?" I'd inadvertently shortened his name. He smiled at me, telling me it was all right.

"Wylend sent me to tell you that the soul shifter is a warlock. We've gone to do a tri-scry on all the places that we're sure a soul-shift happened. It takes three strong warlocks to do a tri-scry. Wylend, Erland and Rylend did this, and determined that it's Karathian in origin. Some of the wizard clans hold enough power to do a soul-shift, and if we dig deep enough, we can get a feel off the power signature. All three of them say it's Karathian."

"But they don't know who." I sat up in bed with a little help from Corolan.

"That's right. The power signature was too old to get that—that part of it fades right away. If they could get to a soul-shift triangle immediately, they might be able to get a power scent. But that's not likely to happen." He shook his head and pursed his lips in thought.

"I appreciate the information," I patted his arm.

"Wylend wants to know if we'll get a night next week." He was smiling, now.

"I can try."

"Try for Two-Day," he grinned. "I want to make you breathe hard again. I want to hear that little yelp you make when you come."

"I want you to move faster when it feels right," I wrinkled my nose at him.

"Now, where's the fun in that?" He laughed and folded away.

Lok was sipping tea when I padded into the kitchen, wrapped in a robe. I'd wakened naked, with towels wrapped around me. I have no idea what Corolan thought of that. He hadn't remarked on it, anyway. Lok didn't say anything, so I put breakfast together for both of us.

"These eggs are good," Lok was enjoying his food.

"Thanks. Where are we going? So I'll know how to dress."

"Edness first, then Dindre."

"Winter to summer?" I lifted an eyebrow at him.

"Easier to take clothes off than put them on."

"You may have a point, sir." I waggled my fork at him. He ate with chopsticks, like all Falchani. Lok has several sets, some of them beautifully carved. He always washed them carefully when he was finished eating. He did use my spoons to eat soup, though.

"You're allowing me some intelligence?"

"I never said you didn't have it. All I've ever said is that you couldn't go a click without getting into trouble. Intelligence didn't figure into that." He lowered his head, but not before I caught the hint of a smile. Too bad, his black eyes sparkle when he smiles.

"You look good in leathers." Lok nodded his approval of my dress —I had black leathers on, with boots, a sleeveless vest and a lined leather jacket over that. I carried a scarf and hat, just in case, with my knife clipped to the back of my waistband and an extra, smaller knife in the top of my left boot. Perhaps I should ask Lendill if he'd consider giving me a Ranos pistol, just in case.

Lok was dressed nearly the same, with a sheepskin jacket over his leathers that fell midthigh. All leather was black, of course. New trainees on Falchan wore white or lightly-tanned leathers or clothing.

The better trained wore brown or dark green. Only the masters wore black. Drake and Drew had shown me how to handle a blade long ago, teaching me the proper grip and such, before sparring with me. For exactly one week. I'd found black leathers lying on my bed shortly afterward, along with a note that said if I moved that fast, then I could spar with Lissa from now on.

I'd never asked Lissa to spar. High Demons were notoriously fast—it was inborn, somehow. Something instinctive, since we'd been designed to combat Ra'Ak or any one of the other creatures native to the Dark Realm. That's why we were immune to any sort of magical or wizard power—there were too many of those races inhabiting the Dark Realm from long ago. When the Ra'Ak destroyed nearly everything in their efforts to dominate, most of those races ceased to exist. Except for the High Demons, who, as Gardevik, Tory's father taught me, sat on their hands, watching it all happen and did nothing. If I'd been alive at the time, those Ra'Ak would have gotten a message from me, even if I'd been the only one hunting their hateful hides.

Edness was bitterly cold. Everything looked gray, too. From the clouds and the stone of the buildings that lined the street to the street itself. All gray. More than glad I'd brought the hat and scarf, I slipped both on and followed Lok, who hunched into his coat and forged his way down the street. Few were out—not only from the cold but because it was Eight-Day on Edness and early, in addition to that.

"This is where they were taken," Lok pulled gloves on before holding his comp-vid out to me—the dot on the electronic map was steady, showing we'd reached our destination.

Edness was the first place that had a witness, and the woman had reported seeing three children instead of the two who'd been taken.

"Was there any description given of the extra child?" My breath frosted out before me as I looked around for any evidence left behind.

"Dressed in a coat and hat—she didn't see the face and since they were bundled up with leggings on, she couldn't determine the sex."

Lok's mouth was set, but his lips were full and sensual, below a beautiful, straight nose. I realized then that I hadn't even seen his tattoos—he'd always worn a shirt around me. It didn't matter, he found me inadequate. Shaking myself, I went back to looking for clues.

The stones of this building were set so well and so closely together, there was barely a seam between, leaving no rough places to catch fibers or anything else. The concrete beneath our feet was hard, gray and frozen, but no snow or sleet had fallen to betray footprints. I leaned back and stared up at the walls of the building—there were no windows on our level, but there were windows running in neat rows two stories up and higher. I remembered that two of the girls on Tulgalan had seemed to disappear, as if snatched from the air.

"Can we get into this building?" I asked Lok. "I want to see the rooms overlooking this spot." Lok now was looking upward, frowning. Probably wondering what I hoped to find there. He tapped Lendill's code into the comp-vid and waited for an answer.

"Reah wants to see the rooms inside the building overlooking the kidnapping site," Lok explained.

"I'll clear it with the authorities; give me a tick or two." Lendill terminated the call. Lok and I both huddled against the building in an attempt to block the wind—any exposed skin was freezing. I turned my back to it; that part was better shielded than my front. After what seemed a click, Lendill contacted us.

"The building manager will meet you outside those rooms—units 224 and 225. Don't waste his time and remember to say thank you."

"We will," Lok promised and shut off the call. I was more than thankful to go inside the building and ride the elevator up to the second floor. We waited outside unit 224 as instructed. I wondered what the manager might say if I asked to see 324 and 325.

The building manager showed up half a click later, key chip in hand. "We rent some units out to businessmen and such who come for short stays," he said, slipping the chip into the reader. "We have three staying in this unit, but they didn't answer when I rang them and the comp-unit inside says that there's no life source there right now.

That's the only reason I gave permission to your supervisor." I had no idea how Lendill had identified himself—maybe he didn't want to frighten the man by saying he was Vice-Director Lendill Schaff.

"Oh, my. This was not in our agreement," the man said as we walked inside. The stench nearly knocked me down. Inside one of the bedrooms, we found the source of the smell. Andree Wirth's decomposing body lay face-down on the bed, the coverlet bunched up around her. I wanted to gag. Lok gripped my arm—hard—telling me to breathe through my mouth. The building manager didn't have as much success—he was vomiting in the hallway outside after running through the door to get away from the girl's body.

"Vice-Director, we have a situation here," Lok said the moment Lendill answered the call. He and Norian were there beside us in ticks.

"This is the first girl taken from Tulgalan," I said, my gag reflex still trying to kick in. Norian was on his comp-vid, asking for local agents and a forensics team to come right away. Lendill went to speak with the building manager, who was still heaving at times, although the contents of his stomach had been emptied long ago.

"So, we need to check the rooms above where she was taken," Lok jerked his head toward Andree's body. Andree, the other two on Tulgalan, the three on Edness and one boy from Farrahn were the only ones that we knew of who'd had been taken next to a building.

"Why did they not consume her?" Lendill asked softly. He'd come back to stand beside me. Norian was now talking to the building manager.

"Perhaps they weren't hungry, or she died too soon?" I asked. "Did she have a medical condition, Lok?"

"It says here that she had an eye defect—partially blind in one eye, but it didn't interfere with much as far as her schoolwork went," Lendill beat Lok to the punch.

"So, nothing really to make her a bad candidate for the soul-shift or for the Ra'Ak's dinner," I said. "Norian, will you make sure they do a rape check?" I turned to him when he walked inside the bedroom.

"Reah, we always do that. But you just frightened me, I think."

I was frightening myself with my thoughts. If the soul-shifting warlock had been an adult male once, there was nothing to prevent him from entertaining or acting upon any of his more prurient thoughts. Andree had been a pretty girl, with long, dark hair and blue eyes.

The forensics team came in while we speculated, and we were moved to the sitting room while the ASD operatives did their job. The other agents were busily searching through the building manager's comp-vid, recording information regarding the three men the suite had been rented to. I didn't think they were going to find anything except a dead end on that idea. Ra'Ak were powerful and could construct aliases that looked legitimate just as well as the ASD could. They were power-wielders in their own right, and only the Saa Thalarr and the Larentii might be more adept.

"The probe confirms semen samples," a forensics specialist came out to talk with Norian and Lendill. "The DNA matches that of one of the boys taken from Dindre. There may be more, but it's degenerated."

"I think we have the information we wanted," Norian nodded at the man, who went back to the bedroom.

"Can we get into the rooms over the street in Tulgalan? Not where Andree was taken—the other two." I turned to Norian. Andree had been snatched for sexual purposes, nothing more, and her boyfriend, who'd been there with her, had been bitten, probably because he tried to defend her. They'd fought long enough to leave physical evidence behind, along with Andree's boyfriend. After he'd been left behind, he'd bitten others. Therefore, the standoff with the spawn in the schoolyard had occurred. I'd said all that aloud, without really meaning to.

Lendill was busy calling the authorities in Targis. We had something set up in very little time. "Let's go," Norian sighed. He folded all of us right back to Tulgalan.

"We had two businessmen renting this unit, and their lease hasn't run out. I do not appreciate this invasion of their privacy." The building manager was a woman this time, and quite snippy with the local constable who met us in the lobby. I wondered if Norian was about to pull out his credentials. He didn't. Probably used to this by now. The woman, whose name was Mirita Proth, opened the door for us. At least the bodies—plural—inside this one were bagged conveniently for us in plastic, since they'd been dead longer. Both girls and both pretty. Mirita was still gagging and pale when the constable led her back into the hall. Norian again called for local ASD. I shivered. Our warlock, and possibly the Strands, too, had a sexual appetite that included killing young girls. I had my comp-vid in my hands quickly.

"Teeg, what do you know about the Strands, and that other one— Hendars Klar? Do you know if any of them liked teen girls—you know—for sex and such?"

Teeg was shocked to hear from me—I could see it in his face. He covered it well, though. "Sweetheart, Darsen and Ansen, two of Lersen's three cousins, are twins, and rumor has it that they love young girls—sometimes to death."

"Do we have any of their DNA on file?" I looked up at Lendill.

"We have Lersen's, and yes—we have the cousins as well," Lendill consulted his comp-vid.

"Reah, what's going on?" Teeg asked.

"Honey, we just found three dead girls. All pretty. I get the idea that soul-shifting and Ra'Ak meals aren't the only things they're snatching these kids for," I sighed. My headache from the day before was coming back.

"Baby, what's wrong?" Teeg was sitting at his desk when I called; I recognized the wide window behind him. He was standing now.

"Nothing, I just have a headache. That's all."

"I'm coming," he said, and shut off the comp-vid.

"Did we tell him where we were?" Lok asked. We didn't have to, Teeg was there in a blink.

"Sweetheart, come out of there." Teeg had taken one look at the bodies wrapped in plastic on the bed and hauled me away.

"The one at the first place was worse," I said, rubbing my forehead.

"Here." Teeg placed his fingers against my forehead and the pain disappeared. I don't know how he does it; not many can. "Now, did you have breakfast this morning?"

"Yes. But I wouldn't mind something to drink. Something hot."

"Let's go to your apartment." He folded us; I didn't have to do anything. He put tea together for us, too.

We were still sitting there, drinking tea when Lendill, Norian and Lok folded in.

"They found DNA from another missing boy and from Darsen Strand. And we got additional evidence from forensics on Edness—that girl was asphyxiated. Probably during the attack," Norian muttered angrily. "They'll give us any DNA evidence on that shortly."

"We've put out information that they may disguise themselves as businessmen, and anyone renting for a short-term lease—less than a full-turn, that is—is to quietly turn the rental information over to the ASD for verification. I don't know if this will help, but for now we have to keep this away from the media." Lendill was tapping information into his comp-vid while he talked. When Lok set a cup of tea down on the island, Lendill slid it toward himself.

I buried my head in my arms at the island while Teeg rubbed my back in gentle circles. I'd changed clothes—into a fleece set, and Teeg's hand was warm and comforting. *I talked with Farzi and his brothers,* Teeg sent mindspeech. *They say they want to stay where they are for now, but they'll tell me if they want something different someday. Just so you know.*

"All right," I mumbled aloud as Teeg continued to work on my back.

"Sweetheart, you need another massage. Your muscles are way too tight." He attempted to work out some of the tightness in my shoulders with a thumb. He was right; my shoulders ached. The images in my head of those three dead girls didn't help much, either.

"You have to cook tomorrow; you ought to get that massage done today," Lok suggested. I thought about throwing my teacup at him for reminding me that I had to work the following day, but I didn't.

"Boss, you should warn us the next time you disappear," Astralan and Stellan were there and taking seats at the island. With their presence, I no longer had much in the way of available seating in the kitchen.

"Send mindspeech," Teeg murmured.

"Reah, how hard would it be to get one of those fruit drinks with rum in it?" Astralan reached over and tugged on my sleeve.

"Honey, for you, I'll make it," I said, sliding off my stool. Everybody ended up getting one—some of them two or more. We'd had a tough day.

"Reah, we'll check all the worlds that have had disappearances— we'll see if there's anything else to find," Norian promised. I nodded at him. Even though our findings had been grim, at least we knew more than we did before the day started. And we would be tapped into the rental market, in case anything else came up. But there was something bothering me.

"Lendill, Norian—none of those places had enough room for six Ra'Ak and several of those children, plus the Strands. Those rooms were big enough for the Strands, maybe, and Hendars Klar. He's probably funding the operation right now, since the Strand's assets are frozen. At least I assume they are." I looked at Teeg. He nodded.

"No doubt. I was thinking the same thing. Which leaves us with the problem of where the six Ra'Ak are staying and what they're doing with their victims." Norian agreed. Obviously he and Lendill had some sort of silent conversation going while we'd been drinking and having snacks that I'd put together.

"They were underground on Bardelus, but they might not do that again." I didn't know if there were records of underground facilities, abandoned or otherwise, across the Reth Alliance.

"Understood," Norian nodded. "I have to go. Lendill, are you coming or staying?"

"I'm staying. For a little while, at least." Norian folded away, leaving Lendill behind.

Astralan grinned and nudged Teeg. Now what? Were they all planning to stay? "I'll be back," Astralan said and folded away.

"Baby, do you have something else to drink?"

"You want more fruit drinks or a tomato spice?" I asked.

"Tomato spice?" Lok spoke for the first time in a click, I think.

"I'll make one for you and see if you like it," I said, and went to the liquor cabinet.

"I like this." Lok finished one off and asked for another, just as Astralan came back, masseuse in tow, with a table and everything.

"Now, our girl gets the massage she needs." Lendill smiled and pulled on his tomato spice drink.

"Oh, no." They were going to undress me right there in front of everybody.

"Reah, I don't think there's anybody here who hasn't already seen you naked," Teeg laughed. Yeah, he was on his way to drunkenness.

"Watch, I can do this," Lendill was almost as drunk as Teeg. He waved his hand and all my clothing disappeared. I shrieked.

"Baby, don't you worry," Teeg was nearly slurring his words. "We'll take care a'you." Stellan had already had one drink, Astralan was working on his first, now. I'd mixed up another double batch in a pitcher, and they were already working their way through that.

"Come on," Lendill lifted me onto the table while I was trying to pull the sheet off to cover myself. "Breah-mul, just lie down and relax. We promise not to give the masseuse alcohol until she finishes, all right?"

"No, don't cover that up," the masseuse was about to lay a towel over my buttocks.

"Teeg!" I was trying to pull the sides of the sheet over me.

"No, baby. We've seen it before."

"Not all at once," I hissed.

"Don't upset her." Lok laid the towel over my hips. I sighed with relief as the masseuse started working on my back. About halfway through, the hands changed. Became firmer. More sure.

"You don't know me, little girl, but I was giving massages to the Dragon Warlord a long time ago. I'm Rik, and I'm Kyler's ai yevu," his voice whispered next to my ear.

"Another Falchani I don't have a chance with," I muttered, my face down. I didn't even look up at him. I'd heard of Rik—his healing hands were almost legendary around Lissa's palace. He'd come to her shortly after Gavril had gone missing. Word had it that he could work wonders.

"Just relax, little girl. We won't worry about stupid Falchani men right now. Let's just worry about our little High Demon who needs better care. See, that little neck is full of knots. Now, how many of these men put those knots there and didn't take them away again?" His fingers on my neck were heavenly. Just the right amount of pressure and gentleness. "Look how pretty these shoulders are," Rik soothed. "Who wouldn't want that?" He worked on those. And then my ribs, hips and legs. Then, because I was so relaxed and boneless I couldn't move; he turned me over and worked on my front. I was asleep before it was over.

"Thanks, Rik." Gavril offered to pay, but Rik waved him off. "She's Aurelius'. She's entitled, just because of that. Do you want me to carry her to bed?" Reah was wrapped tightly in the sheet from the massage table.

"We'll take care of that," Gavril said. Rik nodded and disappeared.

"Want to flip for it?" Lendill asked. They'd all sat around drinking while Reah got her massage.

"I think it's my turn," Gavril observed, lifting Reah. Lok and Lendill watched as Gavril carried Reah toward her bed.

"You staying?" Astralan asked Lendill.

"I want to."

"You get the extra bedroom. Stellan and I will bring bedding in and sleep out here." He gestured at the sitting room.

"Good enough," Lendill nodded to the two warlocks.

"We need to find a house for Reah if she's going to stay here—a big one," Stellan said.

"Maybe Gavril and I will work on that tomorrow," Lendill grinned.

"Reah, I want to stay in bed with you all day." Teeg nuzzled my neck. "I never got to bite—I didn't want to give myself away," he murmured against my skin. "I shouldn't do it now—you have to work today. I want to, but it wouldn't be good for you."

"You bite?" Somehow, I hadn't expected that. Aurelius did, but then he'd been a vampire. I had to remind myself that Gavril had been born a vampire. To vampire parents.

"I got the urge around nineteen or twenty, I think. Dee had to show me how to do it properly."

"I don't know what to say." I sat up in bed, rubbing my forehead.

"You're not getting a headache again, are you?" Teeg sat up with me —he was just as naked as I was. Teeg is a beautiful specimen. I couldn't argue about that. I'd always thought him well-put together and muscular. Working construction had made his shoulders every bit as wide as his father's, too.

"Sweetheart, we have time—don't we?" He put his arms around me when I told him I didn't have a headache.

"Teeg."

"Come on, we do. You know we do. Then we'll have a quick breakfast and I'll take you to work. And one day this week, we'll go skiing and take the reptanoids with us."

"Really?" I hadn't done anything fun in so long.

"Yes. I promise. We'll take all eight of them. They love to ski."

"I remember." They did, from their very first time—Farzi, Nenzi and their brothers loved snowboarding, and could do it naturally from the very beginning.

"Come on, sweetheart. Let's make love." Teeg rubbed himself against my thigh suggestively. We did. And he did bite. He didn't take much and the climax was powerful and immediate. I may have fainted for a short while. Teeg was kissing and nuzzling when I woke; told me so many times that he loved me. Said the taste of my blood was powerful and intoxicating. I didn't know what that meant—Aurelius had never said anything, but then Aurelius hadn't bitten me in a while. Not since I'd lost the baby, anyway. In fact, we'd only made love once since then, a few days before.

"Come on, let's have breakfast," I sat up, looking around for my robe or something suitable to wear. I got a shower before making breakfast for everyone, and then dressed quickly. Teeg folded me to the restaurant and kissed me before seeing me through the employee entrance.

~

Silmor left a note for me on the prep table, asking for the fish stew. Everything was in the keeper already, so I got that started, the stuffed pork roast went into the oven and we started working on the river fish in a creamy citrus sauce. Bread was kneaded and set to rise again —stock was cooked and reduced for the sauce to go over the pork roast. I prepared the rice noodles last of all—Lok would come for those. We worked on the regular menu, too, but much of the prep had already been done for that. When we opened for the midday meal, people were lined up already.

"We have someone asking when you'll serve the ox-roast again," the waitress who'd taken me to Lok's table the first time told me. Her name was Marissa, and she had long, red hair that she tied back while she was working.

"Do you know who it is?" I asked.

"He looks important," she replied.

"I'll go talk to him." Marissa told me which table, so I removed my apron and went out to the dining room. The Governor of the Realm had come, after getting elected for another term.

"Governor, thank you for coming," I nodded respectfully to him.

"You know, there was a time when I thought you were dead to us, Reah." He smiled.

"And I would have agreed with you," I said. "I'll probably serve the ox-roast again next Eight-Day. I think I can fit you in for a reservation if you don't already have one."

"I'll get one," he smiled. "But this pork roast is just as good. The sauce is excellent."

"Thank you, Governor. Is there anything I can get for you? I think we have a bottle or two of Sun Vineyard Red in the kitchen." Sun Vineyard Red was an expensive wine that we served to special guests.

"I'd like that," he nodded.

"With my compliments," I smiled at him and asked his waiter to bring it out.

"I don't suppose I could hire you to work for me again?"

"Sir, I have other interests at the moment, so one day a week is what I can manage. If that changes, I'll be sure to let you know."

"Please do so. Have you met my wife and daughter?" I hadn't, so I smiled as the Governor introduced them. The waiter brought out the wine; I poured it for the Governor and his wife.

"I'll bring something special for you," I told his daughter, who was in her early teens and not old enough to have wine. I went to the kitchen and put a citrus fruit drink together for her and brought it out in a tall glass.

"Mother, this is really good," the girl took a sip and handed the glass to her mother.

"It is," she said. "What's in it?" I described what I'd put in it. It was very close to the rum drink I'd served the night before, without the alcohol.

"Don't forget to contact me if you become available," the Governor reminded me as I said good-bye and returned to the kitchen.

"That was the Governor of the Realm? I didn't recognize him without his formal robes," Marissa whispered.

"That's him," I sighed. I don't think I could ever work in his kitchen again without remembering Master Cook Vyn. Those weren't good memories. I turned back to preparing meals. It wasn't until about a click before closing that Marissa was back, telling me that another table wanted to speak to me. I went out again and got quite a shock. Fes, Aldah and Addah were there. They'd ordered several items off the menu, including the fish stew.

"Did you cancel your engagement with the King of Karathia?" Aldah sneered as I stopped beside their table, my heart thumping in my chest. I tried to breathe through my fear—they shouldn't be able to hurt me.

"No, Wylend and I are still engaged," I said. "He doesn't control every bit of my time and I still enjoy cooking."

"This fish stew is suspiciously similar to what we serve," Addah threw in. Did he think to threaten me? I'd designed the recipe to begin with, and Ilvan and Edan would likely support my claim now.

"Yet it is not the same." It wasn't, I'd added a few things and perfected it. Desh's couldn't lay claim to what I'd done. Where was the family I should have had? There sat my paternal grandfather, accusing me of stealing his recipes, when they'd never been his from the beginning. "Grandfather," I sighed, staring at Addah, "your customers will always come to Desh's. The food is exceptional and you always have a fine wine list and the best in décor and staff. Did you come here solely to make me miserable? Is that what you did? Because I can assure you, there is no need."

"We came to check on the competition." Fes spoke for the first time. "You know we've always done that."

"Yes, I do know that," I nodded. "I might have liked to do it in the past, when I was still at Desh's number two, but I never received anything other than pocket change from Edan. I had to buy all my clothing second hand, Grandfather."

"That blame is Edan's," Addah rumbled.

"No, Grandfather. That blame is yours as well. You sent a child you didn't want off to someone else, because she had no mother. You never thought to check on me or Ilvan or any of the others besides Fes and Edan. Where are your other twenty-two children tonight, Addah? Can you even give me their names? Is there anything else you want from me tonight? I can give you a full sampling of the menu if you like. And you Fes, I envy you. You at least saw my mother when she still lived. I never got that. Even the photographs of her were withheld or destroyed. I never saw those. You have a mother, Fes. A good one. I saw how she treated you, Aldah and Rane. You probably don't appreciate her nearly enough." I turned and walked away from them, wiping tears.

"Reah, what did they do to upset you?" Lok was walking beside me before I got even halfway to the kitchen.

"That's my grandfather and two of my uncles, come to check on their competition," I sniffled. "It could have been worse. Did you get your noodles and your rice wine?"

"Yes. They are very good. Do you need anything?"

"No. I promised I'd send a sampling of the menu out, and I will," I said. "Go finish your meal before it gets cold." I patted Lok's shoulder. He examined me carefully with glittering black eyes before nodding and moving away.

I sent a tray out with a bit of everything on it, and it was dutifully delivered to Addah's table. I hid behind a row of tropical plants and watched as the three men sampled this or that, discussing the food. Eventually I went back to the kitchen and finished everything for the night.

"Sure you don't want to take the bus?" Oris asked when we walked out of the restaurant after midnight.

"You know, I think I will tonight," I said. I was tired and I wanted time to think before going back to the apartment. Now, I'd be going in the same direction that Oris and Danis went. We waited in the cold at the bus stop, our breaths blowing away from us in a strengthening wind. Limited seating was available at this particular stop and the hard plastic slats on the bench would be frigid—I didn't want to sit on that.

We all stood, waiting for the hoverbus to arrive. The familiar noise of the braking system sounded as the bus pulled up, the door swishing open to allow us inside. Warmth billowed out—the bus was heated well, at least. Danis, Oris and I scanned our credit chips as we climbed up the steps and chose seats. Six others rode with us as the door shut the cold out, the brakes released and we lurched forward.

Perhaps it was because I was as tired as I was, or perhaps it was because the visit from Addah, Fes and Aldah had rattled me so much that I kept going over and over it in my mind. Regardless, when the Ra'Ak hissed and attempted to change in the lengthy bus, I still beat him to the punch and killed him in my smaller Thifilatha.

CHAPTER 9

Many passengers were injured—every Ra'Ak dusts when it dies and this one was no different. Chunks bigger than my fist blasted outward when I twisted the head from the body. Some pieces shattered windows and went flying into the street. Four of the six passengers needed medical attention, their injuries caused by flying Ra'Ak dust.

Oris and Danis, who'd been behind me, were spared because my Thifilatha's body blocked anything from reaching them. They were both staring at me in shock, however, when it was over.

Lendill, Norian and Gavin came. I don't know who'd called Gavin, but I was more than thankful. He placed compulsion on the passengers, telling them that it was an accident only. Norian and Lendill were smoothing things with the local constabulary, and I was thankful for that as well. My hands shaking and my entire body quivering in reaction, I sat on the back seat of the bus and let the others handle everything. Lendill brought clothing, shoes and a coat for me—everything had been burned away the moment I went Thifilatha. I'd dressed with shaking fingers in the back of the bus while Gavin placed compulsion.

"Reah, little one, shall I send for Gavril?" Gavin's voice was low and calming. I nodded at his question—I needed someone with me right then and I knew it. Teeg showed up almost immediately.

"Sweetheart, do you want to go to the apartment or come home with me?" Teeg lifted me off the seat in the back of the bus.

"I'll come with you," I muttered. I was still shivering and couldn't seem to get my breath. What had the Ra'Ak been doing on a bus? I didn't normally travel that way—it couldn't have been looking for me. All the people on the bus were adults, too. Was this Ra'Ak even one of the six we were hunting? I couldn't tell. Perhaps Teeg could have, or Lissa, with their perfect sense of smell. But the Ra'Ak was in chunks now and we wouldn't know, more than likely.

"Can somebody let Lok know that I won't be back at the apartment tonight?" I asked Lendill as Teeg carried me off the bus.

"I'll let him know." Lendill pulled out his comp-vid.

"Come on, baby, let's get you home. You're cold and shaking," Teeg murmured and folded me away.

"I should have known sooner, but I was still fretting over Addah, Fes and Aldah showing up and calling me out of the kitchen like assholes," I muttered later as Teeg dumped me in the hot water of his spa behind the palace.

"They showed up and demanded that you come out and talk to them?" Teeg was shocked. So was I, honestly. I might have walked into Desh's to sample the food, but I sure wouldn't alert Addah to my presence. But then Addah wasn't afraid of me. I was of him, though. I drew a shaky breath.

"Addah tried to accuse me of stealing their recipes—said the fish stew was close to what they served. The only reason it's close is because I designed the original recipe. Fucker." I didn't have any kind words for my paternal grandfather. "I'm glad now that I left out three ingredients when I wrote down the yaris fish recipe for Edan six years ago. They can't lay claim to that, either."

"Baby, stop fretting about your grandfather and tell me about the Ra'Ak." Honestly, the Ra'Ak had upset me less than my own family.

"I didn't notice him when I walked past his seat toward the front of the bus," I said. "I was too busy going over Addah's visit. The moment the doors closed on the bus and it started moving, he stood up. I noticed it then and went right to my smaller Thifilatha. I had to twist his head off; he tried to lash out at me but that's a mistake with a High Demon."

"And then he dusted," Teeg added. "Did the dusting hit you, sweetheart?" He ran his hands over my body.

"I ducked and covered my head with my arms," I said. "But I got hit in a couple of places. I'm better equipped to handle that than the other passengers were."

Farzi, Nenzi and six other reptanoids crawled up in lion snake form and all of them plopped into the water. Farzi and Nenzi draped over me as well as they could while the others got as close as Teeg would allow. I think I cried a little while eight lion snakes tried to console me.

"That's Reah." Lendill ran the images from the bus camera back, then allowed them to play again for Lok's benefit. Norian had confiscated the recording to keep it out of the locals' hands.

"That's what she becomes?" Lok was surprised.

"That's the smaller one," Lendill nodded as Lok stared at the golden scales and long white hair flying as Reah decapitated the Ra'Ak using only her hands. "She's about six feet or so in the smaller one?" He looked to Norian for confirmation. Norian nodded. "In the larger one, she's around fifteen feet. And she has her wings tight against her body here," he stopped the image. "They're amazing when she spreads them out."

"So that's what a High Demon looks like."

"When they change, but Reah is the only one with gold scales. The only other female who has ever turned is the High Demon Queen—

Glindarok. Her Thifilatha is white. The males turn Thifilathi and theirs are larger and all black with short horns. Reah doesn't have horns."

"Reah is unique." Lok nodded.

"They can't ever get tattoos," Lendill jerked his head toward Lok's red dragons—it was late and he wasn't wearing a shirt. "The ink burns right off when they change."

"Their clothing burns off, too, if they're wearing any. Reah didn't have time to undress, obviously," Norian ran the footage forward, showing Reah coming back to herself. She was completely nude. "Lendill knew to take clothing when she sent mindspeech to him."

"I can't even see the attack, it happens so quickly," Lok muttered.

"Neither can we. That's how fast they are. Lissa says that the High Demons were made to fight the Ra'Ak and the other creatures that inhabited the Dark Realm. They were designed specifically for that purpose." Norian sighed.

"I was worried about her earlier—her family from the other restaurant—they came in and upset her." Lok said.

"Who was it? Did her grandfather come in?" Lendill was seething, suddenly.

"I believe so—with two others. Her uncles, she said."

"Calm down, Lendill, you can't bring charges against someone for being a prick," Norian said.

"Addah Desh would be at the top of the list if I could."

"That's neither here nor there—we've had a Ra'Ak attack in Tulgalan's capital city. That's unheard of. What are we going to do?" Norian looked at Lok and Lendill.

The reptanoids were gabbling excitedly as we climbed into the reserved snowbus—Teeg had rented one for the day to carry us up the mountain near Campiaa City and back again. Somehow, Teeg had provided several outfits inside the closet he'd set aside for me—all of them ski outfits. Other things were there as well, but I was almost afraid to sort through all of it. Now, we were loading onto a luxury snow bus and driving up the mountain. Unsurprisingly, Teeg and the reptanoids had their own snowboards. Farzi's was black with white stripes, Nenzi's was a bright red. He loves red and wears red shirts often. The others also had their own special colors, ranging from orange to blue. It made me smile to see them so happy.

"I haven't gotten to do this in ages," Teeg slipped dark glasses over his nose and grinned at me. It was at times like this that I felt Aurelius might be right—that Gavril the boy was somewhere deep inside Teeg the man. Gavril might come out to play now and then.

"No, you go, I want to see all of you go down first," I said, shooing Farzi toward the edge. They went, in twos and threes, and it was a pleasure to watch them move so expertly. Surely, it had to do with their supple muscles and bone structure. Teeg grinned at me and followed the reptanoids. I, still a bit unsure and with two skis strapped to my feet, went over the edge after them. I shrieked several times, trying to convince my feet to go in the proper direction. Fell twice, too, but didn't hurt myself. When I made it to the bottom, Teeg and the others were laughing and dusting snow off my jumpsuit. We wore ourselves out, broke for lunch at an expensive restaurant, went back out again and stopped before the sun hung too low in the sky.

"That wonderful," Nenzi sighed, pressing against my right side. The left was leaning against Teeg. Farzi sat across the aisle from us, with the others scattered behind.

"Have a good time, sweetheart?" Teeg murmured in my ear.

"Yes. Can we do it again next month?"

"I'll make sure we have a day," his mouth was warm against my temple, as he nuzzled and kissed his way to my jaw.

Teeg took me out to dinner at the San Gerxon. Guarded by Astralan and Stellan, people whispered as we passed. They were all saying Teeg's name and speculating as to who I might be. Teeg heard every word—he had vampire hearing, after all. He smiled over most of it and put his hand on the back of my neck—there'd been a beautiful dress and a hairdresser waiting when we arrived at the palace. Now, dressed formally and my hair piled on my head, we walked toward the best restaurant in the San Gerxon.

Almost the moment we were seated at a private table, Kiasz was out of the kitchen and in raptures, hugging me carefully so as not to ruin my outfit. The dress was a spring green, almost the color of my eyes and Teeg had likely paid a fortune for it. My Tiralian crystal ring came out of a jewelry box I hadn't recognized and Teeg placed it on my finger before we left the palace. No wonder everybody was whispering. I think a few unauthorized photographs were taken as well.

"Tell me what you want to eat and it will appear," Kiasz was still grinning.

"Right now, I'm so hungry I could eat a moose," I said. "We went skiing today."

"A steak then? Prime rib? Seafood?" Kiasz was ticking down a mental list.

"What do you want, honey?" I looked at Teeg. He drew in a sharp breath for a moment, then gave me a lazy smile, his eyes half-closing in pleasure.

"Prime rib," he replied.

"There. We'll have prime rib," I said. "And can I get some of those sliced potatoes with Vharis cheese crusted over them?" I gestured with my hands.

"Lady, I think you can get anything you want." Kiasz cut his eyes toward Teeg, bowed smartly and went toward the kitchen.

"Reah, I feel like the luckiest person alive right now," Teeg said, sipping the wine Kiasz sent out. The vintage was good. A bottle of a darker red would come with the meal, but this was good with the plates of appetizers we'd been served. Kiasz was choosing everything except the main course and the potatoes for us.

"Going to get me drunk and then have your way with me?" I snuggled into his arms.

"Sweetheart, that is the finest thing imaginable."

∽

"Sometimes, one of ours surprises us," Ferrigar, Head of the Larentii Council sat at Kiarra's kitchen island. He, Pheligar, Renegar and Lenigar had come, setting a chunk of Ra'Ak dust on the granite surface. Kiarra, with her mates Adam and Merrill, all Enforcers for the Saa Thalarr, stared at the chunk. They were more than familiar with what Ra'Ak dust looked like.

"Which one, and how did he surprise you?" Kiarra asked. Pheligar, also her mate and Archivist for the Saa Thalarr, took up the explanation.

"You have never met Nefrigar. He is our chief librarian, you might say. He guards the Larentii Archives with the help of six Larentii—the equivalent of Protectors for the Wise Ones."

"I've heard of the Archives, but I thought that was where all information gathered by Larentii went to die," Kiarra sat beside Pheligar and patted his back—she was teasing him.

"It does not do that," Ferrigar said, holding back a rare smile. "In fact, Nefrigar usually absorbs what is sent. If the Archives were lost, Nefrigar could reconstruct most of it from memory."

"Wow. A living Archive." Kiarra leaned her cheek against Pheligar's arm. He pulled her against him—he liked having his mate close.

"Nefrigar is my older brother," Pheligar smiled down at Kiarra.

"What?" she sputtered, staring at him in surprise. "After all this time, you're only now telling me you have a brother?"

"Nefrigar is much older than I," Pheligar said haughtily, before smiling at Kiarra. "He and I only speak now and then, and usually it is mindspeech. We are busy with our own concerns, Lara'Kayan. Each of us can contact the other easily if there is need."

"Unbelievable," Kiarra rubbed her forehead.

"I would have told you if you'd asked," Pheligar kissed the top of her head gently. "You didn't ask."

"But what does that have to do with this?" Merrill tapped the granite island where the Ra'Ak chunk sat, bringing everyone back to the relevant topic.

"We have Ra'Ak dust in the Archives," Ferrigar replied. "Pheligar supplied some of it, from his earliest days with the Saa Thalarr. When Nefrigar compared some of those chunks with the one taken from Tulgalan two days ago, he found—discrepancies."

"Discrepancies? I don't follow," Kiarra said.

"We find it puzzling as well. Nefrigar brought this to our attention and at first, we thought it irrelevant. Now, we are not sure that was the correct conclusion."

"What did he find?" Adam asked. Normally he was content to listen and observe, but even his curiosity was roused.

"This," Ferrigar *Pulled* in what appeared to be an identical chunk of Ra'Ak dust, "was collected ten turns ago, from another Ra'Ak dusting. This Ra'Ak would be considered normal—healthy." He set it down beside the other chunk. "This one from Tulgalan," Ferrigar hesitated a moment, "to the best of our knowledge, we have determined it to be diseased."

"Diseased? That's next to impossible," Kiarra said, trying to stand. Pheligar pulled her onto his lap and rubbed her shoulders.

"We have gathered additional information, at Nefrigar's insistence. Even the Wise Ones are in agreement. The Ra'Ak who still live, who have been consuming these young ones after they have been subjected to what the Karathians refer to as a soul-shift?"

"What about them." Kiarra asked.

"We have determined that they are, in your own words, mentally ill."

"You're saying that eating children that have gone through a soul-shift makes the Ra'Ak crazy?" Kiarra managed to struggle out of Pheligar's lap.

"Yes. Somehow, this forbidden spell work—a misuse of power, as it is, would destroy the child's mind, if their body did not die so quickly. By consuming this tainted flesh, the Ra'Ak despoils its mental capacity."

"Holy crap," Kiarra muttered. "What are we supposed to do?"

"We believe that this is the reason the Ra'Ak attempted an attack on a passenger bus. This one did not bother to jam the camera signal.

If Reah had not killed the creature, and had Norian not confiscated the vid images afterward, Tulgalan's population would even now be screaming and running for every available exit."

"This isn't good. Honey, have you contacted Belen?" Kiarra looked up at Pheligar.

"Yes. He is very concerned, and he and the others of his kind are attempting to come to an agreement regarding appropriate action," Pheligar sighed. "He will let us know soon."

"How did Nefrigar know to pick up this chunk?" Merrill asked.

"We do not question the Archivist—he searches for his own data upon occasion. We as a race are often enriched with his findings. He is not bound by the Archives, or restricted by the Council where knowledge is concerned, as long as the laws are followed."

"So, you don't lock him up in a dusty library?" Kiarra's dimple showed.

"Our Archives are pristine," Pheligar pulled Kiarra onto his lap again. "Nefrigar sees to that, with his Protectors. He is nearly as old as Ferrigar, you know."

~

"Reah, wake up, sweetheart."

How did my men always wake before me? How? I opened my eyes to find Teeg's concerned face over mine. "What's wrong?" I asked, right away.

"Several things, but you need to get up and get dressed, love. Some of the news can wait a little."

Farzi and Nenzi came to help me in the shower. I was glad—my fingers shook and I was having trouble holding onto a washcloth. Something was wrong, and that frightened me. I was ushered into Teeg's private study—he was already there with all four warlocks and a man I'd never seen before.

"Reah, this is Dee—Dormas, my assistant." Teeg introduced the man I'd heard of but never met. He took my hand and kissed it gently. I nodded to him. Dee had brown hair, gray eyes and an unlined face that still bore the weight of the world in it. He'd seen a lot of life, this one.

"Reah, last night, someone died on Tulgalan." Teeg pushed a comp-vid across the desk toward me. I sat on one of his guest chairs and lifted the device in my hands, terrified, somehow. I was relieved at some level, horrified on another. Relieved that it wasn't Lok or Edan or Ilvan. Horrified at whom it actually was. Addah Desh, my grandfather, had died from multiple stab wounds. Fes, who'd been with him, was in critical condition at a hospital. I watched the vid as Aldah and Rane, Fes' brothers, stood by their weeping mother as she'd been interviewed. Some of the other wives and sons were in the background.

The whole thing would have been bad enough, but what came next was worse. Aldah stepped forward after his mother stopped speaking, saying that I'd had a fight with Addah and was likely the one who'd attacked him. My eyes flew wide and I was staring at Teeg across the desk.

"We're already on this—we have vid and photographs of you with me at the same time the attack was taking place, and Norian and Lendill are handing the information over to the local constabulary. I don't know what the fuck is going on, Reah, or why that idiot is blaming you for this." Teeg was angry—his eyes were tinged with red, and for a vampire, than meant he was furious.

"I don't believe this," I muttered. "How is Fes doing?"

"As well as can be expected. We don't know yet whether he'll live or not."

"This is awful, but what could they possibly believe I'd gain from all this? I'll have to contact Wroth—see if he's got the vid from the restaurant on Eight-Day."

"We have audio and the vid," Dee offered, "and that has also been turned over to the locals."

"And they know you were on the bus the other night," Teeg went on. "Norian turned that information over to them, and since you're ex-ASD, Norian handed your report over, too."

"I didn't turn in a report."

"Norian and Lendill turned in an official report, Reah. Do you want your Thifilatha splashed all over the news?"

"Fuck," I muttered softly. Too much had happened in the past two days. Where was my mind?

"Dee has forwarded a copy of our marriage contract to the Tulgalanian authorities as well, so there won't be any wild rumors. If Aldah Desh wants a war, he can have one." Teeg was growling.

"I need to get back." I was stunned and not really sure what to do.

"If you go back, you'll likely be followed. At least until the media sinks their teeth into someone else."

"Teeg, I don't want that."

"Sweetheart, I know that. Lendill and I found a house for you on the west side. We'll move you into that, and we'll place enough guards there that you won't have to worry about those things."

"But what about the investigation?"

"We may be able to get someone to either change your appearance or work up a disguise," Teeg offered. "I know this is important to you, so I won't try to keep you in the house. You just have to realize that the media, if they learn who you are, are going to follow you to the ends of the Alliance and back."

"I don't believe this." My head hurt now, and I'd had more than my share of headaches, lately.

"If it gets to be too much, baby, go to Le-Ath Veronis. Nobody will bother you there."

"All right." I nodded my acceptance. What would this do to my job? The reporters would be camped outside the restaurant, waiting for me to come to work next Eight-Day.

Teeg was right—news crews had hover-vans parked up and down the street outside the Crown Apartments and outside the house that he and Lendill had purchased in my name. Reporters were shoved aside by Astralan, Stellan, Galaxsan and Celestan. Farzi and Nenzi had come with me, and I thought Nenzi was going to hiss at some of the people who were shouting at me, asking if I'd killed my grandfather. It was horrible. As soon as we made it inside, I looked at Teeg. "Arrange for transport to Le-Ath Veronis," I said, defeat in my voice. He nodded and pulled out his comp-vid.

Farzi, Nenzi, Lok, Corolan and Tory were with me when I boarded the ship to leave Tulgalan. Listlessly I watched the vids of myself entering the ship station. They had nothing to hold me on—Addah and Fes had been attacked outside Addah's enormous estate. Sixteen of his sons lived there, in addition to all five of his remaining wives. Marzi was still incarcerated, and Addah had divorced her anyway. Truthfully, I didn't even know where Addah lived now. I remembered the old house—I had vague memories of it.

So far, too, no weapon had been found. The story went that Addah, Aldah and Fes had stayed late at the restaurant, going over the books for the end of month expenses. They'd been driven home by Landor, Addah's third wife Teena's first son. He had no skill in the kitchen so he worked as Addah's driver. Mostly he drove the wives around. Rane, Farla's third son behind Fes and Aldah, kept the books for Addah. Landor drove Addah, Aldah and Fes home, dropping them off at the front gate while he drove around back where the garage was. It was a shorter walk to the door from the front gate. Aldah said he'd gone inside the house while Fes and Addah talked by the front gate. They'd been attacked after that. Landor said he hadn't seen anything or anyone when he dropped his father and brothers off. No DNA evidence was found either, other than that of the family.

I watched as they played the vid from Dee's over and over again—all of Tulgalan got to see the entire conversation, start to finish. Once again, I experienced Aldah's and Addah's slights. Fes had been the most civil of all of them.

"Baby, don't let them get to you." Tory held me tightly against him inside our private compartment. Teeg and Lendill agreed that folding or skipping away from Tulgalan right then would be a mistake. It would only feed the blaze for those who thought me guilty, even without a bit of evidence to back it up.

Lissa, Gavin, Drake and Drew were waiting for us when we arrived at the space station on Le-Ath Veronis. Lissa hugged me the moment I walked through the doors.

"Don't let them hurt you," she said softly. It was too late for that, but I appreciated her words anyway. "There are a few reporters in Casino City, but we're going past that. They're not allowed anywhere near the palace right now."

"Thank you." I sighed heavily. Dee said he'd contact Wroth for me. I'd agreed to let him handle things. At least I'd get to see Radolf and cook with him.

"Reah, Norian and I have moved into our offices here," Lendill met me inside the private residence wing of Lissa's palace. His and Norian's offices were on the edges of that wing.

"Lendill." I was in his arms and sobbing.

"Don't, Deah-mul," Lendill lifted me off the floor and with Lok, Tory, Farzi, Nenzi and Corolan following along behind, he carried me to Aurelius' old suite.

"Do we need to place a healing sleep?" Karzac appeared as if he'd been called.

"Karzac, can you move me ten turns into the future, so all of this will go away?" I wiped tears from my face. Lendill settled me onto Auri's bed and then sat beside me, while Farzi and Nenzi climbed in on the other side.

"No, little girl. But I will see to it that you sleep for a while, and then wake and eat with the rest of us."

"Reah, I'm going back to Wylend." Corolan said.

"Tell him I'm sorry I didn't make it."

"He knows, love. Go to sleep. We'll see you soon." Corolan folded away. I didn't have time to say anything else, Karzac's fingers were against my forehead and I was out.

"The injured one knows the truth." Smoke was pouring from Kifirin's nostrils. Denevik, Gardevik, Glindarok and Jaydevik had all come to check on Reah. She was still sleeping, but Kifirin had appeared in Lissa's library, where they were having a drink.

"You're saying Fes knows who attacked them?" Lissa looked up at her oldest and most powerful mate. Even he had restrictions as far as interfering went.

"Yes, he knows. And if he does not survive, have your youngest place compulsion on Aldah to clear Reah's name."

"I will, honey. Sit down, please. Do you want anything?"

"Not at the moment. I do not like this persecution of my heart's daughter."

"I want to punch that fool," Denevik growled.

"Denny, stay away from them. We can't gain anything by threatening harm." Glinda placed a hand on Denevik's arm.

"I know, sister. But this makes my blood boil. As if Reah would attack anyone like that. If she were going to, she'd have killed Edan Desh long ago."

"Edan Desh will not be harmed, you know why," Kifirin turned his eyes toward Denevik.

"I know, High Lord," Denevik inclined his head respectfully.

"Do you think we should bring Edan and Ilvan here—for their protection?" Lissa asked.

"It could not hurt," Kifirin agreed.

"I'll look into it," Lissa said, sending mindspeech to Norian.

It took roughly a click, but Ilvan and Edan were brought to Lissa inside her library. "Welcome," Lissa smiled at both of them. "I am Lissa, Queen of Le-Ath Veronis. We merely wished to bring you here for your own protection." Lissa wrinkled her nose at Norian—he'd produced his ID and hauled both of them away from Tulgalan. "We'll bring your clothing and other necessities, and you'll be guests of the Crown. Now, would you like to meet Reah's other family?"

Edan and Ilvan looked around them in shock. The Queen was inviting them to stay, to protect them? And what was this about Reah's other family? "I am Reah's grandfather, Denevik Lith," Denevik rose and offered his hand to Edan and Ilvan. "Raedah was my daughter, that I was unaware I had."

"I know," Edan nodded, taking Denevik's hand. Ilvan shook after Edan.

"I am Glindarok, Queen of Kifirin and Reah's great-aunt," Glinda shook next. "And this is my husband, King Jaydevik."

"Reah is related to royalty?" Ilvan didn't know what to think.

"Reah is High Demon," Kifirin announced, blowing a bit more smoke.

"I don't know what that means," Ilvan quavered.

"We'll explain that later, we just want you to know that Reah is very, very special," Lissa said, lifting an eyebrow at Kifirin. "Very rare. In fact, High Demon females are extremely rare."

"As are female vampires." Norian pointed out.

"No need to worry, you will be safe here," Lissa said. "Come, we will find rooms for you, near Reah's if you'd like."

"Will we be allowed to attend father's funeral?" Ilvan asked.

"If you want," Lissa said. "And Reah will not be prevented from attending as well, if that is her wish."

"But she will be heavily guarded, I do not want any of those fools near her," Denevik blew clouds of smoke from his nostrils.

"How could Aldah even think it possible that Reah could do this?" Edan shook his head. "But then he is somewhat vindictive. He is the reason I left Desh's to work at Dee's."

"He is the least honorable difik," Jayd snapped.

"Difik?" Ilvan asked.

"Idiot," Lissa supplied.

Farla, Addah's second wife, elevated to first after Addah divorced Marzi, watched the vid repeatedly. One part in particular. Farla watched as Reah repeated, again and again, that Farla was a good mother and her sons didn't appreciate her as much as they should. Fes had called her shortly after he, Addah and Aldah had gone to Dee's. Told her he loved her. Farla had been shocked and more than pleased —she felt her sons ignored her most of the time. Something they got from their father, Farla knew. Addah only had one use for women, and if not for the fact that she might be cut off from her sons, she might have left Addah long ago.

There was little love in her husband, unless it was for cooking and making money. Now, Farla hoped her eldest son would wake. Without Fes, Desh's would likely die. None of the others had the talent in the kitchen like Addah or Fes. Edan looked to be a rival, but all along, it had been Reah making Desh's number two so successful. It had crashed shortly after she'd been conscripted by the Alliance, and now number two struggled against two other successful restaurants in Shirves.

Reah was no longer a member of the family—she'd separated herself legally five years earlier. None of the family had any pull with her, and Aldah, the fool, had accused her of killing Addah when date-stamped, tamper-proof vids showed her with Teeg San Gerxon on Campiaa at the time of the murder. Who knew she was married to that one? And still she was engaged to the King of Karathia as well. Reah had done more than well for herself. Had powerful friends, mates and allies. Farla could only see disaster coming for the Desh family. Addah kept the best recipes to himself, suspicious of his children, even, and so refused to share his knowledge. All that died with him.

"Farla, the constables are here again," Teena, now second wife, walked into Farla's sitting room. Teena, Indiva, Hilde and Baretis had each borne five sons for Addah. A few had some skill, but most worked on the business side of the restaurants. Desh's number three, in Cardon, was barely keeping its head above water, although Baretis' eldest, Halde, was very good at stretching a budget.

"What do they want?" Farla stood, prepared to answer even more questions regarding her husband's death.

"They've arrested Aldah. Rane turned him in."

"Just stay back while Karzac wakes her—you don't want to tangle with Farzi and Nenzi." Tory was trying hard not to smile as Edan and Ilvan shrank back after spotting the two lion snakes in Reah's bed. Nenzi was coiled beneath Reah's chin, Farzi was draped over her waist. Both had lifted their heads and spread their hoods when Tory brought Reah's uncles into the room.

Both reptanoids knew Karzac now. They also knew that Karzac would only protect Reah, as they sought to do. Retracting their hoods, they moved aside so Karzac could wake Reah.

~

"Huh?" My voice was thick with sleep and my mouth was as dry as a desert.

"Reah wake now." Nenzi kissed my chin—he'd just turned from lion snake.

"Sweet man," I wrapped my arms around him. Farzi was hugging me from behind now, so I turned my head and gave him a sleepy peck.

Tory cleared his throat nearby. I hadn't realized he was in the room. "What, hon?" I asked.

"Your uh, father and uncle are here."

I turned to see Edan and Ilvan standing with Tory, both not far from my bed.

"Are you awake now? Where's my help in the kitchen?" Radolf stalked in, mock indignation all over his face.

"What are we making?" Farzi and Nenzi scooted off the bed and trotted toward my bathroom—they were naked. Edan and Ilvan watched them go, a bit of shock consuming them, I think.

"Did you explain they're shapeshifters?" I glared at Tory.

"No time," Tory grinned.

"They won't hurt you as long as you don't threaten Reah," Radolf explained. "Now, are you coming to help? I'm trying to put that duck thing together."

"I'll come help with the duck thing if you'll give me something to drink." I came off the bed while Karzac watched silently.

"My heart's love, you sound as if I'll leave you parched." Radolf had a fist at his heart.

"Let me get changed. And since Edan and Ilvan are here, maybe they'll help too." I offered Radolf a big smile.

"I'll come watch, as soon as Reah gets some decent clothes on," Tory grinned.

All of us ended up in the kitchen—Edan, Ilvan, Farzi, Nenzi and Tory. Lok walked in with Lendill, Drake and Drew. Lok looked as if Drake and Drew had been sparring with him.

I put a fruit drink together for all of us, while Radolf and I got five stuffed ducks into the ovens.

"Is this a new recipe?" Ilvan asked. He'd helped put the stuffing together while Edan trussed the ducks afterward.

"We cooked it together for the first time on Karathia," Radolf said. "It turned out great—it just needed minor adjustments. We'll see if we got it right this time."

"Reah?" Denevik walked into the kitchen.

"Em-pah?" I went to give him a hug.

"How's my baby?" he whispered.

"I'm all right," I said, bumping my forehead against his chest. He gave me an extra hug and accepted the drink that Radolf handed over. "How is Jusef?" I asked. "I've missed both of you."

"Jusef is fine and busy herding the help around in Glinda's palace kitchen," my grandfather smiled.

"He's a good cook," I said.

"Jusef?" Radolf asked.

"Amterean Dwarf," I said, pulling Denevik toward a barstool at the island. Tory, Drake, Drew and Lok were already there, having their drinks and a light snack.

"Reah," Lissa and Gavin walked into the kitchen, "your name has been cleared. The police on Tulgalan just arrested Aldah for his father's murder."

CHAPTER 10

The breath caught in my throat and I was paralyzed for several ticks. "But—how? Why?" I couldn't understand this. Fes and Aldah had always been Addah's prize pupils.

"His brother—Rane? Is that right? Turned him in," Lissa explained at my nod. Edan and Ilvan were both just as stunned as I was.

"Did Rane see it?"

"No. He caught Aldah washing one of his cooking knives off in the house," Lissa said. "He saw blood. Aldah didn't see him, and Rane didn't say anything at first. But with Fes in the condition he is, Rane said he wanted justice for his oldest brother."

"That had to be a kick in the stomach for Rane," I muttered. Addah had always belittled him, so Rane settled for doing Addah's books.

"Is it safe to go back to Tulgalan?" Ilvan asked.

"You're still welcome to stay here if you want," Lissa smiled at him.

"I could use a couple of good assistants," Radolf remarked, tossing a hand in the air dramatically.

"Are you serious? Work in this kitchen?" Ilvan sounded thrilled.

"I'm willing, if you're serious about the offer," Edan nodded. "I'd prefer to go back to school and get a medical degree so I can practice medicine again, but since I have no funds, this is the next-best thing."

"What did you just say?" Lissa came around to stare at Edan.

"I'd like to practice medicine again?"

"Yeah. That's the one. Karzac!" Karzac was there in a moment, his light-brown hair a bit ruffled, as if he'd ripped a surgical cap off quickly before folding in.

"Lissa?" He lifted an eyebrow at her.

"Do you have room in your teaching classes for this one? He wants to practice medicine again." Lissa nodded toward Edan.

"What sort of medicine did you practice before?" Karzac was sizing Edan up.

"Pediatrics," Edan admitted. "I worked with a group that provided free medical care to indigent worlds," he added.

"Good enough. I'll fit you in," Karzac said.

"But I can't pay—I have no funds."

"Not a problem," Karzac waved it off. "Tuition here is free to all residents. Cook if you want to earn your pocket money."

"I'll help." The words were out of my mouth before I thought.

"Reah, no. Let me do this on my own," Edan was there and pulling me into a hug.

"Can we plan to go to Addah's funeral?" Ilvan was next to us, hugging us both and sobbing.

"Ilvan, honey, it's all right," I was rubbing his back. This had hit him harder than I thought. With Tory, Drake and Drew helping, we got Ilvan onto a barstool and a stiff drink in his hand. I was rubbing his back still, while Radolf offered a towel.

"I can arrange to send flowers and monetary assistance." Wylend folded in with Corolan and Erland.

"Would you?" I looked at my Karathian Warlock mate.

"Done," Wylend said.

"I'll handle it," Erland agreed.

"I'll write the card," Corolan offered.

"Farla, there's a mountain of flowers in the entry, and this came with them." Indiva handed a thick card to Farla. The envelope was addressed to her and the Desh family. It also bore the royal crest of Karathia.

We wish to express our deepest condolences to you and your family, the card read. *We hope that this contribution will assist you in some way during your time of grief. Sincerely, Wylend, King of Karathia and Reah, Queen to be.* Inside, nestled in a protective wrapper, was a credit chip worth one hundred thousand Alliance credits. Farla fainted.

~

"Wylend sent flowers and a credit chip for a hundred thousand," Dee said, setting the comp-vid in front of Gavril. What do you want to do?"

"Exactly the same," Gavril grinned.

"Wise choice," Dee smiled and went to make it so.

~

"Farla, this just came, along with another flower delivery," Baretis handed over the envelope, this time. This one bore the newly designed crest of the Campiaan Alliance. Farla sat down to read this one.

Reah and I wish to express our condolences on your loss. Please accept this contribution toward your expenses at this difficult time—Teeg San Gerxon, Founding Member, Campiaan Alliance. Another credit chip, also for one hundred thousand Alliance credits, was tucked inside the envelope. Farla fanned herself with this envelope, attempting to retain consciousness.

~

Wylend stayed for dinner, and the duck was perfect. "This is the recipe we'll use in the restaurant," I clinked wineglasses with Radolf. Wylend and Corolan spent the night. They took very good care of me, leaving early the following morning. Radolf was there afterward, and we didn't get out of bed for a while.

"My heart's love," Radolf kissed my hand then pressed my fingers to his chest. His heartbeat was steady and strong beneath my hand.

"Where did you come from, love?" I asked him. "You are a gift to me."

"Just what I always wanted to hear," he smiled, leaning down to kiss me.

"Mother, Fes is waking!" Farla had arrived at the hospital to check on her eldest before making final arrangements for Addah's funeral. Rane had come earlier to sit with his brother.

"Thank the stars," Farla was nearly running down the hall toward Fes' room.

A doctor stood beside Fes' bed, checking his vitals. The physician smiled, his green-gold eyes twinkling a little. "He should be fine now. Let the staff know if you need anything." The doctor left the room.

"Mother," Fes reached out a shaking hand to Farla.

"Fes," Farla was in tears as she grasped his fingers in hers.

"Mother, Aldah has gone mad. He killed Father and then turned on me."

"They've already arrested him," Rane said. Farla was sobbing.

"Fes, do you know why he did this?" Rane asked softly. He couldn't fathom why his brother had stooped to this measure.

"He became angry, because father still refused to share some of his special recipes with us. He accused father of keeping all of us under his thumb by withholding what we were entitled to. Father shouted back, of course. All this happened in the car on the way home. Then, when Landor let us out at the front gate, Aldah pulled one of his cook's knives from its case and stabbed Father. I tried to stop him, that's how I got this." Fes held up his bandaged hands. "When Father fell, Aldah stabbed me. Twice."

"We were so worried," Farla lifted her tear-stained face to her oldest son.

"I think I will be fine now," Fes sighed. "Do you think they will allow me some water?"

"Gavril and Wylend will escort you here," I blinked at the vid-map that Lendill had splashed on a wall of his office. Lendill pointed to a spot on the map showing where the family would be and then where I was expected to sit—nearby but not with the family at Addah's funeral. "Lok, Tory, Erland, Rylend and I will provide security, in addition to Gavril's four warlocks. I believe Farzi and Nenzi may also be there with you, Reah."

"I want them with me," I nodded. Ilvan and Edan were also in this meeting, but they were welcome to sit with the family. I'd separated from them, so I was no longer entitled. It didn't matter—none of those there, except for Edan and Ilvan, would likely recognize me.

"I will sit with Reah," Edan said. "If she'll allow it."

Turning to Edan, I nodded at him. Slowly I was getting used to him. Becoming accustomed to the face that was so different now. Before, Edan would get angry over nothing. This one I had yet to see angry. *What was your name before?* I sent mindspeech. The effort was likely useless, but this was an easier way to ask.

What? How did you? His voice came through clearly.

You have mindspeech. Likely Kifirin gave it to you, I answered.

Come rest your head on my shoulder and I'll tell you, he returned. Blinking at him, I worked to make the decision. Rising from my seat, I went to sit beside Edan on Lendill's sofa. He pulled my head onto his shoulder and kissed my temple. *My name was Eldan, he told me. Not far from Edan, don't you think?*

No. Not far off, I agreed.

I was nearly two hundred when I was brought here, he added.

I'm glad it's you, instead, I told him. He ran a hand over my hair.

"You are allowed to attend under the bereavement clause," the Warden examined Marzi Desh with distaste. She'd kept the last name against her ex-husband's wishes. Marzi was a troublemaker inside the prison —had most of her neighbors in conflict at all times. Even now, she was blinking her beautiful blue eyes at the Warden. He huffed at her pitiful attempts at flirting—his taste ran to males. Of course, she wouldn't know that—Marzi wasn't bright enough to read the signals. She did know how to keep things unsettled around her, however. Warden Brig Andlen pursed his lips at the thought.

"You will have guards around you constantly, you will be cuffed and should you do anything other than what is directed by your attendants, those cuffs will be activated. Do you understand?"

"Of course I do." Marzi's voice was low and sultry as she drew a pattern on her knee suggestively. Brig was thankful she was chained for the interview.

"Spare me—I find it insulting," Brig snapped. "You will have suitable clothing provided, but you will not be allowed to keep it. You will attend the funeral only, and return to the prison upon its conclusion. Do you understand?"

"Yes." Now she was angry and nearly spat the word at Brig.

"Get her out of here," Brig nodded at Marzi's guards.

Marzi called Brig an extremely unkind name as she was escorted to her cell. "There's one on the top floor that sends his greetings," the guard on her left whispered carefully. "He says that the white-haired bitch needs to suffer. He wants you to get close enough." Marzi, who'd done favors for both her guards, smiled.

"I'll owe you," she said sweetly. "Both of you."

"You'll have a heavy coat issued—winter is well-established," the other guard said softly. "You'll find what you need inside a pocket. And we'll expect the usual. Tonight and for the next six moon-turns."

"You'll get that and more," Marzi promised with a smile.

Former Master Cook Vyn Bralnon paced across his cell. The men's prison was located two floors above that of the women's. He wasn't without resources, and he'd watched every bit of news available, as soon as Aldah Desh accused Reah of killing his father. Aldah was the murderer as it turned out, but Vyn still blamed Reah for his imprisonment. He hated her. Would always hate her. Plus, he had ways of acquiring what he wanted. His mother still lived, and anything she could do for him, she would.

Vyn's mother, Stria, had bribed guards too many times to count, just to get a treat or some bit of contraband inside. This time, however, Vyn had two particular guards bribed—or at least his mother did. Reah Desh would attend Addah's funeral—that had somehow been leaked to the press. Marzi Desh, two floors down in the women's prison, would also attend.

Vyn didn't care what happened to Marzi—he only wanted Reah dead. It would be simple—supply Marzi with a weapon and Reah would die. Rumors abounded inside prison walls, but it was no secret that Marzi hated Reah just as much as Vyn did. Vyn smiled. His plan was perfect. Reah would die, Marzi would likely be killed onsite and since the guards would keep their part in this secret, Vyn would achieve his objective with no repercussion. His mood was nearly gleeful as he flopped onto his narrow bed. Now, if he could just find a way to speed through the next few turns of his sentence, life would be so much better.

"We'll wait until after the funeral to have our meeting," Lissa sighed. Kiarra had come to give Lissa information regarding the mentally ill Ra'Ak. "Reah took that one down on Tulgalan, thankfully. She needs to hear this, too."

"Yes, she does," Kiarra agreed. "And we must all be more watchful. Invite everyone connected to this, regardless. The more who know, the better we'll be at recognizing the signs."

"Lendill, Norian and Lok have been investigating more of the sites where children disappeared. So far they haven't learned anything new," Lissa said.

"We need a liaison between the ASD, what Gavril has in place and the Saa Thalarr," Kiarra said.

"Plus Wylend's warlocks," Lissa agreed. "You know, Denevik may be interested—Garde says that he's bored, most of the time."

"I'll consult with Pheligar. If he agrees, then we'll approach him," Kiarra nodded.

"Reah, I realize you may never wear that dress again, but you are beautiful in it." Corolan had a hand at my back as we were escorted into the temple for Addah's funeral. It looked to be a lavish affair. Erland walked ahead of us, Wylend behind with Ry. Cory looked more the part of King of Karathia than Wylend did, and that was by design. Cory was offering himself as a target, allowing Wylend to stand at his side and appear to be a guard.

Teeg was behind Wylend, with all four of the Starr warlocks guarding him and Wylend. Farzi and Nenzi, dressed finely for the occasion and looking quite handsome, walked on either side of Teeg. I pitied anyone who tried to harm the founding member of the Campiaan Alliance. Lok and Lendill had already gone inside; just to make sure all was well inside the temple before we arrived by hover-limo. Edan and Ilvan were walking on either side of Corolan and me —Ilvan would break away and join the family at a prearranged seat, Edan would remain with me.

Love, what do you think they'll find to say about the old bastard? Teeg's voice was in my head.

I don't know, other than he knew how to cook, I replied.

Well, there's that, Teeg agreed thoughtfully.

Tory, Lok and Lendill waited next to our seating area while our company took its seats. Small, complimentary palm-vids were placed on the back of the seat in front of us. By pressing a button, we could pull up information on the deceased, and even record the ceremony or images of guests, if we wanted. Unfortunately, more than a few were trained on us already.

Soft music played while the remaining guests filtered in, escorted by temple acolytes dressed in the accustomed funeral white. Funerals were seldom invitation only, but this had turned into a state affair. Even the Governor of the Realm was there, since Wylend and Teeg had come.

I'd gotten mindspeech from Aurelius earlier—I didn't know exactly where his assignment had taken him, but wherever it was, he'd gotten news of Addah's death. He and I had held a lengthy mental conversation regarding dead parents and lost opportunities.

Once the Governor of the Realm was seated off to the side, the ceremony began. My conversation with Teeg proved to be prophetic —the priest went on at length about Addah's service to his customers and his genius in the kitchen. Very little was said about his extensive family. I glanced across the aisle at Farla and the other wives. Each was sitting on the first row, accompanied by their firstborn sons.

Surprisingly enough, Fes had come with Farla. I'd heard he'd wakened, but I hadn't known that he was fit enough to attend the funeral. His face was pale, but so was Farla's. He looked much like her, with darker hair, though his eyes were Addah's. Farla was in a terrible position—one of her sons was imprisoned for killing her husband. The situation had to be traumatic. I saw her squeezing Fes' hand several times with one of hers as she wiped away tears with the other.

Farla's head rested on Fes' shoulder, too, and he whispered to her now and then while she nodded, wiping more tears away with a kerchief provided by the temple. I held back my sigh of relief when the service was over and we stood when prompted, ready to file out. The family went first, followed by my bunch, in reverse order.

Wide doors at the front of the temple were swung open, allowing daylight to wash over the crowd near the back. We'd almost reached the portal when someone to my left stood. In slow motion I whirled to see who it was, receiving a terrible shock; they'd allowed Marzi to come.

Although she was surrounded by guards and wore shock cuffs, she somehow held a weapon in her hand. One of her guards, moving faster than the others, batted at the hand holding the weapon, which was aimed directly at me. The guard's blow caused Marzi's aim to go wide. Instead of sending the projectile flying at me, it now flew toward Corolan's head.

I may have screamed—I don't remember—all I know is that I moved swiftly enough to leap in front of the warlock, who was too stunned to move. Or perhaps he was moving, as were others around us, it's just that I could and did move so much faster.

As I leapt forward, I felt the bullet hit my neck, effectively deflecting it from Corolan. I heard shouting around me as the front of my beautiful, white gown was splashed with blood. Before everything went black, I recalled in some part of my mind that my carotid artery had likely been hit.

Marzi's four guards forced her to the temple floor quickly, wrestling the weapon from her hand and employing the shock cuffs. She was shrieking and convulsing while chaos erupted around the King of Karathia, the founding member of the Campiaan Alliance and their combined party. All were struggling to reach Reah, who was bleeding profusely.

"Enough." All were thrown back gently as a huge, blue Larentii appeared in their midst, Reah held in only one arm. His other hand was pressed firmly over the wound in her neck, sealing the wound swiftly with quick thinking and power. His clothing was covered in blood—Reah had been soaked in it. Kifirin appeared as well, shocking all the guests remaining inside the temple.

"Stand back," Kifirin growled. "Who has done this to our small one?" He stepped toward the guards, who still held Marzi on the floor. She stared up at him—he was in his smaller Thifilathi, black scales gleaming, wings half-furled, horns curling about his face and dark eyes angry as they glared at Marzi Desh.

"Save me!" She shouted. "He'll kill me!"

Her words caused Kifirin to breathe a billowing cloud of smoke. Marzi and her guards shrank back. "I won't kill you," Kifirin growled. "From this point forward, however, you will only speak the truth." Kifirin disappeared.

~

"Reah? Open your eyes, sweetheart." I heard Teeg's voice from far away. Where was I? My head was stuffed with cotton. There was no pain, but something had gone wrong. I just couldn't recall what it was.

"She's trying to wake—she moved a little." Wylend's voice, sounding hopeful.

"Please tell me she's all right." Radolf fretted.

"Karzac's here—he'd let us know if there's a problem." That was Tory's voice.

"We will give blood if it works for our Reah." Nenzi, now, but what was he saying? What did that mean?

"Young one, her grandfather and her great-aunt have already donated, and we have two more who are compatible and willing to give," Karzac replied to Nenzi's worried statement.

"Karzac?" My eyelids were weighted, I think, it took such an effort to lift them, and they wanted to close again immediately.

"Little girl, stay with us," Karzac brushed gentle fingers down my face. "You've lost much blood; that foul woman hit a major artery. If the Larentii hadn't come, even I wouldn't have been able to save you. You are stable now, so do not fret—we just need to get a bit more blood into you."

"Who?" I was struggling to remember the woman Karzac spoke of.

"Mother." I heard Ilvan's voice but I couldn't see him. Now I remembered. Marzi. Marzi, the one who'd killed my mother had nearly killed me, and probably not for the first time.

"Not for you to worry over at the moment," Karzac was hanging another bag of blood on a pole beside my bed. I didn't know where I was, the ceiling was unfamiliar.

"You are in the house that Gavril purchased for you in Targis,"

Karzac said softly, connecting the blood bag to a line hooked into my arm. "Rest assured that Marzi Desh is spilling everything she knows, not just to the prison Warden and Norian Keef, but the Governor of the Realm is there as well, and all are asking questions. I'm sure it is an unpleasant experience for her, forced to speak the truth as she is."

"Daddy?" My voice sounded lost, even to my own ears. Did Edan remember his mother? Where were his loyalties now?

"Baby, that woman means nothing to me," Edan knelt by my bed and gripped my fingers in his. "I don't know her, I only know of her."

"Em-pah's here, too, baby." Denevik's face appeared above Edan's.

"We had to hold him back for a while, he wanted to kill a few people," Tory grinned behind my grandfather. "And then Karzac and Jeff took some of his blood, so he's calmed down, now."

"Em-pah, if I'd been able, I might have wanted to kill people too," I said, my eyes closing in weariness.

"Come—we won't talk of such things now," Karzac's fingers were warm against my forehead.

"Master Cook Vyn, did you think to come before me a second time?" The Governor of the Realm gave his former head cook an angry glare. Vyn was terrified. How had that woman survived to tell the tale? He, the two guards he'd conspired with and his mother were all being questioned. And what was this regarding threats to a visiting dignitary?

"She fired directly at the King of Karathia's party," the Governor growled. "Are you aware of the charges that result from such an act?" Vyn could only shake his head—he had no idea.

"An act against a visiting dignitary is the same as an act against the Governor of the Realm, here or from any other Reth Alliance world. Now do you know?"

Vyn was unsure whether to speak or not. He knew the answer—it was an act of treason, or in his case, conspiracy to commit treason. And his mother—brought in on the same charges? Vyn was more frightened than he'd ever been in his life. "We have the vid—would you like to see it?" The Governor went on. "It shows the weapon aimed toward the Karathian King's party. I'm sure you were unaware that the original target—Reah Nilvas Silver, once called Reah Desh, is betrothed to the King of Karathia."

"Wh-what?" Vyn stuttered.

"Yes. I speak the truth. Had one of the benign Larentii not come, Reah would be dead. Now, would you care to tell me what kind of revenge you arranged with Marzi Desh, to kill the Karathian King's Queen to be?"

~

"I want to kill you—it's as simple as that," Norian hissed at Marzi. "But I'll let the court system handle this. I'm sure you'll wish you were dead by the time this is over. You're charged with High Treason, did you know that? You fired at the King of Karathia and his party."

"That slut of a girl was not a part of his party," Marzi denied.

"Call her names again and I'll watch you die," Norian snapped. "Reah is betrothed to the King of Karathia. He was there to lend her support. You are charged with High Treason, Marzi Desh, and with what those two guards are saying concerning your trading sexual favors to get your way, I think the term slut might apply to you. You will be placed in solitary confinement, and the cuffs will not be removed. Pass any wall of your cell and they will activate. Your co-conspirators will receive the same treatment, and if I know the Governor of the Realm, all of you will be sentenced to Evensun. Do you know what happens there?" Norian gave Marzi a satisfied smile.

"The death planet?" Marzi's knees went weak.

"That's what they call it," Norian nodded. "Take her." He jerked his head toward the guards in the room. She'd been compelled to answer every question truthfully, and Norian silently thanked Kifirin for that gift. Otherwise, Vyn Bralnon and the two guards might have gotten away. Vyn's mother had also been implicated—she'd been bribing guards to get contraband inside prison walls for years. She would suffer the same fate as the others, when sentence was handed down.

~

"See—when the guard hit Marzi's hand, the shot went wide," Lendill was stopping and starting the vid image. They all watched in horrified fascination as the projectile flew directly toward Corolan's head, only Reah, moving faster than the camera could capture the image, whirled in front of the laser bullet and blood flew as it pierced her neck. "Now, here's where the Larentii comes—do any of you recognize him?" Lendill asked as the Larentii appeared, almost from beneath Reah a blink after she was hit, and he staunched the blood flow with large blue fingers. He settled Reah carefully into Tory's arms before disappearing as quickly as he'd appeared.

"Mom says that his name is Nefrigar," Tory sighed. "He's like the Larentii librarian or something."

"Do we know why he came?"

"No. Not yet, anyway. I don't know how he knew to come." Gavril said. He was angry, although Marzi and the others were likely to be sent to Evensun. In his estimation, Reah had been exposed to too many attempts on her life. Karzac was concerned, just as he was.

"It doesn't matter; he came and she's still alive." Wylend had almost thrown a spell at Marzi Desh; one that could end her life. Erland and Rylend had held him back.

"Karzac says that Reah will be down at least two weeks, with his supervision. Longer without it," Lendill said. He wanted to go to Reah's bedroom and crawl under the covers with her. Whisper that he'd keep her safe. And perhaps he could. While he had guards posted around the house and nobody was allowed in or out without his knowledge or permission. Lok was in charge of perimeter security at the moment—Lendill had seen the anger and grim determination on the Falchani's face—he pitied anyone who might argue with Lok over Reah's safety.

"How many bedrooms do we need to prepare?" Gavril stood and

stretched. "I'm staying—Dee will handle things on Campiaa until tomorrow or the day after."

"I want to stay in Reah's room," Corolan muttered. She'd risked her life for his, when it should have been the other way around.

"Farzi and Nenzi are in bed with her—as lion snakes," Gavril said. "Probably not a good idea to get too close."

"Is there a room nearby?"

"I have the one on Reah's left, Lendill has the one on the right, and Tory is across the hall," Gavril loosened the top button of his dress shirt. He hadn't taken time to change, he'd settled for removing the formal jacket he'd worn to the funeral. Tory had been the one to change clothes immediately—Reah's blood had transferred from her clothing to his. "You can take the room on Tory's left and if Wylend wishes to stay, he can have the suite on the right."

"Wylend and I will stay together," Corolan frowned, rubbing a spot between his eyes that insisted on throbbing painfully.

"Suit yourself. Let me know if you need anything." Corolan nodded at Gavril's words and he and Wylend disappeared together.

~

"We should be spending the night with Reah." Wylend fumed as he tossed his jacket across the borrowed bedroom with an angry spell.

"My King, you are overwrought. Do not distress yourself, I beg you," Corolan sighed.

"Admit it—you want her just as much or more than I."

"I cannot deny it, my love, but we are not on Karathia at this moment. We cannot dictate who she should be with on an Alliance world."

"That makes no difference." Wylend's shirt shot across the room, following the path his jacket had taken. "I am King of Karathia, and I have been usurped by my upstart great-grandchild in everything. He dictates where Reah goes. He dictates Karathia's movements. From the moment we joined the Campiaan Alliance, it has been thus."

"My King, we will have Reah again with us, do not fear. Karathia is being treated no differently than any other world in the Campiaan Alliance." Corolan was beginning to worry about Wylend's reaction. Was this about Reah, or something far deeper? Wylend was prone to fits of anger now and then, and this one came on the heels of an attempt on their lives.

"Corolan, I wish to be alone for a while."

Corolan jerked his head up at Wylend's statement. "Of course, my King." Corolan bowed and folded to an empty bedroom down the hall.

"Reah, sweetheart, would you like a drink of water?" Teeg always had the ability to wake me or put me to sleep, just as Karzac did. I sometimes wondered how he'd come by it.

"I am thirsty," I said, realizing it was an understatement. Dry as a desert was closer to the mark, and as I'd been in a few deserts, firsthand knowledge of how dry that could be was an apt comparison. Farzi and Nenzi, still in snake form, had scooted over to give Teeg plenty of room. He held a glass of water to my lips while I drank. I wanted to sit up for a little while, but Teeg settled me down on the bed again.

"Karzac says we'll get the IV out tomorrow, and we'll feed you." I'd gotten broth earlier—I was coming to hate the stuff. I said it aloud, too. "You said stuff," Teeg teased gently.

"I said stuff," I agreed amiably, lying back and closing my eyes. "Teeg?"

"What, love?" He busied himself with pulling the covers up to my chin, the soft fabric rustling as he resettled it over my body.

"Why am I still alive?"

"What are you talking about?"

"This time—and the time before that. Teeg, nobody survives a Ranos rocket. Even if they are in full Thifilatha. And it doesn't take genius material to know that bitch Marzi hit my carotid when I jumped in front of Corolan. A laser bullet will explode on impact—so that means my throat was likely torn apart. I would have bled out in a very short time. Why am I still alive, Teeg?"

"A Larentii showed up this time. Several showed up last time." Teeg was holding something back, I figured, but if he didn't want to tell me, there wasn't any way to pry it out of him. He could do vampire with the very best of them. "Reah?" he said instead.

"What, Teeg?"

"I wish you'd call me Gavril. Or Chash. At least when we're alone. That would make the past fifty-odd years of life without you bearable, I think."

"Teeg," I slapped a hand helplessly across my forehead. I was still weak and the hand shook, even while it rested on my forehead.

"Baby, I hope someday you trust me enough to believe I was that boy you loved. And all that time I never stopped loving you. I'll admit that I was hardened over the years, becoming secretive and self-reliant because I was forced to. I know it's difficult for you that I don't discuss everything with you like we did before. Dee taught me that trust is a commodity we can ill-afford most of the time. I know it's the same for you, sweetheart. How many people do you trust? Completely?"

I blinked at him for a few moments while I sorted through the people I knew. Who among them did I trust? "Three," I said with a heavy sigh. "Three."

"Are you going to tell me who they are? I'm not naive enough to believe I'm one of those three."

"You're right, and it isn't my intention to hurt you with that information," I said. "I trust Farzi, Nenzi and Aurelius."

"Good choices," Teeg nodded his head. Perhaps he didn't mean to betray himself, but there was disappointment in his voice. Farzi and Nenzi, listening in on yet another private conversation between Teeg and me, shifted slightly on my other side. I reached out a hand, allowing my fingers to slide down smooth scales.

"Be honest, Teeg," I added, "you don't trust me either. Not completely. I think Dee hears all your secrets. Does your mother even get that nowadays? Or your father?"

"Reah, you're right—up to a point. The thing I can trust about you is that you'll do the right thing every time, even if we bully you into it when we shouldn't," he admitted with a slight frown. "You didn't have to show up on Campiaa when the Strands attacked, but you did. Tossed me out of the way and took that Ranos rocket blast instead of allowing it to hit me. And today, you were the intended target, but the guard knocked Marzi's hand aside. That laser bullet would have hit Corolan, and there you were, flinging yourself in front of him, taking the hit. I'm terrified that the next time you do that, we won't be able to save you. That you'll sacrifice yourself for someone else who isn't nearly as important."

"Are you saying that you're not important?" I huffed angrily. "Or that Corolan's life is worthless?"

"No, baby, that's not what I meant." Teeg raked fingers through his wealth of dark hair, ruffling it and aggravating the slight curl. I liked that part of him—the not so polished part. "It's just," he was searching for words, unsuccessfully.

"You know how High Demons choose to end their lives, if they tire of living?" I asked. I know he knew the answer; he just shrugged at me instead. I answered for Farzi and Nenzi's benefit. "They have to throw themselves into Baetrah, the volcano on Kifirin, in their humanoid form. That will kill them. If they jump in while Thifilathi or Thifilatha, the heat and fire have no effect—they climb right back out again. The point I'm trying to make, Teeg, is their lives are their decision. When I tossed you aside, or jumped in front of Corolan, those were decisions I was willing to make, without a moment's thought. Other people tend to decide after the fact whether it was a good or bad idea. As if they can decide for you, in that tiny bit of time you have to make such a decision. People react differently to situations, Teeg. I jumped in front of Corolan yesterday, while somebody else might have dropped to the floor. I'd attended one funeral, I wasn't so keen on attending another, and this one would have been for someone I truly cared for."

"Did you have any feelings at all for Addah?"

"Teeg, I can't really answer that. I think what I have mostly is regret. Regret that I couldn't sit down and talk with him. Try to find out why things were the way they were with him. He didn't trust any of his children. Or his wives, more than likely. And he treated me as someone unworthy of his time. Aurelius and I had a long conversation about that—about missed opportunity on both sides. That if Addah had just relented for a short time, we might have made a connection, as fragile as that might have been. Instead, we have nothing, my grandfather and I."

"Do you know who Griffin is?" Teeg said changing the subject.

"Griffin?" I hadn't heard that name.

"He's my grandfather," Teeg replied. "We have the same sort of relationship. He made a mistake with Mom, before I was born. Now, they don't speak, and I've only seen him two or three times during my life."

"Have you tried approaching him? Talking to him?"

"No. He's Wyatt's father, by the way."

"Teeg, Wyatt doesn't want to be Wylend's heir."

"I know that. But Wylend and Griffin pretty much have their hearts set on it, so that's that."

"You know as well as I do that Wyatt doesn't want the throne. He wants to be a healer. If you want my opinion, here it is; Ry would be the King Karathia deserves. How long does Karzac intend to keep me out of action?" I said, changing the subject.

"He said two weeks at least."

"Damn," I sighed.

"What?"

"We need to be out there hunting the fool who's killing those children," I muttered. "And the Ra'Ak and the Strands."

"I know," he growled miserably.

CHAPTER 11

"There's a note with the flowers." Lok was sitting beside my bed after hauling in a huge basket of blooms. As security, he'd already checked them over, searching for listening devices or anything dangerous. Experiencing a bit of sadness over the fact that things had come to that, I accepted the card from Lok's fingers. No expression lay on his face, but his black eyes were narrower than normal as I plucked the note from his fingers. His touch brushed against mine briefly as I took the card.

Lok has beautiful hands, even if they are scarred from holding blades, in and out of battles. His fingers are strong and calloused. At times, still, I wanted to know what those fingers might feel like if they held mine, or if they touched me with something other than indifference. Sighing, I lifted the square flap of the envelope—it was the palest pink. While everything else was paperless, cards were still around and expensive, because of their plant-based origins.

Reah, many of us in the family held our breath when you were attacked, and breathed a relieved sigh when we learned you would survive. I know this may be difficult for you to believe, but some of us truly do see things differently now. We greatly appreciate the gifts we received, and they will be utilized to support the family. It is an inevitability, I believe, that all six

Desh's will be forced to close. Many of our best recipes were kept in Addah's memory, and number two and number three were already failing when he died. I suppose it is fitting, and perhaps justice for you that things are happening in this way. I watched the vid copy of Addah's visit to Dee's, especially the part where you told Fes and Aldah that they had a good mother and they didn't appreciate her enough. Now I know why Fes called me shortly after that meeting and told me that he loved me. I continue to hope for a swift recovery for you, and wish to express my apologies for years of abuse and indifference on the part of the family. Sincerely—Farla Desh.

I was stunned. The note and the flowers were something I never expected to receive from my former family. I was still weak, but strong enough to write. Farla had included a comp-vid code at the bottom of the note. "Lok, can you get me a comp-vid?" I asked.

Lok didn't reply, he pulled his own from a jacket pocket and handed it to me. He'd come in from outside, just to deliver the flowers and note to me. Now he watched me carefully, betraying no emotion as I took the comp-vid and punched in the code to send text messages only. I was wearied and only wanted to sleep afterward, but I'd written out eight of Addah's most prized recipes on the comp-vid with a short note to Farla.

I worked these out several years ago, I informed her. Since they were Addah's, I was never able to use them in any commercial manner—they were for my private use and for my own enjoyment. If you have trouble reproducing them, please let me know and I will be happy to come once I am released from the physician's care, to demonstrate how to make them. I regret not knowing my family better in the past, but those opportunities have slipped away and left us all in a sadder place—Reah.

"Fes!" Farla shouted. "Fes!"

"Mother?" Fes had just risen—he'd been released from the hospital before Addah's funeral—the hospital staff had been amazed at his near-miraculous recovery. He still tired easily, however, and wouldn't return to work for at least two Eight-Days.

"Fes, I sent flowers and a note to Reah," Marzi exclaimed excitedly. "I told her about the family's situation and that Desh's was likely to close because Addah left us the way he did without giving up his secrets. Look at this, Fes—Reah wrote me back!" Fes still didn't understand until he accepted his mother's comp-vid and stared at the first recipe for yellowfish in wine sauce—Reah had written that one and seven others.

"Mother, I want her to come. I want to watch her cook," Fes declared, sorting through the recipes. "Look—here's the sliced beef in bittersweet sauce!"

"That always takes forever to cook and Addah wouldn't let anyone in the kitchen," Farla reached for the comp-vid. "I want her to come, too. I want to see this."

"Then answer her—there's a code listed here," Fes scrolled down to the end of the message.

"Reah my love, what is the meaning of this?" Lendill was wiggling my comp-vid in his hand and frowning at me.

"Is that where it was? I had to borrow Lok's earlier," I grumbled, reaching out in an attempt to snatch it away. A message waited for me; I could see it on the screen.

"Now see, if you were in better shape, you'd have had this in your hand and I'd be staring at an empty palm," Lendill was teasing me with it still.

"Lendill, please shut up and hand me that," I muttered in irritation. I was sitting precariously on a stool in the huge kitchen, where Radolf had served up a better-quality broth this time, with onion, a hint of spice and bits of beef. I kissed him for his efforts after my first bite. He was going back to Le-Ath Veronis just as soon as he fed me—Ilvan was busy doing prep work in Lissa's kitchen and Edan was already in Karzac's medical classes.

"Here," Lendill gave me a kiss when he handed my comp-vid over. I leaned against him—Lendill has a scent that no other man has.

Perhaps it was his Elvish roots or something. I hadn't gotten close enough to his father to see if he smelled the same.

"Reah," Lendill whispered softly, "I'll crawl into bed with you if you keep that up."

"Karzac said no sex for six more days," Radolf reminded us, forcing Lendill to pull away. Farzi and Nenzi were staring, too. They weren't about to allow anyone else into the bed if it might damage me as a result. I checked my comp-vid message while my cheeks heated up.

Reah, it read, *I can't say how much we appreciate what you sent to us. And if there is some way for you to come and show us how to prepare these recipes, we would be more than grateful. Fes is quite excited over the prospect. We will ensure your safety, but please bring your own guards if it will make you feel safer—Farla.*

I'll try to come in ten days, I sent back. *If anything changes, I'll let you know.*

"Honey Snake," I said to Farzi, "will you and my sweet man take me back to bed?" I was exhausted. Farzi stole a kiss while he carried me to my suite, Nenzi right behind him.

"She calls him honey snake?" Radolf had an eyebrow lifted quite high.

"You should know by now that those two consider themselves Reah's mates. They just can't have sex; they were neutered when they were young." Lendill snorted.

"I'm packing up the rest of this, and there's chicken broth, too, if she wants something different for dinner. I have to go before Ilvan tears my kitchen apart." Radolf laid his apron on the island and disappeared.

"Farzi, Nenzi?" I heard Lendill's voice. It had to be the middle of the night—I was sound asleep with both lion snakes. Wise of Lendill to let them know he meant no harm. I had a tough time opening my eyes—I'd been sleeping comfortably surrounded by the reptanoids.

"What is it, Lendill?" I asked, struggling to sit up. Farzi changed first and helped me.

"Reah, we need you to come—don't worry, someone will carry you. There's a new site on Boodreatis. They've attacked an entire college, there. I'd like to hear your thoughts on this when we go through the place." Lendill told me not to worry, but there was more than worry in his words—he was frightened.

"Farzi, Nenzi, will you come with me?" I asked.

"We come with Reah," Nenzi, now humanoid, was padding across the room to snatch up his clothing. Farzi was already getting dressed. I hadn't realized it, but Lok had come in with Lendill. He found shoes and socks for me while Lendill helped me into jeans and a long-sleeved shirt. Out of habit, I looked around for my knife.

"You won't need a weapon, this is investigation only," Lendill said as Lok lifted me up. "And this is the first time I've attempted taking others with me when I fold, so be prepared."

"You fold?" The words were torn from my lips and left behind on Tulgalan, taking my stomach and my equilibrium with them. We landed safely, thank the stars, in the middle of a gymnasium that direct hits from lightning bolts might have treated kinder.

"I've discovered latent talents," Lendill murmured at my question. I'd forgotten it at the vision that met us. The gymnasium was filled with local constabulary as well as ASD agents. The horrible thing? The place was also filled with bodies, some piled several deep.

"It was a college handball match—the regional championship," Lok whispered softly against my ear. Farzi and Nenzi stood guard on either side of us—it was late afternoon where we were—light filtered through a very large hole in the tall ceiling over our heads. "All the students were expected to attend—classes were let out for this event," Lok went on. "They're all dead."

"How many?" I wanted to weep, my hands and body shaking at the sight of students, professors and attendees littering the floor and surrounding elevated seating.

"More than a thousand," Lok murmured, kissing my temple gently.

"Lok, let me stand," I was thankful my voice only quavered slightly. Lok lowered me to the floor, what little there was of it not covered with bodies, so I could turn around and survey the scene.

"Were there any in the bathrooms or outside, getting a drink of water or anything?" I asked. This was a small, private college, much like one I might have attended had Addah allowed me to go.

"I don't know," Lok answered, placing a hand under my elbow, in case my knees gave way.

"Where you think those things are—bathrooms?" Farzi gazed down at me. He and Nenzi were almost of a height—roughly two hands taller than I.

"Farzi, I think they might be toward the back of the gym. Maybe down some steps or something," I was improvising.

"Then we'll go check." Lok was humoring me, I think. I wasn't sure he or Lendill expected this sort of devastation. We stepped around and over bodies as we made our way toward a doorway at the back of the large gym.

"This it—I smell water," Nenzi affirmed, once we passed through the door. I nodded and gave Nenzi an encouraging smile—the best I could muster under the circumstances, anyway.

We found a set of bathrooms with showers for the athletes. Nenzi was correct; I heard the occasional drip of water from a small shower cubicle off to the side. Looking up, I saw that the ceiling was lower than that outside—it consisted of rectangular, fiber tiles set in a grid. A few holes had been punched through, here and there. No holes, however, were around the concrete walls of the room. I crooked my finger at Farzi and Nenzi. Without saying a word, both came.

"Can one or both of you make your way through one of those holes up there?" I whispered as softly as I could, pointing to the holes in question. Restroom stalls stood against one wall while the showers lined the other. Benches stood against the wall in between.

Both reptanoids nodded at me before their clothing dropped to the floor. Lok and I watched in fascination as they chose a restroom stall, lifted up and climbed on top of cubicle walls. Then, rising gracefully again, they chose a hole in a ceiling tile overhead and slipped inside it. Screaming and shouting began immediately, as six frightened students, anxious to escape the newest threat, fell through the ceiling tiles over the benches.

"Stop there!" Lok held a Ranos pistol in his hand, pointing it at the students. I sent frightened mindspeech to Lendill, who appeared at our side, just as Farzi and Nenzi came down. I handed their clothing to them and held the restroom cubicle door shut while they dressed again. No need to expose them to students, whom I'm sure had just escaped certain death.

"Who are you?" The young man's voice wasn't steady as he stared at Lendill and Lok.

"I'm Lendill Schaff, Vice-Director of the ASD," Lendill snapped. "How in the name of the daystar did you escape that carnage out there?"

We'd found four young men and two young women, and not so surprisingly, they'd sneaked up into the tiled ceiling and sat atop the concrete wall that rose past the ceiling grid so they could pass around a small bag of halucidust. Lendill cursed under his breath; he wasn't sure any of them had seen anything—enough to describe it, anyway.

Lendill and Lok were herding them toward the restroom door when we heard the shrieks from outside. I wanted to shout in frustration—it had been a trap. "Lendill, fold them out of here!" I shouted, indicating the students, Lok and the reptanoids. They wouldn't stand a chance against a thousand other students, professors and the attending locals who'd been bitten by Ra'Ak and then placed in stasis by a sick and twisted warlock.

"Reah!" Lendill shouted behind me, but my adrenalin was already pumping. I had no weapon with me except my Thifilatha, and I sent mindspeech as quickly as I could.

Em-pah, there are spawn, I shouted the mental message, even as I turned, the effort to become full Thifilatha almost bringing me to my knees. Lendill, who asked Farzi and Nenzi to guard the still-humanoid students, came up behind me, shooting as quickly as he could with his Ranos pistol, Lok doing likewise on my other side.

What do you do when more than a thousand spawn turn in your direction, running over one another, almost, attempting to get to you? I wept, I think, realizing that I was too weak to fight off that many at once. What touched me would burn, but Lendill and Lok would be overrun. I knew it as surely as Boodreatis' sun shone overhead. I batted an attacking spawn away; it had almost reached Lok, who was firing methodically into the oncoming mass of former students, their flesh now housing the worst kind of monsters.

Lendill, surprisingly, was firing his pistol with one hand while hurling energy blasts with the other. Latent talent, indeed. I had no time to dwell on that; I gathered what little strength I could and waded into the press. If Denevik, Gardevik, Jaydevik and Glindarok hadn't come, along with a few other High Demons I didn't recognize, I would have lost both Lendill and Lok. Likely, the students we'd found alive would have died as well—I can't say for sure about the reptanoids. If they'd gone to lion snake, they might have escaped. I can't imagine that they'd appeal to spawn as potential victims.

Jayd, Garde, my grandfather and four others were all black scales and death, but Glinda was a shining white. The spawn, thinking her an easy target, shifted as one and went after her. That was a mistake. Glinda was just as deadly as any of the males, and while the spawn shrieked and died, burning after coming into contact with the High Demon Queen, seven High Demon males burned them from behind. They'd formed their own trap, killing spawn indiscriminately.

The few that thought to come after Lendill, Lok and me were either hit with Ranos pistols or burned against my gold scales. The gym was filled with smoke and the acidic smell of burned spawn when it was over. Garde had chased down the last one, which had attempted to escape. Nothing gets away from a determined High Demon. Nothing.

"Reah, turn back, deah-mul," Lendill was coaxing me. I was so dizzy I couldn't understand what was happening or what he was asking for several ticks.

"Baby, come down and talk to us," Denevik was beside him quickly—he'd already turned. It took every bit of my remaining strength to make the change and I almost fainted afterward. My clothing had been destroyed, but somehow Glinda had something ready and she, Lendill and Lok managed to dress me. Only a few locals and ASD agents had survived the mass waking of more than a thousand Ra'Ak spawn, and those had run out the door first thing. They were back now, surveying the burned and blasted spawn dust covering the floor. You couldn't take a step without it crunching underfoot.

"We're going to local ASD headquarters," Lendill said softly. Garde and Jayd skipped the students plus the surviving ASD and constabulary, Lendill folded the rest of us.

"Reah, lean against Farzi and Nenzi, all right, love?" Lok whispered softly. Unconsciousness was still threatening, so I nodded as best I could and allowed Farzi to pull my body against his. Nenzi scooted over until I was sandwiched between them. I closed my eyes and allowed the darkness to take me.

"I don't know how she knew to take us in that direction," Lok said for the sixth time. "She just said she wanted to check the restrooms. Once we were inside, I didn't see anyone. Reah took one look at the holes punched in the ceiling tiles and asked Farzi and Nenzi to go up and check."

"I've sent another team to the college to go through the rest of it," Lendill paced. Norian had come, and he was hearing everything for the first time as Lok gave his report. Right on cue, Lendill's comp-vid beeped. "It's them," he said, punching the button to receive the call.

Both Norian and Lok heard when the commander of the search crew reported that he had Lersen Strand and one of his cousins in custody. Lendill exchanged a glance with Norian and they disappeared. They were back in moments with two prisoners. Lersen Strand and his cousin Darsen were dumped in front of Lok, who cursed and had his pistol waving in both faces in less than a blink.

"Oh, they don't want to escape," Norian grinned at his captives.

"Those crazy Ra'Ak ate Ansen and Morsen Strand and then Hendars Klar, didn't they?" Norian was smugly satisfied by that turn of events.

"Please, anything is better than what we escaped," Darsen was begging and weeping. Lersen elbowed the younger man. "Shut up," he hissed. "If that fool warlock figures out we're not with the others, he'll come looking. Do you want that to happen?"

"No," Darsen moaned.

"Do you have a name for this warlock?" Lendill's arms were crossed over his chest as he stared at both prisoners. They'd been cuffed by the ones who'd found them hiding inside a janitor's cube.

"Delusional, that one," Lersen snapped. "Calls himself the hand of fate."

"And it was fun until he let those worms eat your cousins and Hendars, wasn't it? How many of those girls did you rape before you killed them?" Norian was done playing nice.

"I don't have to tell you that," Lersen spat.

"No, but you have to tell me," Gavril appeared, his eyes red and fangs out. "Tell me everything you know about this. Quickly!"

"Why can't we just take her back with us?" Glinda was tired of waiting until Lendill, Norian and Gavril finished questioning the captives. Reah was unconscious but her breathing was even—Denevik checked after reassuring both Farzi and Nenzi. The reptanoids had Reah pressed close between them and both wore worried frowns although neither spoke.

"We can move her now," Lendill said softly, walking up to the four High Demons. "We want to put the Strands in the dungeons on Le-Ath Veronis, so we'll move Reah there. I didn't know this was going to be anything but an investigation, and the information I had before we left Tulgalan was spotty. I'd never have brought her if I'd known, but I think we're still alive because we did. Thank you for coming to help." He gave a respectful nod to Jayd and Glinda.

"Thank Reah and Denevik, she called him and he asked us for help," Garde said.

"I think I'll wait until somebody checks her over and she wakes," Lendill said. "Farzi, Nenzi, are you ready to travel with Reah? Gavril said he had to get back to Campiaa, and for you to stay with Reah."

"We stay," Farzi agreed, moving carefully so Reah wouldn't fall.

"I can carry her," Denevik approached the reptanoids carefully. Farzi let Reah's grandfather lift her. Lendill, now more comfortable with his newly-found skill, folded everyone, Lok included, straight to Le-Ath Veronis.

"I still remember what to do," Edan said softly, checking Reah's vitals.

"He does, I am advancing him swiftly in his classes. He will have his medical degree quite soon," Karzac agreed, standing behind Edan and watching closely as he examined Reah.

"Dehydrated and weak," Edan sighed. "Will you wake her or allow her to sleep a while longer?" He gazed up at his mentor. Karzac's green-gold eyes smiled just a little.

"What do you want to do?" he asked.

"I'd like to see my baby open her eyes, but you'll know best."

"We'll wake her—I think Radolf has something ready she can eat."

"According to our prisoners, the warlock's plan was to take a few students and get away. The Ra'Ak had other ideas, once they saw how many were at that handball match." Norian shook his head as a comesula offered a cup of hot tea to the ASD Director. Norian spoke with Lissa, Gavin and Tony inside Lissa's private study.

"This just proves how crazy they're getting," Lissa shook her head. "Normally, they'd bite a few, turn them loose and let them infect others. What did the Strands say about placing the new spawn in stasis?"

"They said that one of the Ra'Ak placed a shield around the gym to keep anyone from escaping. Then, after the Ra'Ak bit everybody, the warlock managed to put the new spawn in stasis, making them appear to be humanoid dead. He set a trap, after the Ra'Ak modified the original plan." Norian sipped tea and watched Lissa carefully. He knew, just as she did, that the entire Reth Alliance was devastated by the news of so many deaths. All of Boodreatis was in mourning and donations and condolences were pouring in from everywhere.

"This may be the worst I've seen," Lissa muttered, hugging herself. Gavin moved to lift her before taking her chair and settling Lissa on his lap.

"Little rose," Connegar appeared and knelt beside Lissa and Gavin. Reaching out, the tall Larentii brushed Lissa's cheek. "Those young ones and the others were already gone, once they were bitten," he said gently. "Conner escorted those souls herself. They are safe upon the other side."

"But what about their parents? Their friends and families?" Lissa brushed tears away.

"My love, monsters take lives every day. We do what we can, and what we are allowed to do. Our work lies ahead of us, to destroy these monsters and bring what little peace we can to those left behind. The Wise Ones say Reah is a key element in tracking these murderers."

"Then we need her on her feet soon," Lissa muttered.

Connegar nodded at Lissa's words. He didn't say what he, Pheligar and a few other Larentii had discussed with the Wise Ones—that a power of some kind seemed intent on destroying Reah and allowing mentally ill Ra'Ak to move willfully throughout both Alliances, leaving death and chaos in their wake.

"Breah-mul, put your arms around my neck, love." Lendill nuzzled my cheek carefully after Karzac woke me and stepped away. Edan was there, too and he smiled encouragingly as Lendill moved to lift me up. I was dressed in clothing Great-aunt Glinda had brought to replace what I'd lost after turning Thifilatha. I was grateful—Glinda has good taste and I wasn't clothed in ruffles and frippery.

"Daddy?" I whispered, holding a hand out to Edan after Lendill lifted me.

"Baby, how do you feel?" He took my hand and kissed it.

"Tired."

"I know. We'll feed you and get you back in bed," he promised.

Lissa's dinner table was completely full, and Radolf sat to eat with us as well. Tory and Ry were off on some investigation for Lendill; he said as much when he settled me on a chair and then sat beside me. Radolf had the other side, with Farzi and Nenzi next to him. I wondered how long Aurelius would be out, but knew not to bother him with that question. His assignments took as long as they took, and there was no hurrying them.

"This came just a bit ago from Wylend," Lissa passed an envelope down the table toward me. I hadn't seen Wylend since I woke on the second day after my injury, and he hadn't bothered to say good-bye. I figured he had business to attend to on Karathia.

"Here," Lendill opened the envelope for me and pulled the message out. I opened the note bearing the official crest of Karathia, expecting an explanation. I got it in spades, as Teeg would say.

Reah Desh Nilvas Silver, it began, *Our engagement is hereby ended. We were informed that you spoke against Our choice as heir, naming another whom you deemed more suitable. On Karathia, that is considered treason. Therefore, as a favor to one whom We once considered worthy of Our care, We are merely banishing you from this world, rather than pronouncing a sentence of punishment. We will not welcome you within Our presence from this day forward—Wylend Giraldus Arden, King of Karathia.*

"Radolf," I quavered, handing him the note and rising from my chair. Radolf was still a citizen of Karathia. Was he supposed to stay away from me, too? What about Erland and Rylend? And who'd told? Only one person had heard me say that Wyatt didn't want to be heir—

Teeg. He'd told Wylend. Had Teeg known what the result would be? I was betting that he did. Teeg knew just about all there was to know about everything. Now, I'd been fucked by both of them, and not in any good way. I skipped away before Lendill could reach me.

"What the bloody fuck?" Radolf stood, staring at the letter sent by Wylend.

"What does it say?" Lissa was standing, too, an expression of concern on her face.

Radolf read the contents of the letter to everyone present.

"I'll kill him myself," Lissa threw her napkin down, fuming. "I don't give a damn if he is my grandfather. Did she say this to him personally? And whom did she name instead of Wyatt? My father is behind this, I know it." Lissa was nearly shouting, while Gavin, Drake and Drew were trying to calm her.

"Well, that's it for me," Radolf tossed the letter onto the table. "You are all witnesses—I renounce my Karathian citizenship."

Tory sat at the bar inside Starshine, a popular nightclub on the outskirts of Quezlos, the capital city on Surnath. His sixth drink was in his hand and he was about to toss back what was left of it and order another. He'd gotten information through mindspeech from King Wylend, and although he'd known it wasn't all the information available, he'd recognized the truth in Wylend's words. Things had certainly taken a turn he hadn't expected, and in between searching for information Lendill requested, he'd decided to get as drunk as possible.

"Well, hello, there." She was tall, black-haired, blue-eyed and lovely. She also made a point to brush against Tory as she took the barstool next to his. "What's your name, stranger?"

"Torevik." While Tory was working to get drunk, he hadn't

achieved his objective, yet. Perhaps it was fortuitous that Lendill had sent him and Ry on an assignment, taking him away from Le-Ath Veronis and the other problems going on. He needed that separation, in order to make a decision involving his future.

"Torevik, how would you like to come home with me for a little while?" Her voice was breathy as she made her proposition.

"Can't right now," Tory replied, turning his eyes away from the beautiful woman beside him.

"That's too bad. Jealous wife?"

"Don't have a wife. Never married her."

"Really? What's the holdup, then?"

"Work. For now."

"Well, if you stop working, you know where to find me. My name's Darletta." She handed a small card to Tory, accepted a drink from the bartender and walked away, swinging her hips suggestively. Tory watched her go, blinking in confusion. Perhaps the alcohol was finally taking effect. He sighed.

"Wylend, I never thought to see you punish someone because you employed an eavesdropping spell and picked up on a conversation two rooms away. She didn't say it to you, personally," Erland pointed out. Wylend had eavesdropped on Reah's conversation with Gavril, angry that he'd been shunted to the side after the attack on his intended Queen. "Did she mention a specific name? Not only that, but she wasn't on Karathia when she said what she did. She was on Tulgalan, and subject to Alliance law."

"She did say a name, and I will not repeat it," Wylend shouted. "I cannot countenance a Queen who will second-guess every decision I make."

"As I understand it, this may be the first and only time that occurred, and since when can someone not be honest and speak their mind with a mate? I have said many things to you that could be considered treasonous."

"But you were not my Queen, Erland Morphis, nor will you ever be."

Erland knew there was no arguing with Wylend when he was in this state of mind. Wylend and any other warlock in a female cycle was moody upon occasion. This appeared to be one of those times. Wylend would come around and see sense; it could take a few days, however. The most damage had been done to Reah. Lissa, too, was seething—he'd already gotten angry mindspeech from his mate over the letter Reah had received. If Erland had known about it sooner, he'd have instructed that it wait a few days, considering Wylend was likely to cool down, see the folly of his ways and wish he could take it all back.

Corolan watched helplessly as Erland argued with Wylend. Wylend hadn't consulted with him before writing and sending the letter. As a result, things were in the worst state of affairs. Reah had saved his life, at nearly the cost of her own. She'd have done the same for Wylend, too. He'd gotten mindspeech from Garek, telling him that Radolf had renounced his citizenship in front of witnesses. Wylend would have to grant it again before Radolf could return to Karathia. Wylend had not bothered to think this through, reacting to a perceived slight when no harm was intended. Corolan was about to react as well.

"My liege," he bowed to Wylend when Wylend stopped fuming for several ticks. Erland had settled in to listen to the King vent all his wrath.

"What is it, Corolan?" Wylend snapped.

"I will be visiting family for the next moon-turn." Corolan disappeared.

"What?" Wylend reached out, as if that would bring Corolan back.

"Reah took a laser bullet for Corolan," Erland said softly. "She would have done the same for you. Yet you, in an ill-tempered snit, decided to eavesdrop. We all get what we deserve at times, Wylend. Call if you need something." Erland disappeared as well. Wylend cursed—loudly and long.

Reah? Where are you, sweetheart? Teeg's voice came in clear as the proverbial bell.

Do you think I'd tell you? You couldn't wait to tell Wylend what I said about Wyatt not wanting to be his heir. Now, he's tried and convicted me of treason, and banished me from Karathia. He withdrew his proposal as well. What did you hope to gain from this, Teeg? What?

I wept and shivered as I sent my reply, and refused to speak to him again while Teeg kept trying to convince me to do so. I had to close my mind off after a while—he was bombarding me with questions and denials. He was the only one, besides Farzi and Nenzi, who'd heard that conversation, and the reptanoids would never approach Wylend with information.

Besides, parts of what Wylend heard had never been spoken aloud to anyone else, which meant Teeg had certainly been the one who'd betrayed me. My thoughts, too, were an open book to most, so perhaps I should learn to shield them as well. I wondered, amid my sobs and sniffles, just how to go about it. Had I loved Wylend? That answer was yes. And I was coming to love Corolan. I would have to work through that—resign myself to never seeing them again.

We will not welcome you within Our presence from this day forward. Those had been his words. He was a King, while I was nothing. Just a cook, and a weak and wounded one in addition to that. But I knew, even if he didn't, that my statement was true. Wyatt had said himself that he didn't want the throne when I first met him. Anyone could see that he would glow if he were using his healing skills, and glower if he were serving in some official capacity with Wylend.

If the King of Karathia wished to wallow in his blindness and short-sightedness, then he was welcome to do so. Since I'd been banished from his sight, he no longer needed to worry that someone might question his perfect warlock world. That didn't keep me from rolling in self-pity, however, and weeping pitifully while I did it.

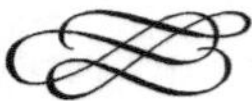

"Where do you think she is?" Gavril was dangerously angry as he paced inside his father's study. Gavin watched his son fret, a hooded expression in his eyes. Gavril had asked to see the letter Wylend sent to Reah, and then almost went crazy. "She thinks I told him, when Erland says that Wylend used an eavesdropping spell to listen to a private conversation. I don't know about you, Dad, but I consider that an invasion of privacy. Anybody else would have kept the information to themselves. Reah won't answer my mindspeech. She thinks I betrayed her. And I can't go to Wylend and have it out with him—the Campiaan Alliance needs his membership. If he's become this petty, he'll pull out at the blink of an eye."

"Son, Erland thinks he'll settle down in a few days and think this through rationally. You just need to wait it out for a while. My concern is for Reah, now—she was weak and still in need of care. Most likely, she's alone somewhere and not getting anything. I wish she'd purge this habit of running away every time someone hurts her."

"Dad, she couldn't before. First, Edan threatened her if she ran away, then the ASD did the same thing, threatening treason if she deserted. Now, Wylend has accused and convicted her of that crime. What would you do, Dad?"

"Son, I don't have a ready answer. This involves your mate and your great-grandfather. I'm inclined to agree with Erland on this and wait a few days. See if Wylend comes to his senses. This is foolishness."

"I could have told you that much." Gavril folded away.

"Little one."

"Honey blue." I stared up at Nefrigar—he'd shown up on day six of my self-imposed exile. On the second day, I'd been forced to go searching for food—I'd depleted the entire pantry on Beliphar. Now I was ready to skip to Tulgalan—I'd promised Farla and Fes that I'd come to cook the recipes I'd given them. I was hoping that more treachery wasn't coming as a result. I was also hoping that Nefrigar didn't have another planet to save or a different objective—my day was planned out already. I still didn't feel completely healthy, either.

"I came to help," Nefrigar settled me on a barstool and placed his hands on my head first, then slowly made his way down the rest of my body. Larentii power was shoring up my fragile health—I felt better when he finished.

"Thank you," I sighed.

"Little one, perhaps it is not wise to be alone at this time."

"Really? What do you suggest? Should I call the one who convicted me of treason, or the one who tattled secrets that led to my conviction? The whole thing is ludicrous."

"Not all may be as it seems," he said cryptically.

"You're a Larentii, so you know everything. I'm just a stupid, gullible High Demon who doesn't have anything near your resources."

"Little one, your emotions are unstable," Nefrigar rubbed my back with large, blue fingers.

"What can you expect? I lost two mates in one day." I tossed up a hand and slid off the stool, walked toward the large kitchen window and stared through it at the unkempt grounds. Once they'd been beautiful, until Beliphar had destroyed itself with greed and neglect. "Tory only shows up when it's convenient for him, Aurelius works constantly, poor Radolf is caught up in this whole mess with Karathia and Lendill has enough to worry about."

"Yet you are one of Lendill's worries," Nefrigar suggested gently. "And the shapeshifters are frightened for you. You were weak and not ready to be on your own when you left them behind."

"Yeah, I know that too. But they belong to Teeg. I don't care how often he says they can do what they want, they're still under his thumb. In the meantime, I've been keeping up with that mess on Boodreatis through comp-vid." I held up the comp-vid in question— I'd seen interview after interview with devastated parents. They'd only been shown the initial attack on the college by five huge monsters and one child, who'd held incredible power. Neither the Ra'Ak nor the warlock had bothered to block the camera images—it was as if they wanted to throw the Alliances into mass hysteria.

The families of the dead weren't told and might never realize that the powerful child in the vids had once been an adult. The Ra'Ak that the warlock worked with were not only insane, they were sick. I'd enlarged images—it looked as if the Ra'Ak were molting, with scales and skin peeling and flaking away. Since I wasn't well-versed on Ra'Ak physiology, I didn't know what that really meant.

"Do you know what this means?" I pulled up the isolated images I'd saved in a separate file I was keeping. I showed Nefrigar the images.

"They appear to be ill—I've never known Ra'Ak to molt—their power keeps their scales and such alive and growing with their bodies."

"If they're ill, why are they ill? What's causing this?"

"Perhaps you should have a meeting with Lissa; I believe she holds this information."

"Really?" I asked, before my face fell. She was mated to Erland, and mother to Rylend. Both held Karathian citizenship. How could I walk onto Le-Ath Veronis? I was probably banned from there, too.

"Little one, things are not so bad as you think."

"How bad are they?" I asked. I was doing my best not to cry.

"Reah, they are not as bad as you think. Go to your family, and then consider meeting with Lissa. She will have good information to pass along."

I rubbed my forehead at his words—a headache was forming. Nefrigar placed two fingers against my forehead, relieving the pressure. "Thank you," I said, and skipped to Tulgalan.

Nefrigar stared at the spot previously occupied by Reah. He would have to tell her soon, he decided, and folded away.

"I'm feeling well," I lied to Farla as she led me into the kitchen of Desh's number one. I hadn't been inside it since I was eight. Many things had changed since then.

"We only opened up again three days ago," Farla informed me as I followed her past prep tables and employees busily preparing the evening menu. The restaurant would open in four clicks. Enough time —barely—to prepare the sliced beef in bittersweet sauce.

"We have the ingredients laid out, we just want to watch," Farla was smiling—the most I'd ever seen her smile during the eight years I'd spent in Targis, believing I was Addah's daughter.

Fes, too, smiled at me as I went over what had been laid out next to the stove and ovens. The two kinds of fruit had been peeled and seeded and the brown sugars were there, as were the tomato puree and spices. The beef was partially cooked as the recipe indicated. Now, we would slice it, simmer the sauce a bit to blend the flavors and then spoon it over the beef slices, allowing it to cook for a while until it was so tender and flavorful it melted in the mouth. It was Addah's specialty, and people flocked in on the nights he prepared it. I was now preparing it in his place. We would see how it all turned out.

Fes watched diligently, as did two others—Rane and Wald were there. If I'd known that Wald would come I might have stayed away, but I forged ahead, ignoring him. He was used to this—he'd watch me before, although he never seemed to learn anything.

"You cut the uyto fruit with a fork?" Fes asked as I worked.

"Or a pastry cutter," I said. "It needs to be in fine strings, instead of cubes. It cooks faster and you get the flavor into the sauce right away. It can go wrong if you use chunks—the sauce won't be as smooth, either. Actually, since it will be easier to acquire gishi fruit, I was thinking about substituting that for the uyto fruit."

"That sounds wonderful," Rane sighed.

"I'll try it soon, if I can get my hands on the fruit. Now, for the pepper and spices," I flung all of it into the pan on the stove with my fingers while Fes watched avidly beside me.

"Want to slice the beef, Rane?" I asked. He looked to be itching to do something. He nodded enthusiastically and did a fine job, layering it in the pan as he should. Once the sauce was ready, I poured it over the six pans of beef and slipped them into the ovens. Then we started on the fowl in white reduction and two other dishes. The fish would cook last—it took the least amount of time.

While we worked on that, I asked Fes if he'd like to serve a special cake as one of the desserts. He did. We swirled chocolate, cream and raspberry into a cake batter, cooking it in a moderate oven. It came out looking and smelling like a dream. Fes prepared the sweet sauce to drizzle over the cake while I told him how to make it. The time to open the restaurant had come and guests were arriving when the beef came out of the oven. Fes dipped out a slice and passed the plate around among us.

"May the stars have mercy, this is better than Addah's," Farla exclaimed. "We may stay alive, my darlings." She hugged Fes and Rane —hard. I watched, feeling a slight twinge of self-pity. I was motherless, and had been my entire life. The cake, too, came out beautifully, and Farla was in raptures, closing her eyes in pleasure with the first bite.

"But this recipe is yours," Fes said, pointing at the now-empty saucer—we'd devoured the slice of cake.

"Use it—I don't care as long as you don't show up wherever I'm working and say that what I'm serving is very like yours."

"Reah, I apologize for that," Fes said. "I didn't know any better. I do now."

"Mother, Garet Howt is here tonight!" Wald was back and hissing —he'd disappeared to help open the restaurant.

Garet Howt. The most famous (and demanding) food critic on all of Tulgalan. He'd decried the absence of the yaris fish dish ever since I'd been conscripted by the Alliance. I quirked an eyebrow at Fes. "Well, why don't we give him a night to remember?" I said, smiling at my uncle.

Garet Howt received a complimentary serving of yaris fish with my own sauce recipe, along with a sampling of the sliced beef in bittersweet sauce, the fowl dish and two others, followed by the cake for dessert. Garet had two people with him, but there was plenty of food to go around. The yaris fish, though, he kept for himself and called for the cook afterward. Fes dragged me to Garet's table.

"I was planning an article, scheduled to come out in two days, over the death of Addah Desh and his restaurants," Garet smiled at Fes and me. "However, it seems that Addah may have been keeping his talent under his thumb. I often suspected him of this. I'll rewrite the column, telling everyone that Desh's has been reborn. This is the best yaris fish I have ever tasted." I noticed he'd cleaned his plate.

"Fes and I worked on it, with help from the other staff and family members," I nodded at Garet Howt. "I think you will not be disappointed, anytime you visit Desh's, sir."

"And your name, lady cook?" he asked.

"Reah," Fes answered for me. "This is my niece, Reah Desh Nilvas Silver." Garet smiled widely, hauled out his comp-vid and dutifully recorded my name. I wasn't sure how I felt about that, but it was too late to take it back.

I worked with the kitchen staff throughout the evening, helping

Fes and the others prepare regular menu items. It was a relief when the doors closed and the last guest went home—I was exhausted.

"Here," Fes handed a glass of wine to me and offered a chair in his office. Farla, Rane, Wald, Landor and several other family members were also inside. He explained to all of them what Garet Howt had said. "After this, we just need to get number two and three back on track, and four through six through a small drought," he sighed. "Wald, are you going to be able to take care of number two? I'll bring Halde in and show him how to prepare these recipes that Reah brought to us. Perhaps number three will reincarnate."

Wald looked at me. And then dropped to his knees. "Reah, I'm so sorry," he said. "I was trying to impress Edan. I wasn't impressing anybody."

"You won't ever impress Edan with that kind of behavior now—he's changed drastically. Did you know he's working on his medical degree on Le-Ath Veronis? I think I've called him Daddy twice—he seems to like it."

"You're joking?" Farla stared at me in shock.

"No. Someday, maybe I'll tell you about gods and things of that nature. In the meantime, here's to a successful night and a positive review," I held up my glass. Wald surged to his feet and clinked my glass with his.

"Are you sure you won't stay with us?" Fes was doing his best to convince me to come home with him and the others.

"No, Uncle Fes. I have some thinking to do," I said.

"Uncle Fes. I like it, Reah. Don't leave us. Visit often. You'll be welcome anytime."

"I enjoyed cooking with you tonight. I'd like to do it again," I smiled up at him.

"Reah, walk into my kitchen whenever you want." His grin widened. "It is my kitchen now, isn't it?" I think it was just sinking in. I wasn't privy to Addah's will, but I felt Fes was probably the primary beneficiary.

"Fes, it's your kitchen." I patted his arm. "Your family, too. Spread the love around."

"I'll call you—I have your code," he patted the pocket where his comp-vid rested inside his heavy coat. Winter had definitely settled in for Targis.

"Any time," I said and turned to walk toward the bus stop. As soon as Fes was out of sight, I skipped away.

Beliphar wasn't my goal for the evening—I was tired, bone tired, and only wanted a warm bed. Perhaps a nice bath. I skipped to the house Teeg had purchased, since all my belongings were still there. He wouldn't think to look for me in such plain sight.

The clanging of swords greeted me the moment I set foot inside the house. It frightened me at first, so I crept toward the large solarium on the eastern side of the mansion. There I found Lok, sparring with Drake while Drew watched from the side, offering smiling advice now and then.

"Don't you know when to stop?" I skipped to Drew's side and watched Lok and Drake attempt to beat each other into submission.

Drew grinned at me. "We wondered where you went, little girl," he said, before shouting at Lok to keep his elbows in.

"I've been here and there," I replied, unwilling to share my hiding place with anyone.

"Everybody's worried sick," the smile disappeared.

"Wylend isn't," I pointed out.

"Wylend's being a jackass," Drew said, keeping his eyes on Lok and his brother. "Where were you tonight? You smell like an entire restaurant."

"I was at Desh's number one, keeping the family from going bankrupt," I said. "Addah didn't share some of his best recipes, so I went to show Fes and the others how to make them. It seemed to go well."

"So, with Addah and the original Edan out of the picture, the family gets along?" Another smile quirked at the corner of his mouth. He and Drake were more than handsome, and reinforced my Falchani fantasy. I'd just have to find a Falchani someday. One who didn't mind if I were shorter, with white hair. I could hold my own against anybody with the blades.

"You're forgetting Aldah and Marzi," I said. "You remember Marzi, don't you—you know, the bitch who tried to kill me?"

"Yeah. Definitely forgot about her. So, without those four, the family likes each other?"

"I think they get along," I said. "Enough that they won't kill each other."

"Reah, how tired are you?" Drake asked as he and Lok clanged swords.

"Tired," I said.

"Then you won't kill Lok too bad. Drew, hand her your blades." Drew was grinning as he placed both his practice blades in my hands.

"But I wanted a bath and a long sleep," I protested as Drew shoved me into the sparring square.

"Get a touch on Lok and that'll happen," Drake laughed.

Lok glared at me, as if I were a bug to be squashed or something. "I'll let you attack first," I said, nodding at the enigmatic Falchani. I was seeing his tattoos for the first time—they were red dragons very much like Dragon's. He was covered in a light sheen of sweat and still looked good enough to eat, his long braid swinging down his back. His eyes narrowed at me. I watched him, keeping my wrists loose, preparing for his attack.

He'd gone to the Dragon school of warfare, I decided, as he came after me as fast as he could. I blocked three of his blows before getting a touch in.

"What the fuck?" Lok stared at me in disbelief. At least they'd practiced with dull metal blades—I'd had the point of one of mine at Lok's throat.

"High Demon, dude," Drew snickered. "Don't ever expect to move faster than one of them. Glinda can put you in the dirt, too."

"Here." I handed Drew's practice blades back to him. "I want a bath and a bed. And if you tell Teeg where I am, I'll kick your ass."

"He'll kick my ass if I don't tell him," Drew called after me. I gave him a rude gesture and continued on my way.

~

"Reah, I didn't tell Wylend. Mom says that he listened in on our conversation using an eavesdropping spell because he was in a snit."

"And how did your mother find out about that?" I pulled the warm cloth off my eyes and stared up at Teeg. I was soaking in a tub of warm water, and was falling asleep when Teeg showed up.

"Uncle Erland told her. He said he had an argument with Wylend afterward. Corolan disappeared and Radolf has renounced his Karathian citizenship in front of witnesses."

"Then I'm glad Wylend banished me. Listening to our private conversation and convicting me of treason because of it? That's the ultimate in jerkdom." I'd used a phrase Chash was fond of, once upon a time. "And you probably shouldn't be seen with me, or he'll cancel his membership in your Alliance."

"Don't care," Teeg dipped his hand in my bathwater, brushing my left nipple with a knuckle.

"Teeg, you can't let sex force you to commit a major mistake—you need Karathia in your Alliance."

"And Karathia may need us, too. Have you thought about that? If he hadn't come on board, he was in danger of becoming isolated. Karathia would be locked into trading with only non-Alliance worlds, and that leaves pirates and Giffelithi Dwarves. He'd be paying through the nose for anything not produced on Karathia. And nowadays, that's a lot."

"Well, gee, maybe he can get one of those dwarf women to marry him," I snapped. Yeah, I wasn't in a good mood where Wylend was concerned.

"Erland seems to think he was just angry and went overboard. He'll come to his senses."

"Well, too bad it's too late where I'm concerned." I moved to get out of the tub.

"No, sweetheart, I didn't mean to upset you or interrupt your bath. Drew told me you spent the day cooking for Desh's, so they wouldn't go belly up."

"And I told Drew that if he told you where I was, I'd kick his ass. He's got an ass-kicking coming his way."

"Baby, don't," Teeg made my nipples peak just by stroking a finger across each one. There are times when I'd like to shout at my traitorous body. Teeg knew what to do, every time, to make it respond to him. Had Chash known when he was seventeen that this was the way it would be? I slid down in the water, just from the thought.

"Come on; don't try to drown yourself now." Teeg pulled me up again, getting the sleeve of his expensive silk shirt wet.

"I need to get out before I fall asleep," I said. Teeg pulled me out of the water. Then dried me off with a huge towel. Kissed me while drying my hair, rubbed his erection against my belly, removed his clothing, settled me on the granite sink and made me come—twice. And he didn't even have to bite to do it.

"You're sleeping with me," he said softly. I thought we'd sleep there at the house. Teeg had other ideas, folding me to his bedroom on Campiaa.

"You need to go see Mom," Teeg informed me the following morning, after making love again. "While I'd like to stay in bed all day, I have meetings. Go see Mom. Promise me." He put a finger against my lips before leaning down to kiss them.

"And what am I supposed to tell her? Does she have meetings, too?"

"I already sent mindspeech—there is a meeting and they're waiting for you now."

"Joy. I love meetings."

"Reah, you promised."

I hadn't, but I wasn't going to get into an argument with Teeg San Gerxon. "What's my last name?" I asked. "Where you're concerned?"

"On paper it's San Gerxon. I'll get it officially changed on Le-Ath Veronis. It'll be Montegue there."

"Joy."

"Go." He swatted my behind lightly. I went.

"Oh, shit." I thought it would only be Lissa and Gavin, maybe. I was wrong. So very wrong. I recognized a few people, but not all of them.

Kiarra was there, with Merrill, Adam and Pheligar, Kiarra's Larentii mate. Nearly all the others I assumed were Saa Thalarr—that race of beings selected and redesigned to combat the Ra'Ak.

Spawn Hunters were foot soldiers in that army—the Saa Thalarr were the elite fighters—they could shapeshift into giant animals suitable for fighting Ra'Ak. Karzac was one of several healers who worked with them and the Spawn Hunters. Rumor had it that Karzac was the oldest healer working with them at the moment, and he was more than fifteen thousand years old. As a physician, he had the experience to back him up, every time.

"Reah, we waited until you could join us," Kiarra stood. She was going to run this, I supposed. I expected Lissa to do it. That meant that the information was generated by the Saa Thalarr and not Le-Ath Veronis.

"You can sit with us," Drew grinned at me. *I owe you that ass-kicking,* I sent to him. He laughed. I sat between him and Drake. The next two hours were taken up in a very educational presentation. At the end, I added my files from my comp-vid to the growing evidence that at least five Ra'Ak were ill—mentally and physically. Somehow, a warlock was doing this to them by feeding them spelled and tainted teenagers.

"Nefrigar told me they were ill," I was pointing out the scale deterioration that I'd recorded and expanded on the screen in Lissa's library.

"You saw Nefrigar?" Kiarra sounded surprised. Her hair was nearly as white as mine and great-aunt Glinda's, but not quite as long. She was beautiful, though, and her mates watched her carefully. Why did some women have all the luck? I had mates who didn't seem to have time for me unless they wanted sex. Somewhere there must be a flaw in me or something. I breathed out a frustrated sigh at the thought.

Reah, there's not a damn thing wrong with you, Drake sent. *Wylend needs that ass-kicking.* He was reading my thoughts, just as anybody else could. I really needed to learn how to shield them and my conversations.

"What are we going to do about this?" A beautiful man with

shoulder-length dark hair, pulled back and tied with a leather thong, stood and asked.

"Lisster, I've had three meetings with Belen, and we still haven't come up with a good solution. This falls outside every rule we've ever made or revised," Kiarra answered him.

Leopard shapeshifter, before he came over, Drew informed me. *Has spots on his back and legs,* he added.

Not tattooed? I asked.

Born that way, Drake was listening in.

"We don't need another incident like the one on Boodreatis," a beautiful, strawberry-blonde stood and said. Her hair was slightly darker than Lissa's, I noticed.

That's our mom, Drake was smiling as he watched his mother.

You mean you didn't spring up from the pumpkin patch? I teased him.

Whenever we papered the house or repainted Dad's dojo bright purple, she accused us of being someone else's, Drew ducked his head to hide the grin.

"The Guardian says this is a problem that belongs to the Dark Realm," another blonde stood.

Conner, Drew said. *She is the Guardian—just not all the time. She speaks for her when she's Conner.*

I need a map to understand that, I replied.

"The Ru'Kani Ne'Vanir says the same thing," a honey-blonde woman stood next.

Aunt Gracie—she's the avenging angel, Drake informed me.

"So the Dark Realm is expected to deal with this?" Lissa asked. As well she should—Le-Ath Veronis was unofficial Dark Realm Headquarters. Before, it was Kifirin, but then the High Demons stood aside long ago and allowed the Ra'Ak to destroy almost all of it.

"That's what I'm seeing." The woman Drew had called Conner nodded.

"As long as I keep this body, I'm limited on what I can do," Lissa said, irritation in her voice. I hadn't heard that—what did that mean? Would Teeg know? I made a mental note to ask him. Drake and Drew were grimly silent on Lissa's statement.

"If I knew where the fuckers were, I'd go now and kill every stinking one of them. And the warlock, too." The words were out of my mouth before I'd even thought to voice them. I was also standing and breathing hard. I don't know if anyone present had seen the carnage at the college on Boodreatis, but I had. I'd certainly seen the interviews with weeping parents, all asking why their child had been taken. I'd wept for days on Beliphar, not just from Wylend's desertion and accusations, but for them, too. Lives lost—and for nothing.

Kiarra stared at me, as did everyone else in the room. "This is the one who can heal cores?" I heard a soft voice near the back.

"Yes. I can heal cores. It isn't difficult," I snapped. "But these murderous things are always a step ahead of me, somehow. I've stood in bedrooms where they've left young girls behind, stinking and wrapped in plastic because they asphyxiated them while they were raped. I saw that gymnasium filled with bodies of students, all changed to monsters their families wouldn't recognize. I don't understand this. What are they hoping to gain from this? The warlock indulges his sick fantasies, even as he leaps from body to body in a soul-shift to stay alive. If I could get my hands on any of them," I didn't finish, my hands were clenched in anger and my voice had become a hiss.

"Then perhaps this assignment should be handed to you," Kiarra nodded. I don't think she understood—it didn't need to be handed to me—I'd already taken it, with or without permission.

"You keep talking," I made a motion with my hands at the crowd in general. "I'll start looking." I skipped away.

"Do you see how simple her solution?" Belen appeared, seemingly satisfied about something. As one of the Nameless Ones, he was prevented from interfering with any of Kifirin's races. Officially. He shone, there in Lissa's library. The Saa Thalarr were accustomed to his presence. Lissa and one or two others knew of him but hadn't seen him very often.

"You mean just go off and hunt them?" Drew asked. "Without permission?"

"What you do with your own time is your affair," Belen replied. "Unless you break the primary rules."

"Dude, I don't think this breaks the primary rules," Drake grinned at his brother. Both disappeared.

~

The warlock was so weary he barely remembered his name. Shifting from one body to the next, with the resulting residual memories, had a multitude of names crowding his mind. What he clung to now was the knowledge of the spells—the ones to keep him alive and skipping from body to body to remain that way, leaving dying bodies in his wake to satisfy the growing demands of five crazed monsters.

The warlock couldn't put his finger on the cause of the insanity, but he slept with one eye open at all times. He'd watched while Ansen and Morsen Strand, followed by Hendars Klar, had all disappeared down thick, scaly throats. He couldn't escape the Ra'Ak, either—they watched him closely, expecting him to keep their hunger for young flesh sated.

What he needed, the warlock decided, was to perform more forbidden spellwork. Perhaps he might get away from his self-appointed wardens if he tapped a core. That would give him a tremendous boost in power. When he'd first thought to ally himself with these creatures, he couldn't have imagined the consequences he now faced. He realized it was likely due to his skipping from the bodies before allowing the monsters to devour them, but how could anyone have known? It was an experiment that worked, until the terrible side effects had come. Now, to decide on an appropriate world to tap the core. The warlock searched his mind, smiling a nasty smile. One world owed him, he thought. And his monsters could get him on and off without notice. Yes, that one would do nicely.

"We go," the warlock announced to the five, who'd just fed and were now back in their humanoid forms.

"Where?" The one who still held verbal capability asked.

"Put up your strongest shields," the warlock smiled. "We travel to Karathia."

CHAPTER 13

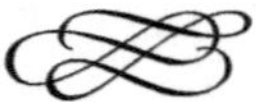

"There's some kind of a disturbance around Didge. I want you to go there and search for the source," Wylend pointed a finger at Wyatt. "And if you find the cause, I expect you to provide punishment."

"Em-pah, punishment is yours to hand down."

"Wyatt, do not argue with me. As my heir, it is time you handled some of our more difficult situations," Wylend snapped. "Now go. I expect a full report when you return."

Wyatt wanted to grumble as he folded to the small village that housed perhaps three hundred witches and warlocks. These preferred the old ways and were mostly old themselves, the youngest at least thirty thousand years of age. Wyatt didn't know what to say to them—Wylend had received a brief call for help through mindspeech and then nothing.

When Wyatt set his feet on the narrow, stone street, the village looked deserted. That shouldn't be—bread in the bakery was burning, too—Wyatt could smell it. Why would they walk away from their business? It didn't make sense. Wyatt put up his strongest shield as he cautiously stepped down the narrow lane between archaic shops.

"Help me," someone called weakly. Wyatt began to run.

"Something's wrong!" Lissa shouted, just as the Vampire Council was seated for a meeting. Flavio jerked his head in her direction; he knew what that meant, even if the others didn't. Lissa always knew. She disappeared in front of the others, causing gasps and shouts among the crowd. It couldn't be helped; something or someone needed Lissa's attention immediately.

The man looked very ill to Wyatt, but he couldn't get a reading through his heaviest shield. He'd found the man sitting on the stoop of the butcher shop, his head bowed. His clothing looked ragged, too, as if he'd been in some sort of conflict. Where were the others? People should be all around.

"What is wrong?" Wyatt called out, approaching slowly.

"We were attacked," the man lifted his head to stare at Wyatt. "Now, all are dead."

The kitchen on Beliphar was filled with images splashed on one wall. Comp-vids littered the island as they projected scene after scene of child kidnappings and murders. The last were the images from Boodreatis—the inert bodies of teens littered the floor, with dashes of adults, here and there. I was adding one final comp-vid, that held a pinpointed map of the solar systems attacked and in what order, starting on Bardelus. Then I went backward from there, searching for data on missing children prior to that point. What I found not only disturbed me, it frightened me so badly I went weak at the knees. I needed to talk to Teeg. And to Astralan or some other warlock who knew about soul-shifting. I was shaking already when the terror came over me, dropping me to the floor while I screamed in horror and pain.

≈

"I can help you." Wyatt lowered his shield and reached toward the man. To Wyatt's eyes, it looked as if the man's skin were flaking and sloughing away. Had he been burned? What was causing this? Wyatt couldn't tell without putting his hands on the patient.

"Would you? I don't feel well," the man muttered. Wyatt nodded, moving close enough to place his hands on the injured man. As Wyatt used his healing ability to search out a cause of the disease, he closed his eyes as he often did, searching inwardly to track the source. He missed the pupils in the eyes becoming slitted instead of round, and when the skin roughened under Wyatt's hands, Wyatt was already screaming in pain.

Every part of a Ra'Ak's body is poison while in serpent form, and Wyatt had both hands placed firmly on the man's shoulders as he changed. Wyatt jerked and spasmed beneath the Ra'Ak's monstrous body, no longer able to scream—the poison was too strong and virulent. The Ra'Ak lifted his head and roared his victory, just as Lissa appeared. Without wasting time, she went to mist and swept inside the Ra'Ak's brain, blowing her mist outward. The Ra'Ak's head exploded as he roared his last breath.

≈

Wylend knew his heir was dead the moment he folded to Didge. Amara, there before him, was weeping and moaning in her grief. Her only child—the one she'd waited for so long, was dead in her arms, killed by Ra'Ak poison. Griffin sat where the Ra'Ak had previously sat, had he but known it, his head in his hands. Lissa stood nearby, tears streaming down her cheeks. She wanted to comfort Amara but was unsure of her welcome. Wylend, escorted by Erland, went to his knees and wept as well.

≈

"You gave him prophecy, and Wylend chose to persecute you for it," Nefrigar had come to lift me off the floor. "At times, we can only say what we can. What the listener does with the information is out of our hands, Lara'Kayan." I was only hearing half his words; I knew Wyatt was dead. Somehow, I'd felt him die, in terrible pain and alone. I wept harder at the thought, Nefrigar's loosely-woven tunic gripped in my hands as my tears drenched the fabric. "Little one, it pains me to hear you weep," he said softly. "Cry this out, and I will place the healing sleep."

"Falchani, do not let the opportunity slip away." A huge blue Larentii was placing a sleeping Reah in Lok's arms, her pretty face tear-stained. Lok knew the likely reason—he'd gotten word from Lendill of the Karathian heir's death at the hands of a Ra'Ak associated with the rogue warlock. He'd also been informed that Lissa had killed the Ra'Ak responsible for Wyatt's death, but hadn't gotten details. He hadn't known a vampire could kill a Ra'Ak. He was still learning things, he admitted to himself as he gazed down at Reah's sleeping face.

"Opportunity?" Lok ventured to ask the Larentii.

"Reah is your opportunity," the Larentii pointed out. "Will you toss it aside, because you desire darker hair?"

"No," Lok sighed heavily. "I was the biggest fool, saying that to her. How was I to know that everything I might want would come in such a package? I know now that it is beautiful. I was allowing my mouth to betray me."

"Wise," the Larentii agreed. "I will go, now. She will wake in four ticks—let the others know where she is. Now is not a good time for them to worry more than they should."

"I will—I'll send out messages as soon as I get her into bed."

"Very good. I will see you soon, Falchani. We may have things to discuss."

"All right." Lok nodded, even as he wondered what a Larentii might have to discuss with him. The Larentii disappeared.

Lok did send out messages—to Lendill, Gavril and Lissa, asking them to share the information with anyone else who needed it. He'd sent it from his comp-vid as he lay beside Reah—he'd pulled on silk sleeping pants and crawled in beside her after settling her as comfortably as he could. He'd been left at the house in Targis, keeping the guards around it and investigating anything that came along that might be connected to child disappearances. He couldn't regret being left behind on Tulgalan—the Larentii had brought Reah to him instead of one of the others.

"Little snowcat," Lok leaned down and nuzzled Reah's jaw, kissing it gently. Moving carefully, he settled her head on his shoulder, wrapped his arms around her and went to sleep.

My waking was disoriented—I couldn't say where I was, and then came the pounding heart, followed by pain and fear—Wyatt was dead. Is that how it is? You wake, and then you remember? Where does sleep take you, that you can leave things like that behind for a time, only to come back to consciousness and find it waiting, like a tiger crouching to pounce?

"Reah, hush now, the pain will pass," a soft voice, from above my head. My cheek was pressed against someone's chest, hardened with muscle. Opening my eyes, I blinked to bring red dragon tattoos into focus.

"It's just me, your Lok," he murmured gently against my ear. And then kissed and nuzzled the sensitive spot behind it. When had he become my Lok? When? I wasn't going to argue, relaxing against him instead with a sigh.

"See, you can relax, little snowcat." I lifted an arm to twine it around his neck. I'd wanted to do that so many times. But he hadn't wanted me. I almost pulled my hand away again.

"No, Reah. Don't pull away from me. I am yours. There is no

doubt. And forget what I said about preferences. I can be every bit as foolish as the next one."

"Lok?" I leaned back so I could see his black eyes.

"Hmm?" The black eyes were smiling at me.

"I always wanted a Falchani. I watched the vids over and over again when I was in school, about the Falchani warriors. You don't know what those images did to a fourteen-year-old who was beginning to see boys differently."

"Now you have your own Falchani," his smile widened. "What are you going to do with him?"

"What does he want to do with me?" I asked, flushing slightly.

"He wants to make love to his little snowcat," he said, and lowered his head to kiss me.

"I need to talk to Teeg," I said later, after serving breakfast for Lok. Lok nodded, dipping into his shaved ham and eggs on a breakfast roll. He was eating it with his fingers, which was more than acceptable. Those fingers had stroked my skin earlier, and every fantasy I'd ever had about a Falchani warrior had come true.

"Lok," I went on, staring at my plate of food, "We may be in terrible trouble if what I think about this warlock is true."

"That idiot warlock managed to tap Karathia's core," Lendill appeared at my elbow. "Do we have more?" He eyed my plate of food.

"Take this, I'll make more," I sighed, slipping off my stool. "And I guess it's too bad that Wylend banished me, isn't it?"

"Reah, he just lost his grandson and heir." Lendill chastised me gently.

"I know." I rubbed knuckles against my forehead. "Will somebody contact Teeg to see if he has time for me today? I have to talk to him—ask him and Astralan some questions."

"What do you mean, see if he has any time for you?" Lendill huffed.

"I have to take what I can get from all of you," I said, putting more eggs on to cook. "We have sex and then you're off to work. I don't get any days where we get all day, now do I?"

Lendill dropped his fork. "Is that what you think?" He asked, lifting the fork again and cutting into his meal.

"It's what I get. What else am I supposed to think? When have we gone shopping, Lendill? Or went anywhere just for fun?"

"Did we wake grumpy today?" Teeg appeared with the requested Astralan. Lendill must have sent mindspeech.

"Sit down, I'll have a plate ready for you in just a few ticks," I said. I busied myself at the stove, preparing three more plates. I didn't tell Teeg what I thought until I placed his plate in front of him. Astralan was smiling as he ate—I hadn't cooked for him in a while. I almost missed those early days with Arvil San Gerxon—at least I'd seen Teeg and the others every day.

"What did you want to talk about, sweetheart?" Teeg asked as I took a stool next to his.

"I need to ask Astralan a question first," I said, cutting into my egg. Astralan gave me an expectant look. "How long does a soul-shift take, once you have the triangle drawn out?"

"Only a tick or two," Astralan frowned at the question.

"And does the targeted body have to be right there next to the warlock?"

"As I understand it, never having done it, of course, you have a bit of space—perhaps thirty or forty of Teeg's feet," Astralan replied.

"Teeg, how big were those rooms at the hotel in Sharaan, on Kareed?"

Teeg blinked at my question. And then blinked again. "Maybe twenty feet across, or so," he whispered. Yeah, he was about to become frightened, too. "What are you saying, Reah?"

"Here." I drew a comp-vid over and pulled up the information I'd compiled. "Child disappearances, occurring after Zellar's death on Kareed, including one from the same hotel around the time of Zellar's recorded death. Everybody assumed the boy ran away, but they never found a trail to follow. All the other disappearances occurred on non-Alliance worlds at the time, so the information wasn't disseminated.

But," and I pressed a button to pull up other information, "look at this. Before, adults came up missing, here and there. Always six at a time, spaced three days apart. Now, maybe I'm wrong, but I think normal Ra'Ak feed every third day."

Teeg was staring at me now, as were Astralan, Lok and Lendill. "We may have killed Zellar's body on Kareed," I said flatly. "But Zellar's soul is still alive and living inside a child's body somewhere. He hasn't been tapping cores to throw us off track and make us think it was somebody else. He's desperate now, since those creatures are crazy, and I think he may be trying to get away from them. That's why he tapped Karathia's core."

"Oh, my toes and stars," Astralan breathed in alarm.

"What's this?" Norian appeared, followed closely by Lissa, Gavin, Erland, Kiarra and a roomful of others.

"Our warlock is Zellar." Teeg tossed his fork onto his plate and stood. "We thought we had the fucker, and he fooled us every step of the way."

"Willem said somebody was tapping into the Telling Winds, and that things were happening that shouldn't be," Lissa said. I stared at her—I hadn't heard this before. Willem Drifft—the Prince of a lesser house of Elves and Ildevar Wyyld's assistant, was an Elvish seer. Few were able to tap into the Telling Winds—Lendill said that they were often referred to as Akashic records on many worlds, but a very rare seer could see forward and backward in the Winds. The enemy was reading our every move and staying one step ahead of us as a result.

"Then one of those Ra'Ak fuckers is doing it, or was doing it," I snapped, angry that information had been withheld, for some reason.

"That makes sense." Willem appeared—Lissa had likely sent mindspeech. "If a Ra'Ak turned a humanoid who could read the Winds, and nurtured it instead of letting it fight and die with the others, they'd have a weapon in their hands," he said. "This is awful."

"Awful doesn't begin to describe what this is," Lissa rubbed her forehead.

"Here, now, little one." One of Lissa's Larentii appeared, lifting her and placing gentle fingers against her forehead. I knew he was removing the headache for her.

"So, now that the warlock has tapped Karathia's core, he may hit others," I said, my stomach rebelling. "He'll keep trying to get away from these Ra'Ak, but as long as the one who can read the Winds is alive, he'll lose that battle." I thought I was going to be sick. Pheligar appeared, lifting Kiarra and rubbing her back. I felt dizzy now, in addition to feeling nauseous.

"Little one, this stone floor is not a pleasant place to fall," Nefrigar's voice came from far away.

"Huh?" I stared up at him. How was I in his arms? When had that happened?

"And you must eat, Lara'Kayan. Bearing twins is never easy on a female's body. You must take better care of yourself."

"Twins? You're joking," Teeg was standing next to Nefrigar now, even as my eyes filled with tears. "I mean, I knew she was pregnant again, but twins?"

"Hush now, Reah," Nefrigar said, and then began to hum. I'd heard rumors about the Larentii trilling, but I'd never heard it before. I was asleep in very little time.

"They're Tory's," Teeg muttered, watching Reah's eyes close as Nefrigar held her.

"Do not fret, young vampire," Nefrigar said softly so as not to wake Reah. "Yours will come someday. The High Demon race is in peril, and Reah must help rebuild it. Do not begrudge them this. You will get your child."

"I will?" Teeg's voice nearly cracked, he was so surprised.

"When the time is right," Nefrigar's eyes were unfocused for a few moments.

"But what about Karathia's core—Wylend has banished Reah. Even if he lifts that banishment, she may not be willing to go back there," Lissa voiced another concern.

"Unless he wants Karathia to die, he'll be forced to lift the ban. But that will have to take a back seat for now—his heir is dead," Astralan observed.

"Something else that was not supposed to happen—not like this," Willem said quietly.

~

"Tell me how great a fool I am." Wylend gave Erland a hopeless glance. Erland was helping Wylend into dark robes for Wyatt's funeral.

"Love, we all make mistakes."

"But this mistake cost Wyatt his life. If I'd just listened, instead of demanding my own way. Amara has left Griffin. She'll come for the service, but she'll sit with Lissa's group—she's already asked for that favor. Griffin and I were so set on Wyatt having this that we overrode his feelings in the matter. Belen took away the Oracle's ability to see the future where his son was concerned. Now, Griffin and I pay the price."

"I asked Gavril to tell Reah that you've rescinded the sentence and the banishment," Erland said softly.

"Erland, it's too little too late, and everything we do from now on will be suspect. She doesn't know me as you do—she doesn't know to wait out these little fits of paranoia and jealousy. And I'm afraid that I complicated things further, before her words and thoughts became a painful truth to me."

"Love, what did you do?" Erland lifted Wylend's face with a gentle hand.

"I listened in at other times. I heard her tell Gavril that Torevik was too young in her estimation, when he fathered her first child. She and Gavril discussed Tory's maturity since then. I'm afraid I only took those words of hers regarding his immaturity to my great-grandson. I had to send Corolan yesterday to find out what sort of damage that might have done."

"Wylend, you didn't." Erland backed away, a concerned frown on his face. He hadn't yet told Wylend that Reah was pregnant with Tory's twins.

"Erland, I don't know what possessed me to do it. Reah will pay for private thoughts and words."

"What has Torevik done?" Erland was almost afraid to ask the question.

"You will find out at the funeral, I'm afraid. It's a good thing Reah isn't planning to attend."

Erland shivered. If Tory were plotting some sort of revenge against Reah for Wylend's invasion of her privacy and reported half-truths later, Erland didn't want to witness it.

A four-hundred-year-old clock ticked in the background inside Merrill's study. Griffin sat at Merrill's desk, gazing at the lawn outside the window without seeing anything. Although Griffin and Merrill had barely spoken for years, he and Amara still lived in the old mansion Merrill owned in Kent. Until Amara left him after Wyatt's death, anyway. Griffin brushed wetness away from his face. His mate and his son—both gone in a blink. He couldn't even *Look* to see if Amara might come back to him eventually; that ability to see her future had been taken from him after she'd left.

"Now you get to experience a little of what you handed out to others," a woman's voice snapped. Griffin turned quickly before rising in a blink, claws and fangs out. It had been years since he'd let the vampire in him loose, but the fangs and claws disappeared quickly. There was no mistaking this one, shining brightly from across the desk.

"Mighty One," Griffin bowed his head.

"You need to get your ass back in time and help your daughter. At least you can kill the Ra'Ak threatening her and her children, if you couldn't manage to kill the one who took Wyatt."

"What?" Griffin blinked in confusion as the woman shone brighter. Images filtered into his mind before he was flung backward in time.

"Reah, he's lifting the ban, so of course you should go. You were the last one to stand up for Wyatt, when he was alive. Why shouldn't you go to his funeral?"

"Teeg, it's not that simple and you know it. I thought of Wyatt as a friend, but there will be others there who are his family. You're part of that. I don't want to interfere with this in any way." I didn't add that I thought Wylend had selfish reasons to lift the ban—Karathia's core had been tapped, so he had to make nice if he wanted me to fix it. I would, but it wouldn't be for him. It would be for Corolan, Erland, Rylend and Radolf.

"Then come as my mate. As my support in this." Teeg was begging me now. We were having this conversation inside my suite at the house he'd purchased for me in Targis. Lok was outside, making sure the guards assigned by Lendill were doing their job.

"Little one," Nefrigar appeared at my elbow—I'd been combing out my hair as I talked with Teeg.

"Honey blue?" I looked up at him. When we were like this, he was nearly twice my height.

"Reah, as a gift to my love, I will place a shield around your words and thoughts. No other will be able to tap them or employ spells to eavesdrop, unless you wish it."

I was still staring at him. Someone had told me when I woke what Lara'Kayan meant—Nefrigar had been calling me *forever love* in Neaborian, a nearly dead language.

"Thank you," I sighed, wishing that gift had come sooner than it did.

"I wish it had come sooner as well," Nefrigar smiled sadly. "I did not lock myself out, but then neither I nor any Larentii will ever seek to harm you with your own thoughts and words."

I nodded, staring at the floor. I still didn't understand why Wylend chose to damage me in this way. What had he hoped to gain by it? Wyatt had paid the price for all this, and that made me sad and angry at the same time.

"I must go; send mindspeech if you need me," Nefrigar's large blue fingers tilted my chin up. "I love you," he said, his bright blue eyes gazing into mine with what looked like worry before he disappeared.

"Come with me, Reah," Teeg said softly at my back. I nodded and went to find something suitable to wear.

Lissa had offered her palace as a neutral space for the funeral, after Amara had come to her. I was just learning that Amara, Griffin's mate for millennia uncounted, had left Teeg's grandfather after Wyatt's death. She wasn't speaking to Griffin or to Wylend. I was with her regarding Wylend. I'd never met Griffin, but he'd been pushing Wyatt, too. It was all a waste—Wyatt was a good healer. I knew that.

"Here—we'll sit with Mom and Dad," Teeg steered me toward a row of comfortable chairs set up in the circular rotunda of Lissa's palace. Flowers were everywhere near a spot at the front, and a podium had been placed there. The chairs in the center aisle at the front were empty—the immediate family would come in last.

I looked down our row while Teeg sent mindspeech that the dark-haired, beautiful woman sitting beside Lissa was Amara, Wyatt's mother. Lissa had an arm around her shoulders and was trying to console her. Drew sat on Amara's other side, Drake next to him. Gavin and Tony sat on Lissa's other side.

I was seeing too, a few that I had only seen a time or two—Lissa's daughter Nissa and her two mates, Toff and Trikleer. Toff was not only a modified Winged Vampire, but also a Grey House Wizard, as was Trik. Behind us were Lissa's other mates. Rylend would come in with Wylend and Erland, I was sure. I hoped I hadn't damaged Ry's relationship with Wylend, just by saying that he'd be the better King.

Wyatt hadn't wanted to be King at all, he'd said so himself when I'd first met him. I'd tried to get him to discuss his wishes with Lissa at the time, but he'd never done it. We were back to the missed opportunities that Aurelius and I had discussed. I missed Auri and wished he were with me, on my other side.

Perhaps Tory would come instead, so I could lean on his strength. Teeg squeezed my hand when Kiarra appeared next to a piano near the front. I hadn't know before then that she sang. Gavril explained that this was what she'd done before becoming one of the Saa Thalarr. The language was from old Earth, and Gavril had to interpret for me, but it was beautiful. The title, he said, was *Time To Say Good-bye*.

Corolan's face was pale as he walked into the antechamber to collect Wylend, Erland and the others. A full contingent of Karathian royalty had come from Wylend's court. He'd seen Reah come in on Gavril's arm. This wasn't going to turn out well.

"What's wrong?" Rylend hissed. He'd been watching his grandfather, his uncle Griffin and all the others, trying to anticipate what might be needed and working toward making things happen to ensure everything went as smoothly as possible. He'd already sent two home who'd shown up inebriated.

"Reah's here," Corolan muttered.

"Please, no," Ry moaned, leaning against the thick double doors leading into the rotunda. "I can't seem to talk my fool brother out of this stupidity yet and we both know how much effect my power has on a stubborn High Demon. There's no way she'll miss this." Rylend rubbed the knot between his eyes.

"This will ruin everything," Corolan muttered.

"What's wrong?" Erland walked up to his son.

"Reah's here."

"Could things possibly be worse?" Erland sighed. "Wylend has plans to go to Tory in the next few days and tell him that he didn't give the whole truth in this matter. Now, even if we can convince Torevik, there's no way to explain this to Reah. She'll never come back to Karathia."

"We haven't told Mom either, and you know what that could mean," Ry looked at his father.

"Son, we'll consider that problem when we get there," Erland sighed.

~

Kiarra was finishing a second song when Wylend, Erland, Corolan and a contingent from Karathia filed in and filled the center row of chairs. Someone was also moving past Teeg and me to sit in the empty chairs between us and Gavin. If Teeg hadn't gripped my hand—hard—I'd have skipped away. Tory was there, pulling a beautiful, dark-haired woman behind him. She was nearly six feet tall, in Aurelius' measurements, and looked perfect. Tory, for effect, kissed her before he helped her into a seat next to him. My mouth was open in shock, I'm sure. Teeg's jaw was working furiously, but he didn't say anything, he merely gripped my fingers tighter, refusing to allow me to leave.

Once everyone was seated, Merrill walked to the podium. Amara and Lissa had asked him to speak. I kept swallowing painfully, trying to hold back the tears that threatened. I was pregnant with Tory's twins, and he was doing this. Jealousy or not, this wasn't the time to flaunt a mistress. I had multiple mates; he was entitled as well. But my hand went to my belly. The last time we'd been in bed had resulted in my pregnancy. Was this his way of telling me what he truly thought of fatherhood? If so, he'd lied to me. He'd said he was ready.

I barely listened to Merrill's words. Wise words, I'm sure—he was an old vampire and had seen much during his lifetime. Amara sobbed quietly now and then. My eyes kept returning to Tory and the woman at his side. Solicitously, she held his hand in hers. I wanted to sob, too, just not for the same reason as everyone else. I did come back to the present, however, when Pheligar took Merrill's place.

Everyone in the crowd was watching—I mean, how often did you see a Larentii appear at a funeral to speak? "We do not do this often," Pheligar announced in his deep, mellow voice. "But it was requested this time, by someone higher than I. I agreed. Here are the images." I was shocked when three-dimensional images appeared in front of all of us—I recognized this scene just as well as Gavril did beside me. He stiffened. He was twelve and looking over a fence at the bus track below while snowflakes fell around us in Targis. And there I was, talking to Wyatt. The tears came, then.

"I wish I were twelve again," Wyatt said, nodding toward a young Gavril.

"Whatever for?" I asked. I'd been nineteen then. So young, and without Tory's claiming marks on my neck.

"I didn't have all this looming over my head," Wyatt muttered. "Em-pah keeps telling me what I need to do to take his place one day."

"You don't want that, do you?" My younger self asked.

"No," Wyatt replied. "I want to be a healer, like my mother. But Em-pah won't even listen to me. He just keeps pushing me in the direction he thinks I should go."

Amara sobbed when Wyatt admitted that he wanted to be a healer, like her. Wyatt's and my conversation went on, until I said, "Wyatt, if you don't tell him soon," meaning Wylend, "you may regret that decision." Pheligar ended the images there. I was grateful; I'd suggested afterward that Wyatt go talk with Lissa, his half-sister. He hadn't ever done that, and he probably hadn't fully expressed himself to Wylend. His body now lay in state before us, dressed richly and placed inside an elaborately carved box.

I wished I hadn't been a part of that transmission—things were bad enough between Wylend and me. I figured that as soon as I repaired Karathia's core, I'd be banished again. It was just as well, I would never come to Wylend again. He'd invaded my privacy and used my private words against me. I couldn't have a mate who was constantly policing my thoughts and conversations, searching for any sort of slight or insult. Wylend and I were finished.

Kiarra sang once more before Merrill invited everyone for refreshments inside the Council Chambers. Wyatt would be buried the following day on Karathia in a private ceremony. Only family would attend that. "Reah, come." Teeg stood and led me away before Tory could brush past us again, hauling the beautiful woman along with him.

"I don't want to go to the Council Chambers," I was wiping tears away one-handed as Teeg pulled me after him.

"You see those journalists and cameras, Reah?" Teeg muttered, dragging me toward the huge hall where the Vampire Council met, "We have to present as good an image to them as we can. They won't be inside the chamber itself, so hold your head up and let's get there with as much dignity as we can."

I wanted to argue with him, but I didn't. Perhaps I should have—mentally, of course. Wouldn't do to let the news-vids have a field day with Teeg and me, speculating whether we were on the outs or not, when it was Tory and me, and Wylend and me, who would have made the juicy news.

Teeg kept me against the back wall, shielding me from the cameras pointed at this guest or that as attendees filed into the chamber. When the door was shut, Teeg breathed a sigh of relief but still kept his hands on me so I couldn't get away.

I saw Tory in the distance, talking easily with this guest or that, his arm draped comfortably around the black-haired woman's waist. I said nothing, letting my gaze drop to my shoes. I'd worn a black dress with a matching beaded jacket and low-heeled black shoes. Tiny jet earrings were in my ears—I didn't want to stand out or draw attention. Not so with Tory's companion—she'd gone for both. A strapless gown with a wrap in such a deep red as to be nearly black, and heels that would have caused me to teeter precariously. She was used to wearing them that high, I could tell.

"Well, Reah, I guess I'm not too immature after all," Tory drawled, forcing me to jerk my head up. How had he come to be in front of us so quickly? And what was he saying? I blinked stupidly at him and the woman standing beside him. "Oh, this is Darletta, my wife," Tory introduced the brunette. We'd never married, Tory and I. He'd never asked—he'd just stuck his teeth in my neck while in his smaller Thifilathi.

"Tory," Teeg was growling and his eyes were going red. I looked from one brother to the other.

"Torevik Rath, you idiot!" Lissa was there and hissing in a

heartbeat. "We didn't tell you, because Lendill said you were on a sensitive mission. Reah is pregnant with your twins, and this is how you choose to come home?"

Another tear slipped out and Teeg couldn't hold me this time; I skipped away.

CHAPTER 14

Gavin placed compulsion on Darletta, who was now humming distractedly in a corner. Erland had come to attempt to explain Wylend's part in this, but it wasn't coming out very well.

"You mean to tell me you married her without a prenuptial? That you were getting back at Reah because she said you were too young the first time?" Lissa's hair was a mess. This was the last thing she'd expected at her half-brother's funeral.

"Mom, Wylend sent me mindspeech."

"And it didn't bother you that Wylend was listening to private thoughts and conversations? That he didn't give you the full conversation I was having with Reah?" Gavril's fangs still threatened. His eyes were red and had been from the beginning.

"Young one, I am very close to removing your claiming marks from Reah's neck," Kifirin appeared, smoke billowing from his nostrils. Tory's eyes widened. And then he turned, going immediately to his smaller Thifilathi, who cringed and fell to his knees before the Lord of the Dark Realm. The howl that came from his throat was mournful and nearly earsplitting. Darletta looked up briefly, before turning away again. She would remember none of what she was seeing—Gavin had made sure of that. Gardevik, coming from a meeting in Jaydevik's court, glared at his son, who knelt before Kifirin.

"You have shamed the High Demon race; The Wise Ones say that Reah's twins will be daughters. Where will their father be, Torevik Rath? You married that creature," Garde jerked his head toward Darletta. "Now, you are stuck with her. Only one kind of woman will marry someone after a first meeting. She knows who you are, and more importantly, who your mother is. You are bound to this marriage, child, and all because of an angry fit."

"Turn back," Kifirin commanded. "Leave my sight, or I will find another High Demon for Reah. And take your wife with you."

"I don't want to bring this to him right now." Erland spoke softly to Corolan and Garek. "Things are bad enough as it is."

"It would have been better if he hadn't done this. What possessed him?"

"He felt slighted. You know how he gets at times when he's in a female cycle."

"He has snits in male cycles, too," Garek pointed out.

"Yes, there is that," Erland admitted. "He and Griffin are in there together, getting blindingly drunk. At least Dragon and Crane volunteered to stay with them." The four men were inside Wylend's private study.

"Why would Wyatt admit to Reah that he didn't want to be King, and never say it to anyone else?" Garek shook his head.

"Come on, we all knew it," Corolan said. "The minute he could get away from Wylend's chores, he was off helping his mother. We all knew; we just knew not to say anything to Wylend. Until he tapped into Reah's conversations. He'll never get her back. Not now." Corolan mourned that fact—he loved her—more than he could ever admit to the King of Karathia.

~

"I'm not kidding, Lendill." I paced in front of him. "I want to separate myself from Torevik Rath. I don't want him to have any parental rights to these children." He'd taken a small bit of information, blown it out of proportion and gotten married to have his revenge. I didn't want my children exposed to that. And I was rethinking my willingness to heal Karathia's core. Wylend was at the bottom of all of this.

"Reah, Alliance law won't let you do that," Lendill pointed out patiently. "Even though you were never married to him."

"Yeah, how about that?" I felt nauseous and hugged myself, trying to calm my stomach. "He never asked me. Yet he picks up the first woman he can find who is tall, beautiful and willing. Well, I won't be willing. Never again. He and Wylend are gone. Period."

"Reah, I know this isn't a good time," Rylend appeared from nowhere. "But Em-pah Griffin and Great-em-pah Wylend are pretty much drunk right now. If you heal the core while they're plastered, then we won't have to make excuses or explanations later."

"Are you sure that warlock fucker Zellar is far away? I don't want to lose twins this time," I snapped at him.

"I will come—they will not get past me or my Protectors," Nefrigar appeared. Two other Larentii were with him.

"You promise?" I looked up at Nefrigar.

"I can promise this to my love—Larentii are allowed to protect their mates."

"Then let's go." I didn't feel good, but then I probably wouldn't ever feel good about this. Lendill called Lok in somehow, so I ended up going to Karathia with Lendill, Lok, Rylend Morphis and three Larentii.

~

"Boss, Reah's healing the core on Karathia—I got mindspeech from Ry," Astralan whispered to Gavril.

"Then let's go," Gavril gave Tory one last glare before allowing Astralan to fold him to Karathia.

Gavril stared at the three Larentii who had come. Nefrigar he recognized, but not the other two. "Two of my Protectors, who also happen to be my two oldest sons," Nefrigar explained, as Reah seated her full Thifilatha onto the ground where Zellar had tapped Karathia's core.

"You have more than two sons?" Gavril's voice held awe. He'd only heard of Larentii having one, perhaps two children, and two was extremely rare.

"All born before Ferrigar's decree," Nefrigar smiled. "Four of them. All four work with me now, plus two others—sons of my eldest friend who separated his particles long ago."

"Working in the Archives keeps us young," one of Nefrigar's sons offered. "I am Serrigar, and this is my next eldest brother, Valegar."

"Very pleased to meet you," Gavril nodded respectfully.

"We have all the information on the Campiaan Alliance, from the beginning," Valegar grinned. "We and father found it fascinating. That is how he learned of his mate, you know. Serrigar gathered information and brought it to Father, not long ago. The moment he absorbed her image, he was lost."

"And after all this time, too," Nefrigar agreed. "Let us watch her now—this is more than fascinating."

"I have the shields set, Father," Serrigar announced. "Everything is clear and none shall break through."

"Good. Thank you, child."

I settled myself as comfortably as I could, and focused on Karathia's daystar. Karathia had barely been tapped—as if the tapping had been interrupted. What did that mean? I pulled energy from the star and went to work.

Zellar glared at the Ra'Ak when he thought the creature wasn't looking. This one only spoke using mindspeech now, and seldom communicated with Zellar. Zellar was frightened—this one had pulled him away from Karathia before he could gather enough energy to effectively escape those he now saw as his captors.

He'd thought them allies at first, when he'd offered his services to Hendars Klar. He was no longer under any illusions regarding who was captor and captive. Zellar wondered if he shouldn't start soul-shifting with adults. His current body was fourteen turns in age and would feed the Ra'Ak soon—it was time for another shift.

Zellar was worried, too, that the four remaining Ra'Ak were planning something. He wouldn't be included in those plans, that was a given. Zellar walked toward the cages that held six teens, the oldest of which was seventeen. That would be his next body. Zellar pulled the chalk from a pocket and knelt to begin drawing runes.

The moment I'd stood after healing the core, the dry heaves began. Nefrigar placed one hand on my forehead and the other on my belly. I felt blessed relief quickly. Someone lifted me, I can't say whom, and transported me to Tulgalan. Radolf was there, waiting with food.

"Here, now, you've had a long day, we'll do a light soup first," Radolf slid a bowl in front of me while Teeg propped me up. Nefrigar and the two he'd brought with him made themselves smaller so they could sit at the island with me.

"I want to sleep after," I mumbled, lifting the spoon.

"We'll make sure you sleep," Teeg murmured against my ear. Radolf fed me as much as he could, but that wasn't much. Teeg rubbed my belly carefully while I ate, sending me mindspeech. Telling me he'd make sure the twins wouldn't lack for fathers. I brushed away tears when he said that.

"Our Reah upset," Farzi and Nenzi came, ferried by Stellan. I wrapped my arms around Farzi while Nenzi stroked my hair.

"Lion snake shapeshifters? Father, this is a very good day," Valegar said, smiling widely.

"We take Reah to bed," Nenzi announced. Lok, Lendill, Gavril and the Larentii followed while Farzi carried me to my suite.

"Here is the information—her father is Dantel Schuul, a minor politician on Quezlos," Norian handed the comp-vid to Lissa. "And he's ambitious, he just doesn't have the clout or charisma to rise above his current position. He must think he's hit the jackpot, marrying off his daughter to your son." Garde stood behind Lissa, blowing smoke. "He's gotten his wealth from manufacturing chips that control assembly robots—every Alliance world does business with his firm. That doesn't help him in his political aspirations—he needs extra support for that, since the population sees him as too wealthy. They don't trust that, so he needs someone behind him who is already respected in the political realm. He looks to you to provide that, through your son."

If Tory had bothered to talk with either parent, they might have gotten to the root of this. As it was, he hadn't and in an act of mindless pettiness, he'd married. If Tory filed for a writ of detachment, Darletta would own half his holdings, and he half of hers. But, as Norian had pointed out, Darletta, having reached her majority, had nothing unless it was through her father. Tory, on the other hand, had holdings granted on Le-Ath Veronis and Kifirin, in addition to his and his parents' reputations. Darletta could damage all of it if she didn't get her way.

"Even if she asks for the writ, it's still split evenly down the middle, so this is a no-win scenario," Garde grumbled.

"Why doesn't the Alliance have an annulment option?" Lissa sighed.

"It's supposed to force them to think before they marry, but you see where we are," Norian said.

"It's neither here nor there," Lendill folded in. "Reah says she's done with Wylend and Tory. And she means it."

"I pray that Kifirin does not remove Torevik's claiming marks," Garde said. "I also hope she doesn't forget that I will be a grandfather to those children."

"I don't think her argument is with you," Lendill nodded toward Garde.

"Great-Grandfather, I brought Reah to heal the core yesterday." Rylend spoke softly; his grandfather had a terrible hangover and neither Wyatt nor Amara would ever be available again to heal his aches and pains. Griffin had disappeared after Wylend passed out the night before.

"Can you find a healer on this gods-forsaken planet to heal a headache?" Wylend moaned.

"Here," Ry touched Wylend's head with careful hands, removing the headache. "I can get tea or coffee if you want it."

"Of course I want it. Do I have anybody left in the palace willing to make it?"

"I just sent mindspeech; it'll be here shortly," Ry said.

"Where's your father?"

"In Didge, with Corolan and Garek, trying to convince sixteen warlocks and seven witches that it's all right to come back."

"Is that all that's left there?" Wylend wanted to moan again.

"Yes—the Ra'Ak and Zellar either killed or ate the others."

"Including Wyatt."

"Including Wyatt. I'll miss him, Great-Grandfather. He was a good friend, as well as my uncle. Your tea's here." Ry took the cup from the kitchen helper and passed it to his grandfather. "Dad should be back soon. Send mindspeech to him if you need anything else."

"Reah healed the core?"

"Yes. I watched, as did three Larentii. I think they would have said something if she didn't get the job done right."

"That wasn't what I meant."

"Then what did you mean, Great-Grandfather? I asked her to come and she came. She's pregnant with Tory's twins, and that might be wonderful, except Tory became angry for some reason and married the first woman who came along. He doesn't care anything about Darletta, but he's stuck with her now. Reah says she's done with Tory. She's walking away and Kifirin threatened to remove his claiming marks. Now, who would take an already tenuous situation and push it past the breaking point? Tory's my brother, and Reah is my sister. She belonged to both my brothers, until a few days ago. I'm renouncing my Karathian citizenship, Great-Grandfather, in front of the ultimate witness." Rylend folded away.

"Erland, I'm not about to tell our son that he made the wrong decision." Lissa accepted a fruit drink from Ilvan, who loved working in the palace kitchen with Radolf.

"Wylend is about to have a breakdown," Erland snapped. "He loses Wyatt and then our son renounces his citizenship? What would you do?"

"I don't know," Lissa shrugged. "Maybe think I fucked up somewhere? At least I did talk our child out of jumping into a six-year, full-time sign-up with the ASD."

"He what?" Erland was about to get furious.

"I said I talked him out of it. I told him that wouldn't be any different from Tory running out and marrying Darletta. He said that he saw my point and went off to visit Gavril on Campiaa. Erland, we have family dinners and gatherings to look forward to with Darletta. Are you happy about that?"

"Of course I'm not happy about that," Erland huffed angrily. "But Ry could have waited until Wylend was past the mourning period."

"I'm not disagreeing with the action, but he could have waited a few days," Lissa agreed reluctantly. "Wylend should have waited, too, don't you think? Before going straight to Tory with only a half-truth, knowing it would likely set him off."

"Lissa, he's under a lot of pressure," Erland took Lissa's arm and led her out of the kitchen. "He was faced with joining either the Reth or Campiaan Alliance or doing business with the pirates and cutthroats of Giffel, Deandrus or their newly-acquired world of Lidrith. You know what would happen if we didn't join one or the other—warlocks and witches hired out to pirates and assassins, just to keep the trade flowing. Wylend has held strong through thousands of years, and now he's being forced to change. He imagined a slight, that's true, but he's worried that Karathia will be viewed as only one among many, and not nearly as important as it once was."

"Then why hasn't he spoken to Gavril about this? Gavril sees Karathia as the cornerstone of the Campiaan Alliance," Lissa said.

"Wylend sees Gavril as a young great-grandchild, who doesn't have near the experience that he does at ruling," Erland sighed.

"Do you think Gavril doesn't have enough sense to ask if he finds himself in a difficult situation?"

"Gavril may be one of the most intelligent people I've ever met," Erland admitted.

"And Wylend doesn't see that?"

"Wylend is afraid to admit it," Erland said.

"Erland, there's something else Wylend doesn't see." Lissa said.

"And that is?"

"That Reah was correct—Rylend would have been the King Karathia deserved."

～

"Reah, we got another hit on our warlock and his Ra'Ak." Lendill slid his comp-vid over so I could take a look. Lok was there with Farzi and Nenzi—Teeg had gone home with Astralan and Stellan. He had work to do.

"Hon, I think it's the crazy Ra'Ak and their slave warlock now. I don't think Zellar ever thought he'd find himself in this position." I set plates of food on the island. Lok watched me, his eyes never missing anything, although he didn't speak.

"Norian and I think you're right—I can't imagine that he ever thought he might be in charge of those monsters." Lendill bit into his breakfast roll. I scrolled through Lendill's information—three young men had disappeared on Horxx. What was a bit unusual was the oldest one had been twenty.

"Do you think he's going for older bodies, attempting to get himself out of this mess?" I asked.

"It's a possibility," Lendill nodded. "If he caught the Ra'Ak not looking, did a quick shift and then released or folded the prisoners away, they'd be scrambling after all of them, not realizing that the one left behind at the hideout wasn't him."

"And he could slip away if there were enough to go after," I saw where Lendill was going with this. "Do you think we ought to watch for a greater number of disappearances?"

"Yes." Lendill turned to his food before it got cold.

I didn't say what else I was thinking—that even if we did find more missing young men than normal, we still wouldn't have the warlock's location, and if his plan succeeded, then we'd have two targets to hunt instead of one. "Has your father ever gone hunting Ra'Ak—or a warlock before?" I asked Lendill, tearing a chunk off my roll and stuffing it in my mouth.

"He might be able to track a warlock if he had something that belonged to him; something that he wore or something—That's how my father found you," Lendill ducked his head, smiling guiltily.

"But we've never found anything of his." Lok pointed out. He'd been doing his research. He was right, up to a point.

"Lendill, does your father freak or gag easily?" I asked.

"My father could be a Larentii if he were taller and blue," Lendill snorted.

"I'll take that as a no," I said. "Do we know what they did with those bodies on Bardelus?" I asked. "I mean, Zellar lived in those bodies—at least for a few days. Can your father work with that?"

~

Kaldill Schaff walked around the body lying on the frigid, steel table. At least the corpse was cold and didn't smell so terribly bad at the moment. Lendill watched his father carefully—Norian stood beside Lendill, staring in a fascinated manner—Norian had never seen an Elf work. Kaldill murmured words that Norian failed to understand; he assumed that they were in the Elvish tongue that Lendill used occasionally, mostly to curse.

"I have the signature," Kaldill sighed, looking at both Lendill and Norian. "It may take a day or two, at the least, but I will track him after that."

"Good. We'll have people ready to go as soon as we get a lock on this. Lissa will come, as will Garde, Reah, Denevik and Gavril. Lendill and I will come as well," Norian nodded his thanks to Kaldill Schaff.

"I do this for my child and his mate," Kaldill nodded at Lendill. "Someday, perhaps my son will know of his worth to his race."

"Thank you, father," Lendill breathed a respectful sigh to his one remaining parent.

"I will send the information the moment I have it." Kaldill Schaff disappeared.

"This will work? How reliable is this?" Norian turned to his oldest friend.

"You can bet everything you have on it," Lendill replied.

~

"Have you heard from Tory?" Gavin dropped his shirt on the bed. He'd always dressed well as a vampire—Aurelius had instilled in him the necessity of looking his best at all times. The only times he'd dressed otherwise in the past were when he'd been undercover for the Council and different dress was required.

"No, honey. And Gavril and Ry are pissed. They can't even get an answer from him. I don't understand this." Lissa rubbed her forehead.

"I fail to understand it as well. Reah will bear his children. He will not get any with that woman."

"Gavin, I don't think she's mature enough to be called a woman. Did you hear her chatter? I have no interest in who her neighbors are, or that their son drinks too much."

"I wanted to place another compulsion not to speak," Gavin grumbled in complete agreement.

"Garde told him under no circumstances could he reveal the Thifilathi to her—it's just too dangerous. I can see Darletta announcing that to the entire Alliance. Jayd will have a cow if that happens." Lissa removed her earrings and set them on her dressing table.

"Jayd is right to hide what Kifirin truly is. Just as Ildevar Wyyld hides his otherness from the Alliance. Some things are better kept hidden." Gavin sat on the edge of the bed and removed his pants.

"Yes. Things might stay safer, that way."

"Little mate, Larentii can provide energy sex, along with more traditional methods," Nefrigar smiled down at me. "The Wise Ones say that a High Demon will be able to handle energy sex until the final two months before the birth."

"Really?" I was learning many things from my Larentii.

"Really." His smile widened. "And as we will have energy sex this first time, I am inviting your two lion snake mates to experience it with us."

"Huh?" Now I was confused. Farzi and Nenzi sidled into the room —Nefrigar had taken me to Beliphar for what I thought to be coupling. Farzi and Nenzi were now with us.

"Nefrigar say we have what we never have before, with him and our Reah." Nenzi looked so hopeful. I knew then just how much I loved both him and Farzi. The other six I thought of as my brothers, but Farzi and Nenzi were more than that. I swallowed and nodded at both my lion snakes. Nefrigar made sure we were all comfortable on the bed and then surrounded us with power. I didn't have to do anything, Nefrigar guided me through the entire thing, pulling energy from himself and then from me, allowing it to mix before slamming it back into both of us. The result was a mind-bending climax that rocked the floor beneath the bed, the backwash hitting Farzi and Nenzi, who experienced the first-ever sexual encounter they'd had in their lives. When I woke from the brief faint after the pleasure, it was to find a smiling Nefrigar, watching while two eager reptanoids stared at him and me, fully expecting us to repeat the performance.

"I informed Amara that I will not consider this while she is still upset and in mourning." Belen stared at Griffin. Amara had come to him only the day before, asking to be released from her long life. Belen wisely had refused, recognizing the pain behind the request.

"Tell me she will come back to me." Griffin was begging the nameless one for hope. The moment Wyatt died, Griffin could no longer see into his own or Amara's future.

"I will not peer into that future for you, Oracle. Had you or your father listened through the years, you would have experienced a different outcome. Wyatt was meant to be a healer. Would have been invited to join the Saa Thalarr quickly, had things turned out otherwise. Kifirin gave a gift of prophecy to Reah, his child. Yet you and your father chose to punish her after her final gift to you. Wyatt tried to heal the Ra'Ak there at the end—the creature was asking for help. But true to his brutal race, the Ra'Ak turned when Wyatt lowered his shield, poisoning your child."

"I hope you didn't tell Amara that when she came to you." Griffin wiped tears away.

"I did not; she is suffering enough as it is. If she comes to me again in a turn, and asks for death again, I will not deny it."

"Please, no," Griffin moaned.

"Bro, you can do more for me than you think." Gavril sat at his desk, looking at Rylend. "Everything you touch turns to gold, and everybody you meet ends up eating from your hand, one way or the other. You can be Prime Minister or Ambassador, your choice. Neither Dee nor I have much patience with some of our members. You can smooth the way for the Campiaan Alliance."

"And it will pay very well," Dee added. He was standing beside Gavril's desk.

"Will I stay here or elsewhere?" Ry asked, his dark eyes going from his brother to Dormas, Gavril's assistant.

"Ry, stay wherever you like. If you don't like it here, we'll build something just for you. Dee and I have plenty of experience in that."

"Yeah. I'll find some plans and see if you can put something together for me on top of one of these mountains." Ry sighed softly.

"You didn't have to renounce your citizenship."

"Yes I did. I had something to say about the laws of Karathia, and that was the best way I knew to say it. Banishing somebody because of words spoken in private? That's ludicrous and you know it."

"I can't hear Reah's thoughts anymore; Nefrigar has blocked them to all except the Larentii. Did you know that?" Gavril didn't sound happy.

"Nobody ever taught her how to shield before, and that's probably our fault. Tory should have shown her how, at the very least, but he just let things go on, and when he upset her when she was pregnant the first time, well, that all came out, didn't it? He knew better. And I'm inclined to agree with Reah a little—he wasn't ready to be a father. Now, with Darletta fucking everything up, he still may not be good father material."

"I hope that's not the case."

"We will see that Reah's children are cared for." Gavril blinked at Dee's words.

"Darlie, this is going to be the best thing that ever happened to us," Dantel Schuul offered Darletta a drink inside his private office. Darletta's new husband was moping out by the overly large pool at the back of Dantel's obscenely huge estate. "His mother is the Queen of Le-Ath Veronis, His father is Prime Minister on Kifirin, his great-grandfather is King of Karathia and if my sources are correct, his brother is the founding member of the Campiaan Alliance. Nobody could ask for better connections than that. We'll get everything we can before we start putting the pressure on." Dantel gloated while his daughter smiled and sipped her drink.

"My father says he's gotten a lock twice, but they moved again before he could even send mindspeech," Lendill paced in front of me. We were sitting in Aurelius' spacious home on the light half of Le-Ath Veronis. Lendill had spent the night with me. He was treating me so carefully since he'd learned I was pregnant. In the two weeks since Wyatt's funeral, I hadn't heard one word from Tory. Neither had his parents. He'd made a choice, and it was to ignore his daughters and his family.

"Not surprising, since Willem said that one of the Ra'Ak could read the Winds." I'd done some research on what Willem could do, in the form of asking Lissa for information, along with Cheedas, the former cook-turned-vampire. Both knew a lot.

"So, that one is predicting our moves." Lendill raked fingers through his hair in a frustrated gesture.

"It only makes sense—they've been ahead of us by a step or two, right down the line. I was hoping that their illness would have affected this somehow, but something is keeping them in line." I was as frustrated as Lendill was over this. At least they were taking males now—Zellar's way of covering his bets, I think. Sex was no longer the objective—getting away from his captors was.

"Yeah, ever since that one attacked your bus on Tulgalan, they've reined in the insanity."

"Wait a minute," I said. "Nefrigar!" I shouted.

"My love?" He was there in an instant.

"You picked up a piece of that Ra'Ak, didn't you—the one I killed on Tulgalan?"

"This piece?" He held the chunk out to me. It was bigger than my fist.

"May I borrow this?" I asked.

"You may have it, I have three more." He was smiling widely at me.

"Lendill, can your dad zone in on this sort of abnormality?" I handed the chunk over. "There's only four more now with this sort of illness, and they should all be together."

"Might be possible—would you like to see where my father lives?" Lendill was smiling too. That's how Lendill, Nefrigar and I all ended up in the Elven Kingdom, somewhere a High Demon had never been before.

"This is fascinating," Kaldill Schaff took the chunk of Ra'Ak dust from Lendill. "I'm not sure I've ever held such as this." We'd been transported to the hidden Elven lands on Wyyld, and stood inside Kaldill's beautiful, private study.

"You may keep it, Elf King," Nefrigar smiled as Kaldill handled the chunk of Ra'Ak dust. "Reah may have one of the other pieces if she wants."

"I don't need it, Honey Blue," I smiled up at him.

"You know, I think I can place a tracer on this," Kaldill grinned. "It was difficult with the other, since he changes bodies so often. I had to rework the spell every three days, using the essence signature. I won't have to do that with this malady, it will give off a vibration peculiar to the sufferers."

"How long?" Lendill was almost breathless in anticipation.

"Two—three days. After that, I can track them even if they're folding from one spot to another."

"I know where Zellar will strike next." Willem had come to Lissa. "The Ra'Ak don't go with him when he gathers his victims, but he knows they'll track him if he doesn't return quickly. Lendill is correct in that he's trying to gather several and then use what power he has left to scatter them, after placing something of himself with each one. What we have to do is give him a surprise when he lands in the next spot, so he'll run back to the Ra'Ak for protection. Then, Reah and the others can be waiting."

"But I thought you weren't allowed to say things like that." Lissa blinked at Willem in surprise.

"Kaldill knows my talents. He gave permission." Willem was smiling. "Be ready tomorrow afternoon, around second bell. I will take you where you need to be."

"You got it," Lissa nodded.

"Is everybody ready?" I looked up at Norian—he was running the command center himself while the rest of us geared up for battle. Drake, Drew and Dragon were coming with us and Teeg stood at my side, a Ranos rifle slung over his shoulder as if he were used to it. My rifle was in my hand and I was checking the charge.

Gardevik had come, with Em-pah Denevik and two other High Demon males. Rylend was also there, and he gave me a heart-stopping smile from across the room. Farzi and Nenzi hadn't been willing to stay behind—they were coming as lion snakes. Lendill had asked them to bite anything that still appeared human and they'd readily agreed. Astralan and his brothers had offered to come, but Teeg asked them to stay behind with Dee, in case something happened. Dee would carry on with the newly-formed Alliance if anything happened to Teeg. I was determined that nothing would happen.

We were waiting for mindspeech from Lissa—she and Willem had some errand of their own. They'd been secretive about it; we only knew that when the signal came, we would know the right time to go. Kaldill Schaff was better than any bloodhound, I learned. He'd gotten the information for us, just as promised. Our quarry had folded to Lidrith, barely a click before Lendill had gathered all of us together. I figured that Lissa and Willem meant to interrupt Zellar in his kidnapping efforts, chasing him back to the Ra'Ak for protection. That would put them all together in a knot. Now, all we had to do was catch them in those bare blinks before they folded to another location. *No problem.*

Zellar, in a twenty-year-old body, stood beneath the awning at the train station on Lidrith. Since the pirates had taken over, Lidrithi went to work as before, for little or no pay. They were rationed food and utilities. Zellar saw them as rats, continuously searching through a maze for small rewards in the form of food and housing. Zellar had long ago lost anything closely resembling a conscience, not even blinking when he saw children waiting to take the train to work alongside their parents. The ones he took might even think it a blessing when their sorry lives ended abruptly.

"Zellar?" A woman stood beside him, smiling. And were those? Zellar stared at the Queen of Le-Ath Veronis, her lengthy claws extended, one lethal nail sliding beneath his chin. Zellar gulped in fear and screamed as he folded away.

Now! Lissa shouted in mindspeech.

Pandemonium. Perhaps there's a better word to describe what happened when we hit the ground inside a cavernous grotto hidden inside a mountain on Lidrith's northernmost continent, but I couldn't dredge it up in my mind, I was too focused on what we had to do. Dragon, Drake and Drew became dragons immediately, doing battle with three of the four Ra'Ak. Garde, Denevik and the other High Demons had turned and were chasing the fourth.

I wasn't sure what was keeping any of them from folding away, until I saw Lissa and Ry. Somehow, between the two of them, they'd shielded the entire cave. The enemy couldn't escape. That made me smile.

It was easy enough to see that Zellar had done a soul-shift with all the humanoids inside the cave, and Farzi and Nenzi were whipping about, biting as many of those thirty humans as they could. Lendill and Teeg were shooting with deadly aim, killing what got away from the reptanoids. But Zellar? He was wrapped inside a spell that he thought to stay safely hidden inside. He'd tapped Lidrith's core shortly before he'd gone hunting more victims, and employed that vast power to hide himself while his Ra'Ak captors died. Did he think his spell would keep him from my sight? I pulled the knife from the sheath clipped in my waistband and made my way carefully toward the other side of the cave.

Three Ra'Ak dusted while I edged around the others, avoiding Ranos shots and humanoids dying of lion snake poison. One man dropped at my feet and stared helplessly up at me as he quivered and died on the dusty cave floor. I felt a brief moment of pity for him, but he was dead anyway—Zellar's soul-shifting had seen to that. This was a quicker and more merciful death—lion snake poison paralyzes everything. You feel no pain at the last.

I stopped not far from Zellar, who was invisible to all except perhaps Lissa and me—the other High Demons were attempting to help three dragons wrestle the last Ra'Ak. Zellar had been hiding for a very long time, and now that I'd stopped moving, seemingly embroiled in watching the last Ra'Ak fight off the others, he turned his attention to that as well.

He never saw me change. My smaller Thifilatha would do just fine for this. Faster than Zellar could see, my arm snaked out and grasped him by the throat. I held back the ability to burn him—I wanted to watch his eyes as he died. Zellar gurgled and struggled in my grip, even as the last Ra'Ak died behind me, some of his chunks pounding me in the back. I barely felt it. Here was the one I wanted. The one Teeg had been sure he'd gotten before. I knew it was Zellar, and he knew that I knew.

"Shall I do this, daughter?" Kifirin had come from somewhere, and he glared at my prisoner, who was still struggling in my hand. I held him tight enough that he couldn't escape, but not so tight that he'd die. At least not yet. The others, their work finished, gathered around us.

"No, Father, I will do this," I said. Zellar whined, poised to beg for mercy when I drew my knife across his throat, relieving him of his head.

~

"I was asked to deliver this to you, my King." Corolan settled the box on Wylend's desk.

"Do you know what it is?"

"I do."

"You're not going to tell me, are you?"

"It's better if you discover it for yourself."

Wylend used power to open the box, folding the top and sides down, much as a flower might open to the sun. Inside was the perfectly preserved head of a young man. Stuffed in the mouth was a note. Cautiously Wylend removed the note and opened it to read.

Wylend Giraldus Arden, King of Karathia, I give you the final head of Zellar the warlock, to keep with his first inside your treasury. I hope you find it a comfort as you rule Karathia. I would also like to take this opportunity to renounce the citizenship you gave back to me. I have no further need of it—Reah Desh Nilvas Silver Montegue.

~

Kifirin sat on the edge of Baetrah, satisfied that few bothered to come to the volcano nowadays unless it was a High Demon, prepared to end his life. Only a few female High Demons remained, and those few were watched carefully, not just by their mates, but by the race as a whole. If those females were lost, there truly would be no future for the race.

He worried, too, about a long-dead race that had somehow resurfaced. The race looked to be subtly influencing events, much as it had in the past before it was destroyed. As it was a dark race, his promise not to interfere hampered him. Rumblings of anomalies in the GodRealm had also come to him, but nothing overt had come to light.

Rumors of an old, outlawed practice had also come to his ears, but he couldn't imagine why any of the powerful might employ a mindcloud. There were other ways to influence things, and if the one or ones placing the mindcloud were too obvious in their efforts, retribution would surely come swiftly. He held not the power to do anything about it, anyway. Kifirin had to shove those thoughts aside and focus on a more pressing issue instead.

A curl of smoke was coaxed away from his nostrils by a gentle surge of heat from the volcano below. He'd made a promise to Jaydevik, to save the High Demon race. At the time, he was depending upon a promise made to him by the one who'd created him in the beginning. Reah represented that promise, and he'd made plans around her after she appeared—plans that included her High Demon mate, Torevik Rath.

Reah's and Tory's relationship had fractured, due to unforeseen influences and events. Kifirin had pushed his rule of noninterference to the limit in the past, and now faced that dilemma again. It would involve isolating Reah, and that would bring her more pain. Kifirin closed his eyes, regretful of the path her life would take.

"I must," he spoke absently to himself. Rising, his shook his Thifilathi and unfurled black wings that might encompass the Dark Realm.

"What might I do about any of this? I have never had direct dealings with any of the created races," Hanlekidus Frebell, a member of the Koh'Ahmari and only lesser in power than the One and the Three, stared at the Shining Messenger before him.

"Then it is time you made your acquaintance. Your help will be required in the future; therefore, I suggest you travel back in time to become familiar with them—dark and light. We have an assignment for you, and we know you may be trusted."

"This is not my desire," Hanlekidus pointed out.

"Yet you will have great reward, should you do as we bid."

"I will do this because you ask, and not for any reward."

"We know this about you. That is why the reward will be great indeed, should you accomplish these things for us."

"Of course, Messenger." Hanlekidus bowed respectfully and disappeared.

The End